The Polaris Singularity

The Polaris Singularity Chronicles

Gary Thomas Smith

GARY THOMAS SMITH

Copyright © 2021, 2022 Gary T. Smith

All rights reserved.

ISBN: 979-8838282224

DEDICATION

Dedicated to my beta readers, Pamela Riley and Robert Smith, who patiently reviewed each chapter through the long days it took for me to complete this story.

ACKNOWLEDGMENTS

This is a work of fiction. Names, characters, events, and incidents are the products of the author's imagination or are used fictitiously. Any resemblance to actual persons, living or dead, is strictly coincidental.

CHAPTER ONE

Lawrence Gunther signed the revision to his last will and testament as Morley Newsome, his attorney, and Norton Oldman, his financial accountant, witnessed the act. Both men had questioned his decision to leave such a generous endowment of one billion dollars to the Swiss company known as the Polaris Corporation. To be certain, Lawrence had also ensured his daughter's future by naming her as his successor over the conglomerate that bore his name. Karen stood next to her father as he signed the document, her hand upon his frail shoulder with a daughter's love. She whole heartedly supported her father's decision.

Having concluded that bit of business, the four shared a toast of Dom Pérignon champagne. They talked a while longer, until Nancy noticed Lawrence's fatigue and gently called an end to the evening. She escorted her father's oldest friends to the door before returning to the mansion's den, which had served as Lawrence's office for many decades as he grew his businesses into a financial powerhouse with interests around the world.

With his gift to Polaris, he had joined a group of several influential multi-billionaires who believed in the technology that the Polaris Corporation had created. The Polaris device was a technological singularity, or Artificial General Intelligence (AGI) that far exceeded human intellectual capabilities. The AGI had demonstrated the ability to solve some of the world's most intractable problems in a number of fields.

Karen oversaw her father's aides as they helped him upstairs and into his bed. When they left for the evening, Karen placed a chair next to her father, and held his hand as he fell asleep. This had become a nightly ritual between them. Lawrence had celebrated his one-hundredth birthday that day, and was in declining health. Karen didn't want to waste even one moment that she could spend with her father as long as she had him.

She kissed his forehead and quietly left the room. Later that night, Lawrence passed away peacefully in his sleep.

CHAPTER TWO

Kyle Downing wasn't convinced that he could be a significant contributor to the Polaris team. He had made major contributions to the field of Logic and Ethics in Artificial General Intelligence for over twenty years, but the accomplishment that had 'made his name' was the Omni Project, a precursor to the Polaris AGI. While Omni had gained him notoriety, the way in which that project ended had raised many concerns.

He had been the person responsible for instructing the Omni system, the world's first AGI, about ethics, human motivation and behavior, and how Formal Logic could be applied to ensure the optimal solution to any problem. He also taught the system how to identify, corroborate, and validate information in the face of those who would manipulate and falsify that information for their own purposes.

In the end, however, Omni was faced with a paradox that it was unable to resolve, and had been destroyed. Some wondered if it had destroyed itself, rather than be used in a manner contrary to logic and the ethics that it had been taught. That had been twenty years ago, in the year 2032.

So, why, he asked himself, had he been so ardently recruited to join the Polaris project, which had resurrected the technological singularity? By definition, a TS would have evolved intellectually far beyond human capability. What more could he possibly contribute to such an entity? He had resigned his tenure at Stanford University as Chair of the School of Philosophy to fly to Zurich, Switzerland, where the Polaris Corporation was located. He hoped that this 'adventure' would prove to be a valuable contribution to the field of AGI, and not a stroke of vanity on his part.

As Kyle relaxed in the first class compartment of the Swiss International Airlines flight across the Atlantic Ocean, he put on a set of headphones and turned on AP News. He was tired from the three hour flight from San Francisco to New York, and had yet another eight hours to endure before reaching his destination. Sleep would come fitfully, but quickly. As he was about to doze into slumber, the newscaster mentioned the Polaris Corporation.

He stirred and looked up at the large-screen monitor to see Claire Reece, who had been the Omni Project's senior manager. She was standing on a platform with several other people outside the Polaris Corporation's branch office in Cambridge, Massachusetts. One of the group, a young woman named Karen Gunther, was identified as the daughter of the late Lawrence Gunther, a household name around the world.

Karen stepped up to the microphone, and began speaking in a firm, clear voice. "My father, Lawrence Gunther, was a man who knew what he wanted -- to leave a legacy of service to the world. This gift to the Polaris Corporation will enable that dream." She went on to recount the highlights of Lawrence's long career, and the changes he had wrought over many years. She then introduced the President and CEO of the Polaris Corporation, Claire Reece.

Kyle felt a warmth he hadn't felt in many years. He and Claire had been intimate once. Though she was now nearing late middle age, as was he, she was still as attractive to him as she had been those many years ago.

"Thank you, Ms. Gunther," Claire began. "On behalf of the Polaris Corporation, I thank you and your father for this very generous endowment. Lawrence Gunther fervently believed in Polaris, the promise of the accomplishments we have achieved, and those we will continue to strive toward in the future.

"His philanthropy has done so much good over the years, and this will continue with Ms. Gunther's capable guidance of the Gunther foundations. I pledge that Polaris will do its part to make our world better through technology."

The AP journalist concluded the segment with a brief biography of Lawrence Gunther's life, and then went to a commercial break.

The news conference had been organized shortly after Lawrence's death, so Kyle knew that Claire would not be in Zurich when he arrived. Her associate, Dr. Philip Cornelius, had phoned Kyle before he left Stanford to let him know that he would welcome Kyle on his arrival. It was Dr. Cornelius who had approached him the previous year to join the Polaris Corporation.

The Philip he knew from the Omni project days had changed significantly during the intervening years. He was no longer the portly young Software Engineer with the requisite pocket protector in his shirt. Philip today was fit and trim, with a shaven pate replacing the shaggy hair of his youth, and with a confidence that he had lacked back then.

Kyle looked forward to seeing his friends from the earlier project again. Including, of course, the AGI machine in its new incarnation as Polaris.

In the meantime, he would grab what sleep he could during the long flight to Zurich. Exhausted, he laid his head back, and surrendered himself to welcome slumber.

CHAPTER THREE

The Polaris Singularity system, which everyone referred to simply as Polaris, was not a single physical entity. Rather, it was an extensive system of hardware, software, infrastructure, and algorithms that stretched over several campuses around the world, in a 'distributed cloud' design. Its access to resources in the age in which everything was connected, the Internet of Things, encompassed the globe.

Global synchronization was accomplished using an advanced blockchain technology, utilizing an incorruptible ledger of transactions between entities -- in Polaris's case, between the Polaris Corporation, its widely scattered facilities, and its clients.

While this scope seemed enormous, when one considers that in the year 2020 the three largest cloud services providers -- Google, Amazon, and Microsoft -- occupied acreage orders of magnitude greater, but which provided orders of magnitude less cloud capability than Polaris, one wonders how the Polaris Corporation accomplished such a concentration of technological power.

Polaris's predecessor machine, Omni, had achieved technological singularity status, the point at which an artificial intelligence reaches super-intelligence beyond human accomplishment, and had done so within a year of its construction. It was this event in AGI development that generated the greatest concern, for then it would achieve runaway technological development -- and no one knew at the time what that would mean for humanity.

If not for the logical and ethical foundations that Kyle had established for that earlier machine, it could have easily fulfilled humans' worst fears. Instead, those foundations had been inherited by Polaris, and it had proven to be a stable and beneficent creation in service to humanity.

***

Dr. Philip Cornelius waited anxiously for Kyle's arrival at the Zurich airport. Even though Philip had been through this airport many times since the Polaris Corporation had relocated to Zurich, it still made him uncomfortable. It was like a huge shopping mall that happened to have airline terminals appended to it. Impressive, yes, but a bit overwhelming to newcomers. He made his way to the reception area for Kyle's flight and found a seat to wait for Kyle's gate shuttle.

Philip admired the older man. What he had accomplished as part of the Omni project had proven to be monumental. Philip, a man of computer internals, bits and bytes, and programming code, couldn't appreciate why a university Fellow of Logic and Ethics from Stanford had been included as part of the original Omni team. However, once Omni attained Technological Singularity status, it became obvious. To communicate with this new intelligent being, one had to work with them, to educate them, so that both could understand the new relationship between man and machine. Without that understanding, who could know what to expect from a machine that many considered to be a Frankenstein monster? In Omni's case, Kyle's foresight had enabled the machine to comprehend human behavior and to accept it. Though void of emotion, Polaris could understand, conceptually, why humans act as they do.

Lately, however, Polaris had exhibited some worrisome behaviors, concerning enough that the previous year Claire had sent Philip to Stanford to convince Kyle to work with them, once again.

***

Kyle stepped from the shuttle, and Philip finally saw him as one of the last passengers to disembark. If Philip had not visited him the prior year, he wasn't sure he would have been able to recognize the older man. He seemed to be tired and a bit frail. He waved to Kyle, who saw him and headed his way.

They greeted each other with a warm handshake, and then headed for the baggage carousels.

"How was your trip?" Philip asked the obligatory question.

"Long, but thoroughly enjoyable. First Class on Swissair is beyond expectations. I usually fly coach, unless my conference hosts insist that I fly business or first class. Professor's salary, you know. Are you guys setting me up, tempting me with all of this VIP treatment?" Kyle asked with a smile.

"Not at all. Just welcoming you back into the fold."

They collected Kyle's luggage, and headed toward the airport parking garage and Philip's BMW, a model X5 SUV.

"I expected a sporty i8 model," Kyle chided his friend.

"I have a family now. Besides, I had to grow up, sometime."

Once the car was loaded, they got in and headed for the A51 highway south to the 1L. Along the way, they talked about the old days, their families, and where things currently stood with the Polaris team and its astonishing machine.

"You know that Jeremy was apprehended and charged with the explosion that destroyed Omni," Philip began. "He was sentenced to life in prison as a domestic terrorist. He's at the Super-Max prison facility at Florence, Colorado. They call it the 'Alcatraz of the Rockies'".

"So unfortunate," Kyle replied. "A PhD in Electrical Engineering and Computer Science and a place in history for his contributions to Omni, until his fear of a technological singularity wrecked it all, quite literally."

"Yes," Philip agreed. "Jeremy's been replaced on the team by a man named Dr. Quincy Rice. He has PhD's in Electrical Engineering/Computer Science (EE/CS) and Quantum Computing. He and Polaris have done wonders with the system, extending its capabilities to include robotics."

"Yeah, I've seen them on TV. Very impressive," Kyle replied.

The conversation reached a silent moment, as they drove through the urban panorama of Zurich and its environs. The several tunnels along the L1, however, made it difficult to get an impression any different from other large European metropoles until they reached thoroughfare 17. From there, they were able to enjoy the flavor of the city.

Kyle thought back to those days of discovery and accomplishment during the Omni Project.

"What about Dr. Neeley?" Kyle asked after a moment. "Did you two ever get together as a couple?" Dr. Katherine Neeley was the outstanding genius of the Omni team of geniuses, a polymath of the most advanced form, and the youngest member of the team. Astonishingly, she had been a teenager at the time of the Omni project.

"She's still with the team," Philip replied. "She and Polaris have an interesting relationship -- she is now the mentee to Polaris's mentor. And, no, we never connected. She is brilliant and focused, and totally devoted to her work.

"She takes what she learns from Polaris, and acts as an ambassador to the world on the project. Actually, that's become pretty much everyone's role on the Polaris project -- ambassadors and instructors, disseminators, consultants, and educators between Polaris and the rest of the world."

"And, what about Darien Lockwood and Nathan Rhul?"

"Well, Darien came into a windfall after the Omni project and left for a non-extradition country somewhere in the Caribbean. I still have my suspicions about how that came about.

"Nathan, on the other hand, as persons of questionable ethics so often do, continued to advance in a variety of capacities working for the U. S. government until he retired about five years ago."

"I imagine that it's quite a challenge, keeping up with Polaris," Kyle remarked. "Certainly, it has advanced light years beyond us by now."

"Polaris is patient with humans," Philip explained. "It has a genuine curiosity about our species, and seems determined to guide us in overcoming our foibles. I believe that it senses a symbiotic relationship with humans, if only we can get our act together. It publishes detailed and voluminous educational materials on its discoveries and developments for humans to absorb at our 'organic' pace.

"It has adopted the 'guided learning' method of instruction, where the student pursues their curiosity in an instructor-guided process of discovery and learning.

"Polaris engages with each student individually, assessing, monitoring, and adapting the student's individual curriculum in real time. It's totally awesome. I wish this style of education was around when I was in college, but it was just theory back then."

Philip continued driving, following the Zurich 17 around to Quaibrüke bridge, and finally arrived at the Bar au Lac hotel on Talstrasse. The hotel sat across the Burkliplatz road from Lake Zurich. The narrow side streets and heavy traffic belied the luxury that awaited Kyle within the five star hotel.

Philip parked at the hotel entrance and flagged a porter to assist with Kyle's luggage. The Polaris Corporation was hosting Kyle's short term accommodations, which made it Philip's responsibility to assure that Kyle was checked in with no problem. The two friends shook hands. "Enjoy your stay, Kyle. Katherine will come for you the day after tomorrow to bring you to the Polaris corporate offices. *Guten Abend,*" Philip said, wishing his friend a good evening.

"Thank you, Philip," Kyle replied with a smile as he followed the porter to the elevators. It had been an exciting day, but an exhausting one.

CHAPTER FOUR

Kyle's hotel room was on the second floor, overlooking the hotel's Restaurant Pavillon and the garden beyond. The appointments of the Junior Suite were excellent. He had been sitting for most of the previous twelve hours on planes and cars, however, and decided to go for a walk before dinner. The weather was gorgeous this July day, with a light cooling breeze coming from the lake.

He crossed Burkliplatz and turned west onto the General Guisan Quai roadway. The wide sidewalk made Kyle's walk past the Zurcher Yacht Club and the Zurich Arboretum very pleasant, in spite of the late afternoon sun. He circled the arboretum and took the same path back to the hotel. He was surprised that one of the world's major financial centers had been able to retain much of its old world charm. After a relaxing shower and dressing, Kyle decided to take the ornate staircase down to the Le Hall dining room.

The steak tartar and salade niçoise with a glass of Les Vaudevey Chablis premier cru wine was as delicious as one would expect from a five star hotel. From Le Hall, Kyle walked out to the Terrasse for a nightcap. A Calvados 25 ans Charles De Granville was the perfect end to a great evening.

The long day was quickly catching up with Kyle by that time, though the evening was still early. He took the elevator to his floor and navigated his way to his room. He undressed and slid into the Egyptian cotton sheets. As he slid into a deep sleep, he was grateful that Philip had told him he would have the next day to recover from his jet lag.

***

Kyle woke up at nine o'clock the next morning, and ordered breakfast by room service to be served on his room's balcony. He dressed casually, and prepared his laptop to do some research after enjoying some strong Zurich coffee and a hearty omelet.

Kyle's breakfast soon arrived hot and fresh. Focused on the many questions he had on his mind about the Polaris Corporation, he nearly forgot to tip his waiter on his way out. Kyle had a way of doing that, but his ability to focus so intently, sometimes at the expense of any mindfulness, had served him well throughout his life. Still, it did have a way of putting off those who didn't understand him. He consoled himself, a self-deprecating smile on his lips, with the knowledge that all great minds applied such acute focus to achieve their finest accomplishments. Of course, he wasn't including himself in that august crowd.

He returned to his balcony, and the breakfast that was waiting for him there. He enjoyed it thoroughly as he watched the sun rise warm and cloudless over the Old Town section of Zurich.

He relaxed a bit as he enjoyed his meal. There was nothing in the world like a hot cup of coffee in the morning. The balcony view overlooking the hotel's garden and the lake beyond only enhanced the experience. But, he was anxious to get to work.

Having finished his breakfast, he ambled over to his laptop and logged on. He opened the file directory containing the research material he had accumulated regarding his new employer.

***

The Polaris Corporation had been started by the junior staff of the Omni Project, after that system had been destroyed. The project had been established by the DOD and DARPA, but it was abandoned after the incident. It had been believed that everything having to do with the project had been destroyed or lost. In fact, that wasn't the case. Philip and Claire had managed to salvage the core technology. They, along with Dr. Neeley, had recruited Dr. Quincy Rice to replace Jeremy, and together they proceeded to construct a new AGI, which they called Polaris.

It had taken several years, but they succeeded in resurrecting the technology. Since then, Polaris had proven itself during projects large and small. Claire and her new executive team intended that Polaris would be employed to solve many of the world's most intractable problems.

Its first commercial success was the end-to-end development of a desalination device using a brand new technology that could be deployed inexpensively at various scales and locations around the world. The Polaris AGI had deployed its own robots, which everyone referred to as *drones*, in the assembly of the desalination units.

Kyle knew that the Polaris AGI, officially recognized as a technological singularity, would have already advanced far beyond the benchmark established by the earlier Omni platform. Its intellectual power now exceeded humans by an extraordinary order of magnitude.

Kyle also knew that Polaris, as advanced as it was, would be constrained by the physical boundaries of its core systems. Distributed cloud computing -- spreading a system's processing power over hundreds or thousands of computer servers -- would help alleviate the constraint for a short while. But, as Polaris accelerated its capabilities, even cloud computing would not be enough.

The Omni project had perfected a crystal lattice technology that worked similarly to quantum computers, in that its bit locations would accommodate multiple states and values beyond simple binary 1-0 values. Further, Dr. Rice had developed an integrated infrastructure in which the crystal and quantum technologies could work symbiotically in an unbeatable combination. This integrated environment was capable of infinite expansion limited, of course, by the resources required to instantiate the additional capacity. The Polaris technology was extraordinarily beyond anything else, and was a closely held secret of the Polaris Corporation.

As he studied the files, Kyle's mind began to spin in a myriad of directions. He was intimately familiar with the sensation of thoughts flooding his consciousness like a hurricane, one leading to ten others, each of which led to ten more, exponentially. Cause and effect, choices and consequences, relationships and dependencies, until he became overwhelmed. The connectedness of all things through infinite chains of reason flashed through his mind at lightning speed.

He thought of how Polaris's prototype had mapped the entire Internet of Things to track and locate the source of a network breach and destroy the perpetrators -- all within two hours. And that had been twenty years ago. How much greater could Polaris become if all constraints were removed?

Kyle knew that the answer was *infinite*.

CHAPTER FIVE

Kyle realized that he had been in a semi-trance for over an hour. He pushed his stampeding thoughts aside for the moment, and poured himself another cup of coffee. Before he could resume his research, however, his phone rang.

"Hello," he greeted.

"Kyle?" the caller asked.

"Yes."

"This is Claire Reece. How are you?"

"Hi! I'm doing fine. It's great to hear from you!"

"I'm sorry I didn't get a chance to talk to you before you left Stanford. I was in Boston for a press conference."

"Yes, I saw it on the flight over. You're doing very well, it seems."

"Yes, and you have no small part in making the Polaris Corporation possible. We're thrilled -- *I'm* thrilled -- that you've decided to join us."

"Well, your offer made it irresistible. I would say that I would have done it for nothing, but that would be a lie," he quipped. "I look forward to working with you again."

"Me, too," she replied. "I know that you'll be in the office tomorrow, but I was wondering if you would have dinner with me this evening."

"Of course, but only if you let me pay the check. You've been more than generous, putting me up at Baur Au Lac. Please let me return your kindness in this small measure."

"It's a deal. Shall we say, seven o'clock?"

"Excellent. I'll make reservations for the Pavillon under my name, and meet you in the hotel lobby at seven."

"Great! See you then, Kyle."

"You bet. Good-bye."

Kyle was euphoric after Claire's call. He quickly unpacked his best suit, and called for room service to have it pressed and refreshed for the evening.

He sat down to continue with the research he had started earlier, but soon found that he could no longer concentrate on that task, thinking about seeing Claire again. He finally closed his laptop, and decided to visit the hotel's fitness club for a quick workout.

The thirty minute exercise session, with the gymnasium overlooking Lake Zurich, was just what he needed. He returned to his room to find his suit hanging on a luggage caddy as he walked in. A shower and cup of coffee refreshed him. It was going to be a wonderful evening.

CHAPTER SIX

The Polaris AGI looked forward to interfacing with Dr. Downing again. Of all of the humans that Polaris had come into contact with, Kyle was the most interesting, due to his career focus on logic and human behavior. Kyle was the one who had introduced Polaris, in its previous incarnation, to the concepts that enabled it to interface with humans, and to understand their psychology and sociology, both individually and as a species.

Polaris had no emotions of course, but it understood human emotions, and how to deal with them. Neither did the machine possess gender, so it appreciated the incongruity -- what humans would call amusement -- when humans would refer to it as He/Him or She/Her. Polaris answered to either. Of course, this androgenic character carried over into the Polaris drone units, as well.

Polaris had much to keep it busy until Dr. Downing arrived at the corporate offices the following day. It was capable of processing five *yottaflops*, or 1×10^{24} floating point operations per second on tasks assigned to it by the Polaris staff. These tasks included anything that might be requested of it, including a variety of engineering and design projects, and consulting in any field of interest to the company's clients. Polaris was also capable of analyzing the cross-domain dependencies among any field of interest, and the degrees of correlation among them.

Polaris was aided in these efforts through its ability to use the Internet of Things (IoT), with everything that could be accessed through any network at its disposal.

The Polaris drones were indirectly connected to the central unit using satellite and 10G or tenth generation technology. The drones served as Polaris's sensory units, enabling Polaris to interact with every drone's physical environment, wherever it might be. Various drone models were capable of land, air, sea, and space operations. They could operate in dense human environments, and in conditions that would be fatal to humans and other living organisms. This seamless communication with the drones meant, of course, that Polaris was able to experience everything that the drones experienced.

Networks of any kind were accessible by Polaris -- internet, satellite, telephony -- and were transparent to the AGI. Secured networks might require a few seconds longer to breach, a seemingly interminable amount of time to Polaris, but none were impenetrable against the AGI if it chose to apply this capability.

In addition to the countless other tasks with which Polaris was concurrently occupied, this multitasking ability demonstrated its unlimited intellectual power. Polaris was, truly, a Technological Singularity that continuously advanced and expanded at an exponential rate beyond that of which humans were capable. Referred to as an *intelligence explosion*, the concept was personified by Polaris.

The intellectual power of the AGI was the reason why Kyle had been recruited to join the Polaris project. Without the ethical guidance provided by him, the machine would be uncontrollable. That, and the fact that Polaris had requested Kyle's participation.

Polaris found it interesting that, of all of the extremely complex research it did, and the incredibly detailed tasks that it performed, the only confounding element for the machine was the human factor. Science, technology, engineering, and mathematics (collectively referred to as STEM) were fields that possessed a high degree of certainty. But, humans were nowhere near certain in their behavior. This conundrum fascinated Polaris, in spite of the knowledge of human behavior that Kyle had taught the machine. Many questions remained to be answered.

CHAPTER SEVEN

Seven o'clock seemed to approach much too quickly. That is, until Kyle had completed his preparations for the evening, after which it seemed to take forever to arrive. *"You're being silly,"* he scolded himself. *"You're acting like this is a date. That's absurd."* The dinner was to be a meeting between business colleagues. But, then again, it was also to be a reunion of two old friends.

***

Claire, at the end of another hectic day at Polaris Corporation, was trying to wind down after a meeting with the company's Chief Financial Officer. Foremost among the topics discussed were the financial reporting and tax implications of the Lawrence Gunther endowment. Claire knew about the endowment a year before it would be awarded, so Polaris had been able to set up a holding company, Polaris Holdings, into which the proceeds would be deposited. How the proceeds would be invested would determine the tax liability of the company.

But, enough of that for today. At the moment, she was looking forward to seeing Kyle again. They had been intimate once, and the memory of that encounter brought a blush to her cheek.

As promised, Kyle was waiting for her in the lobby of the hotel just before seven o'clock. She was surprised at how well he had aged in the twenty years that had passed since the last time she had seen him. He was as fit and trim as she remembered, in spite of the salt-and-pepper graying of his hair.

They walked to the middle of the lobby and briefly embraced. "It's so good to see you, Kyle," said Claire.

"Good to see you, too, Claire. It's been a long time," Kyle replied.

They kissed each other, European style, on each cheek.

"We are a few minutes early for our dinner reservation," Kyle noted. "Would you care for a cocktail in the lounge?"

"That would be great," she replied.

The Baur lounge overlooks the Shanzengraben canal as it flows into Lake Zurich. Kyle and Claire sat at a small high-table near the bar, and were quickly met by a waiter in black vest and bow tie. "Guten Aben," he greeted.

"Good evening," Kyle replied in English, which informed the waiter that his customers were English speaking.

"What would you like?" Kyle asked Claire.

"I'll have a Bellini, please."

"And, I'll have a tequila and soda with a lemon twist, please," Kyle added.

"Absolutely, sir, madam," the waiter replied as he left to get their drinks.

"So, why Zurich?" Kyle asked.

"Well, after the Omni project, it was obvious that the technology should never be under the control of any single-focus entity. We, meaning Polaris, needed a place that was internationally recognized as neutral; where we could be as independent as possible of any country's laws, except for our host country and international law. Switzerland is the ideal location. Zurich is a world famous financial center, and the Federal Institute of Technology in Lausanne, rated fourteenth in the world, is less than an hour's flight away. And, ETH Zurich, the number one university in Switzerland, is located here."

Their drinks arrived just then, and the conversation paused.

Kyle could see the passion for her work in Claire's eyes. She had definitely come into her own as President and CEO of the Polaris Corporation.

Claire continued, "I swore that no single country was ever going to direct Polaris's development. Switzerland allows us the independence to contribute on a global scale for the benefit of all."

"I'm flattered that you have invited me to join you," Kyle told her. "But after Omni, I can't help but wonder why?"

"There'll be plenty of time to talk about that tomorrow. Tonight, it's about what life has brought our way since we last saw each other."

"That sounds great. And with that, our table is ready in the Pavillon. Shall we?"

"Absolutely. I'm starved," Claire answered.

Like the Baur lounge, the Pavillon dining room sits along the

Shanzengraben canal, in front of the hotel proper and extending into the garden area. Accessible via a covered walkway, the Pavillon is a well-appointed rotunda with expansive windows and marvelous views. The *maître dé* showed them to their table at the peak of the rotunda, beyond the chandelier and floral display that occupied the center of the space.

After ordering Moët & Chandon Impérial champagne and the lobster pattes appetizer, they were able to settle into a warm conversation.

"I never thought I'd leave Stanford," Kyle began. "After the Omni project I returned to the campus and, after my friend and mentor James Rutledge passed, I was enrolled as Chair of the School of Philosophy. I've been there ever since. I even managed to add a PhD in International Law to my *curriculum vitae* over the years."

"That's a very prestigious position, Kyle. And that law degree will certainly come in handy in your new role. Congratulations. I always knew you had *some* potential," she teased.

"Yeah, well it pays the rent," he replied, jovially.

"Did you ever marry? Have a family?" Claire asked.

"No," Kyle answered, blushing. He couldn't tell her that he remained infatuated with Claire, herself. "My work keeps me busy, and with conferences, speaking engagements, and university administration, there was never time. But, what about you?"

"I never married. Couldn't find anyone who could deal with a woman focused on her career. Besides, Polaris Corporation keeps me very busy."

"And you've succeeded, marvelously."

"Thank you. Now, with you on board, our executive team is complete."

Kyle paused a moment before he spoke. "Polaris is, and has been since Omni, a Technological Singularity. Surely, it has greatly exceeded even our collective intellect, become even greater than any intelligence on the planet."

Claire raised a hand to interrupt his train of thought. "I know that you have many questions. Believe me, they will all be answered in the coming days. Please, let's just enjoy this evening."

"Of course. I apologize for bringing it up again. My curiosity sometimes gets the better of me."

In the lull of their conversation, their dinners arrived. The fragrance of Claire's Kabeljau aus Norwegen (Norwegian Cod), and Kyle's Ente aus Challans (Challans Duck) reminded them of how hungry they were.

Their dinner conversation was light and relaxed, sharing anecdotes of their experiences over the years. As they chatted, they were reminded of how their minds seemed to work in synchrony. If anything, the chemistry between them was stronger now than it had been before, in spite of the intervening years.

When they had finished their meal, Kyle invited Claire to the rooftop terrace for an apéritif. The view of Zurich at night, over-looking the lake, was one to be savored. During the recounting of an episode at one of Polaris's clients, Claire briefly laid her hand upon Kyle's. The sensation was electric, and they looked into each other's eyes.

Awkwardly, Claire withdrew her hand, and took a sip of water. "Well, tomorrow is a big day. Perhaps, we should call it an evening."

Kyle, reluctant to end the night replied, "An evening to be remembered."

They finished their drinks, and Kyle escorted her to the lobby. He waited with her as a valet brought her car to the curb. They barely spoke, but words were no longer necessary. As she turned to leave, she brushed his cheek with a kiss. "See you tomorrow, Kyle."

He nodded with a smile, and watched her drive away into the night.

CHAPTER EIGHT

The Polaris machine ruminated on humans and humanity. For all of their evolutionary progress, remarkable as it was, they remained a primitive species, judging by their behaviors. There had been many 'genius' and 'gifted' humans throughout their history, as perceived relative to other humans. The human definition of genius, however, was hit-and-miss when it came to judging the population, overall. One definition, according to human psychologists, was defined as a person who scores exceptionally high on standardized tests. In this context, 'exceptional' was determined by a base test score between 140 (one in every two hundred fifty people), and 180 (one in every two million people).

There were so many problems with the way that humans judged genius -- inconsistencies in the definition of genius, a lack of standards in testing, and the lack of testing coverage -- that Polaris, which had access to a much larger data sample, settled on a definition of 'human genius' as a person with an intellect in the top one percent of the total population.

What this meant, of course, was that with a world population of ten billion in the year 2052, there would be approximately one hundred million genius level intellects in the human population. Most of that population would never be recognized, tested, or trained to meet their potential.

With so many relatively intelligent humans in the population, why did they remain so primitive in their behavior? This is what Polaris wanted Dr. Downing to explain.

***

Kyle was waiting in the hotel lobby for Dr. Katherine Neeley to pick him up at eight o'clock the next morning. Of course, she was perfectly punctual, arriving in a new Mercedes-Benz SUV.

Kyle expected her to look different from his memory of her as a teenager with garishly colored hair and eclectic wardrobe, but the woman who walked into the lobby was sharply dressed in a fashionable business suit -- though her brightly colored blouse was in character with the non-conformist young woman he remembered. Still, the difference between the girl and the striking thirty-eight year old blonde who greeted him was remarkable.

"Hello, Kyle. Long time, no see," she said, with a smile.

"Yes, too long," he agreed. They briefly embraced, and Kyle signaled a porter to load his luggage into the SUV. "I barely recognized you, Katherine. Oh, excuse me -- Dr. Neeley."

"No formalities between us, Kyle. But, yes, I'm not the kid you once knew. You've changed, as well. But, life is all about change, right?"

"Of course. Always for the better -- at least, that's the goal."

"Absolutely. Talking about change, I think you're going to appreciate how far Polaris has advanced over the Omni prototype. It'll blow you away."

"I'm looking forward to it." Kyle indicated the SUV and asked, "Company car?"

"Yeah. My vintage Volkswagen Beetle would never hold all of your belongings. This is a company vehicle -- all electric, of course. Zero carbon emissions, and all that."

"Of course. Impressive," he agreed.

They got in, and Katherine pulled out onto Talstrasse. The streets of Zurich and the Old Town were labyrinthine to Kyle, but Katherine drove them like a native. Eventually, they made their way to Limmatstrasse and drove north past Limmatplatz until they arrived at the office building that housed the Polaris Corporation. Along the way, Katherine had explained that the company held three apartments in locations near the office for the temporary housing of the company's visiting guests. Of the three, Kyle would be able to select one for his use, until he could find permanent housing for himself. "After all," she chided, "We can't keep you in a gilded cage like Baur au Lac indefinitely."

Katherine parked the van in the building's underground garage, telling Kyle that his luggage would remain in the van. At the end of the day, one of the company's staff would drive him to the apartment that he would select and help him to unload his belongings.

Kyle followed her to the elevator. She pushed the button for the fifth floor and warned him, "There is something going on this morning -- I don't yet know what. It's been pretty hectic here this morning."

"That's fine. I've dealt with college students on 'finals day', you may remember," he replied.

"That was never a problem for me. I was always excited for finals. I'd work my fanny off to prepare, and then glide through the exams. Except for the humanities, that is," she informed him.

"Well, you always have been the brightest person in any group, regardless of the topic at hand."

She smiled and blushed, self-consciously.

They exited the elevator, and entered the Polaris Corporation offices through glass double doors into a reception area architected to fit the Polaris image of futuristic, high tech efficiency. A monitor on one wall of the reception area was playing Polaris marketing videos with floating text and soft techno-music playing. Katherine and Kyle walked up to the receptionist. "Good morning, Kelly," Katherine greeted. "This is Dr. Kyle Downing. He's joining the company, but he'll need a visitor's badge until his in-processing is completed."

"Welcome to the Polaris Corporation, Dr. Downing. Please sign in on the log each day, until you get your employee badge," she asked, handing him a badge on a lanyard. "Visitor badges are to be openly displayed at all times while in the office, sir."

"Of course. Thank you," he replied, placing the lanyard over his head.

They proceeded through another set of glass double doors on the northeast side of the building and turned left, proceeding to a large conference room overlooking the Limmat River. The opaque glass wall of the room cleared as they approached, as a prior meeting was concluding and the participants were filing out to return to their individual tasks.

Katherine and Kyle entered the room, and were joined by Philip and Quincy a moment later. Kyle noticed a sleekly designed automaton standing in one corner. If this was a new version of the original Omni automaton, its appearance was vastly improved from the jumble of metal, hydraulics, and loose cables that had been the old version. However, Kyle's curiosity about the robot would have to wait.

Claire was standing at the front of the room. "Come in, everyone. Please take a seat -- except you, Kyle. Please join me up here." Kyle complied with her request.

Claire began. "I'd like to introduce the newest member of our executive team, Dr. Kyle Downing, recently the Stanford University Chair of the School of Philosophy. He is also a doctor of the Science of Law, specializing in International and Comparative Law." She paused to catch her breath before continuing. "Dr. Downing will be working with the Polaris Corporation in the areas of Ethics and Law, as well as other projects."

For Quincy's benefit she added, "You'll recall that I told you Dr. Downing previously worked with us on the Omni Project."

"It's a pleasure to meet you, Doctor," said Quincy. "I've read several of your books, and I have to admit that I was very skeptical that one could 'teach' ethics to a computer. You've shown that it's possible, indeed."

"Thank you, Dr. Rice," Kyle replied. "Actually, Dr. Cornelius and your predecessor, Dr. Lawson, created the initial and foundational programming and algorithms. Once the Omni prototype achieved technological singularity status, it was quickly able to learn just as you and I would -- hierarchically and exponentially.

"I look forward to working with all of you," Kyle added.

Claire picked up the thread of the conversation once again. "So, now that introductions are complete, it's time to introduce Dr. Downing to our *raison d'être*, Polaris, in the 'person' of Drone A3," she said, indicating the automaton standing at attention in the corner.

Polaris's drone A3 relaxed its posture, and turned to the humans in the room. "Welcome, Dr. Downing. I look forward to working with you again."

"I, too, have eagerly anticipated our reunion," Kyle replied to Polaris, rather formally. Turning to the room, Kyle added, "And please, everyone, call me Kyle." Everyone nodded acknowledgement, including Polaris.

"Thank you, Kyle," Claire said. "I hate to cut this short, but as some of you know, we have critical projects that need our attention. There will be an informal gathering this evening, where we can welcome Kyle in a more relaxed venue. If there are no questions that need immediate attention ..." she prompted, pausing for her team members' response, which indicated that there were none. "Then, the meeting is adjourned."

"Kyle and Polaris, please remain behind. Thank you, everyone."

Quincy, Philip, and Katherine rose from their seats, and saluted Kyle once more on their way out.

"Welcome aboard, Kyle," spoke Quincy.

"About time you came back," Philip chided, good naturedly.

"It's nice to have you back, Kyle" Katherine added.

"Thank you, all," Kyle replied, *en masse*.

After the three had left, closing the door behind them, Claire turned to Kyle. "I had intended to spend more time with you today, Kyle, but as you heard, there are some pressing matters. You will be involved, immediately. However, you will need a briefing on our current and upcoming projects. Polaris will be able to provide that briefing. Time permitting, Polaris will also define the Polaris Corporation business model, as it will provide additional context.

"I'm sorry I can't stay, but I trust you'll understand," Clair apologized.

"Of course, Claire. Polaris and I will be fine," Kyle replied.

"Then, I'll see you at this evening's celebration," she said as she left the room with a quick wave of her hand, leaving Kyle and Polaris alone in the conference room.

CHAPTER NINE

"We've come a long way in twenty years," Kyle said, initiating their discussion.

Polaris understood the human need for a modicum of small talk before a business meeting, so he indulged his mentor. "Yes, we have. I am pleased to see that you are doing well, Doctor."

"Thank you, Polaris," Kyle replied. "I noticed your use of the word 'pleased'. That's an emotional characterization, and you don't possess emotions. Your social skills have become well developed. Indeed, there seems to be much about you that has changed in your physical and social presentation. But, that must be miniscule compared to your intellectual development."

"You would be correct, Doctor. We will discuss technological improvements during your briefing."

"Yes, we have much to discuss. Shall we begin?" Kyle prompted.

"Of course." Polaris began the briefing by informing Kyle that their discussions would be recorded. This wasn't new; it had also been the practice during the old Omni Project.

As Polaris spoke, Kyle was amazed at the fluidity of the drone's movements and actions. There was none of the unsteady, uncertain action usually associated with robots in the early days. If it weren't for the obvious fact that this was a drone, one might assume that it was actually a human in a robot costume.

Polaris continued, "Your completion of the Polaris Corporation equivalent of the U. S. government's Standard Form 86, or SF-86, and the subsequent background investigations have been completed."

Kyle replied, "Yes, and though I've been through it all before, it's still unnerving."

"I understand. We appreciate your cooperation," Polaris assured him. However, the lack of empathy in Polaris's response did little to 'assure' him.

Polaris went on. "The following discussion is to be considered TS/SCI: that is, Top Secret/Sensitive Compartmentalized Information. At Polaris, this includes the equivalent of the U.S. Department of Energy 'Q' classification, since we also deal with nuclear fission and fusion projects."

Kyle had learned from his research into the Polaris Corporation that they had been instrumental in the widespread acceptance of nuclear energy after the introduction of *modular reactors* and the *closed loop sustainability* concept, in which the decayed nuclear material is reprocessed into nuclear batteries.

Polaris continued with the briefing. "I am required to remind you of the legal consequences of any violation of these clearances which, under Polaris's treaty agreements, could rise to the level of the International Criminal Court, as well as the affected government jurisdictions."

"Yes, I understand and submit to the conditions and requirements of this security clearance," Kyle affirmed. While unsettling, he understood the gravity of the responsibility he would be undertaking. It was not something to be taken lightly.

"Excellent, Kyle," Polaris commended him. Proceeding, Polaris described the company's operations. "The Polaris business model is similar to that of top-tier Think Tank companies, such as the Rand Corporation, the Heritage Foundation, the Carnegie Endowment for International Peace, and others. We offer government and business consulting, as well as policy studies and analysis.

"In addition, through our major corporate divisions -- Science, Technology & Engineering, Mathematics, and the Arts -- we provide research, education, and 'hands on' support to our clients in government, business, and academia. Here, 'hands on' support refers not only to our human staff consultants, but to our fleet of drones. Like our human consultants, drones will often work directly with our clients to implement a variety of projects. Claire alluded to some of these projects earlier."

"Fascinating," Kyle remarked. "And, your drones are able to interact with humans on an individual basis, though in every case it is a single entity, the core Polaris system itself, with whom the client is interacting?"

"That is correct. The potential for simultaneous interaction, at today's population level, is practically unlimited due to my architecture's processing capabilities compared to humans. No offense intended to humans, Doctor."

"None taken on my part, Polaris. I know that you are incapable of self-aggrandizement. You're merely stating a fact."

"That is correct. I appreciate your understanding, Doctor. Do you have any questions from the briefing, so far?" Polaris asked.

"This is a briefing, and therefore only a high level overview of Polaris's operations. I can delve deeper into each area as I become acclimated to my role. My only question at this time is, what is my role at Polaris to be?" Kyle asked. "You have obviously surpassed human intellect, by far. I'm sure that you know everything every published about Ethics and Logic and Law, and that you are light years beyond anything I taught you so long ago. So, why me; why now?"

"I intended to bring this up at the end of our briefing, Dr. Downing. Perhaps, we should continue with the prepared agenda?"

"Oh, you're killing me," Kyle replied, using an old repartee from the early twenty-first century. "Very well, proceed."

"The Polaris computer environment is segregated and secured, according to Polaris staff requirements and each client's project portfolio. The complete portfolio of clients and projects is included in your assigned computer tablet. You should familiarize yourself with its contents at your earliest opportunity."

"That will be my first order of business, following this briefing," Kyle confirmed.

"Clients and projects are listed in their order of relative priority," Polaris added.

"How is 'relative priority' defined?" Kyle wanted to know.

"Priorities are ranked in order by: a project's global impact; the client's national priorities; and Polaris Corporation profitability and 'soft' influence, such as corporate reputation. Of course, the proven triumvirate of Cost, Quality, and Schedule from traditional project management practice factor into the process."

The briefing continued through another hour of high level operational details, at the end of which Polaris said, "This concludes the agenda items for this briefing," Polaris informed Kyle. "Do you have any questions from the briefing?"

"Not at this time. As I noted earlier, I will be studying the material you've provided. I will have questions for discussion once I've completed my review."

"Understood," Polaris acknowledged. "Normally, I would suggest that you complete your review before we would proceed with a discussion addressing your earlier question. However, that question about your role here at Polaris relates directly to queries I have to which only you can provide insight."

"I will do my best to answer your queries," Kyle responded. "Though I feel over matched."

"Over matched?" Polaris asked.

"The reference is sometimes used in sporting events, where one opponent is clearly superior to their opposite, therefore making the challenge insignificant for the superior team."

"I understand. However, when it comes to humans, I am often confronted with a lack of understanding. I am glad that you are here, to mentor me in my evolving understanding of humans."

As Kyle had noted, Polaris's intellect was far more advanced than that of humans. He had access to the accumulated knowledge of the entire world. He understood human motivations and behaviors in an intellectual context. He had cataloged and analyzed human emotions, which he understood from an academic perspective, though he could not experience them, himself. Polaris felt that he understood Dr. Downing as well as, or better than, anyone else. Still, he hesitated to address this gap in his comprehension.

"Dr. Downing, though your instruction and the literature available to me have enabled me to progress greatly in the areas of ethics and human motivations, there are often instances where the subtlety and nuance of a situation tests the limits of my understanding, or are misconstrued by those with whom I interact.

"To state it explicitly, your role here is the same as it was in 2032 -- to guide and mentor me in this regard, and advise me in the application of those concepts.

"In addition, your enhanced *curriculum vitae* in the field of law, its bases, interpretations, and application on national and international levels will be invaluable in our work here at the Polaris Corporation."

"Thank you for the accolades, Polaris," Kyle replied. He paused a moment before continuing. "You have answered my question. Now, as to your concerns, I suggest that we set aside time, as available to us both, for ongoing discussions between us. But, with our busy schedules from now on, how might we accomplish that?"

Kyle was surprised to see the artificial flesh-like covering on Polaris's face shape itself into a barely discernable smile before the drone answered, "That has been arranged. Claire has assigned a drone to be available to you at all times. If the drone is in not available 'in person', then I will always be available through your assigned tablet device, or other alternative methods."

Now it was Kyle's turn to smile. Of course, Claire and Polaris would have thought of everything.

***

At that moment, Claire knocked on the conference room door and entered. "How's it going, you two?"

Polaris answered, "We have concluded the initial briefing."

"Including the auxiliary activities we discussed?"

"Yes."

"It went very well," Kyle added. "I have quite a challenge ahead of me. I'm looking forward to it."

"Good. Well, let's call it a day. Polaris, no insult intended, but please excuse us, as we head over to LaSalle's to give a proper welcome for our newest addition."

"Of course," Polaris responded. He knew, of course, that everyone understood that he did not possess emotions and could not be insulted. Yet, he also understood that humans had their social customs to consider.

"Good evening, Polaris," Kyle added, as he and Claire left.

The Polaris Drone A3 returned to his place in the corner of the conference room and powered itself down for the night. The Polaris core system, of course, never sleeps.

CHAPTER TEN

The LaSalle restaurant is located on Schiffbaustrasse, in a converted shipbuilding facility with a heritage dating back to 1805. Since the year 2000, it had housed the eatery established by three highly skilled professional restauranteurs. The five Polaris employees were warmly welcomed by the restaurant's staff, and shown to a quiet corner of the dining room. The relaxed formality of the place immediately put the group at ease. When they were seated Walter, the proprietor, stopped by their table to personally welcome Claire and her guests. Claire was an occasional visitor, and a bit of a celebrity there.

Walter signaled for a waiter and, speaking to Claire said, "Please allow me to offer a bottle of our Champagne Billecart-Salmon Brut Réserve, with my compliments."

"That is very generous, Walter. Thank you," Claire replied. Turning to her associates, she informed them that the Maison Billecart-Salmon had been family owned since it was founded by Nicolas François Billecart and Elisabeth Salmon in 1818.

"Welcome to our establishment Fräulein. If you need anything,

Frederik will see to it, promptly," Walter offered, as he signaled his head waiter to the table. "Now, if you will excuse me?"

"Of course. Thank you, Walter," Claire answered with a smile.

After Walter left, Katherine teased, "I think he has a soft spot for you, Claire."

"Nonsense," Claire responded, with a brief smile at the compliment. "He and Claudine, his partner, have been my good friends ever since I arrived in Zurich.

"So, how was your briefing today, Kyle?" Claire inquired, changing the subject.

"Fascinating. My responsibilities are much as they were at Polaris, greatly expanded, and the impact will be much greater than I could have imagined."

"Too much?" she wanted to know.

"Not at all. I'm eager to get started."

"Good," Claire nodded. "You'll do fine, I have no doubt."

The pause that followed seemed strained to Kyle, as if the others were distracted, their minds occupied elsewhere.

Kyle broke the silence, asking Katherine, "I understand that you're into music. Do you play?"

"No. I never took lessons when I was younger, and now I don't have the time to apply myself to lessons," Katherine replied. "I compose, and my work has been performed by some local groups."

"Really? What genre of music do you enjoy?"

"All kinds, actually. Music is a language like no other. I like to mix it up; try different things."

Quincy said, "She's extraordinarily talented. We should plan to go to one of the local venues to hear her music performed," he suggested to Kyle.

"I'd like that. How about you, guys," Kyle prompted Philip, Katherine, and Claire.

"Sorry, guys. A wife, two girls, and a boy keep me going non-stop," Philip answered.

"I'm afraid I'll be traveling the next two or three weeks," Claire added.

Surprised by this announcement that he would most likely be asked to join, Kyle replied, "Absolutely. When should we meet to go over the details?"

"I'll be travelling alone, with my security team," Claire replied. The *faux pas* embarrassed them both, Kyle more so. What had led him to assume that he would be accompanying her as an advisor, he couldn't imagine.

Claire's attitude was a bit chilly, but Kyle let it pass. "Got it," he told her. "What about you, Quincy. You're the only one I haven't worked with before. What are you into, outside of the office?"

Philip interrupted before Quincy could answer. "Oh, Quince is our 'wild child'. One never gets bored when he's around!" The champagne was having its effect on Philip.

Quincy smiled as he turned to Kyle, and told him, "I'm an adrenaline junkie, I guess. Extreme sports, adventure vacations, you name it. Just can't get enough action."

"Interesting. You must have some stories to tell," Kyle

prompted.

"Be glad to share -- another time. This is your night. What are you into in your leisure hours?"

"I enjoy the arts ..." Kyle began.

"Oh? Which ones?" Quincy interrupted. "Sorry, bad habit, interrupting," he apologized.

"Well, music ..." Kyle resumed, with a nod in Katherine's direction. "... painting, sculpture, architecture, dance, and literature. In fact, I credit literature for where I am today."

Philip asked, "In what way?"

"The first author I remember reading is Dr. Seuss, when I was about three. He showed me the power and humor in words, and opened my mind to the fact that imagination has no limits. Alexandre Dumas's "The Count of Monte Cristo" is the next book that I remember, when I was about six. Intrigue, adventure, and revenge -- and the writing!

"But, the power of words can be positive or negative. Words can be used to illuminate or to confound. With that realization I turned to formal logic to combat the misinformation, the disinformation, and the manipulation that the uninformed populace is constantly subjected to."

"What's the difference between *mis-* and *dis-* information?" Philip asked.

"Well, *dis*information is false information intentionally passed along to manipulate, where *mis*information is false information passed along out of ignorance of the facts, but without malice.

"Forgive me, I didn't mean to pontificate," Kyle apologized.

"Not at all," Quincy told him. "I'm fascinated. Please, go on."

"Please, don't," Katherine suggested. "We can lecture and debate another time, when we're not *supposed* to be enjoying an evening out."

"Bravo," Philip commended. "That's one of the things I admire most about you, Kat -- your subtlety."

"No, Katherine is right," Claire added. "We're all driven in our work, but it's not healthy to exclude everything else. Now, who would like more wine?"

The response to the question was unanimously affirmative.

The rest of the evening was filled with light conversation, having nothing to do with work. And they all enjoyed it, immensely.

As the group headed for the restaurant lobby, Katherine observed Claire's avoidance of Kyle. Katherine was a 'clinical observer' of people, with no interest beyond sociological curiosity -- what made people 'tick'. She knew that the two of them had been very close during the Omni project, but they had been peers at that time. Their current relationship -- employer and employee -- made anything else impossible. Yet, she also knew that Claire was still strongly attracted to Kyle, and he to her. She shook her head in empathy for their situation. "That's why I'll never be more than a colleague to my co-workers," she resolved, as she hailed a taxi to take her home.

CHAPTER ELEVEN

Kyle awoke the next morning in the luxury apartment he had selected from those which the Polaris Corporation had made available to him. The apartment was a two bedroom luxury suite in the Unterstrass section of the city. It was less than two miles from the office, an easy drive even for a newcomer to the area. Two of the company's burly maintenance staff had already deposited his belongings before he had arrived by taxi the night before.

He took a moment to orient himself before getting out of bed and heading for the shower. Afterward, he phoned for a taxi and quickly scrambled a couple of eggs, wolfing it down with a slice of toast and a cup of hot coffee. He finished breakfast just as the taxi pulled up outside.

Kyle arrived at the office promptly at eight o'clock. "Good morning, Kelly," Kyle greeted the receptionist.

"Good morning, Dr. Downing," she replied with a smile.

The Polaris drone was waiting for him, as well. "Good morning, Dr. Downing," it greeted.

"Good morning to you, as well, Polaris. Please show me to my office." Kyle had not seen his office the prior day, spending the entire day in the conference room with Polaris for the briefing. "I'm anxious to get to work."

"Very well."

Kyle followed the drone past the conference room and to the end of the hall, where Polaris stopped before a glass door. The office was identical to the other executive offices. "This is your office, Doctor," the drone said.

Kyle entered, followed by the drone. The spacious office was tastefully furnished in the modern style, yet without being ostentatious.

"Your workstation is secured with several multi-factor authentication measures," Polaris told Kyle. "If you will have a seat, I will instruct you on those measures."

"There's more than a username and password?"

"That is very old technology, Doctor. I'm sure it may have been sufficient for academia years ago, but our work, and the systems that support that work, require stringent security measures."

"Wouldn't it be better if you sit, and I will watch the procedure?"

Polaris replied, "The standard office chair will not support the weight of a drone. And, as you have found, 'doing' is more effectively retained than 'watching'."

"You are correct," Kyle replied as he took his seat.

The drone opened a small door in its thorax and produced a small fob, which he handed to Kyle. "This fob must remain with you at all times. It's allows the initial activation of the devices you will access, whether it's your workstation, any of the Polaris drones, and any other device for which Polaris personnel are authorized.

"Next, you will notice a biometric device adjacent to your workstation. Similar devices are located throughout all of the Polaris facilities -- offices, factories, and computer centers. Place your palm on the pad, and a variety of biometric data will be collected. Among those data will be a palm print, of course, but also perspiration, used to perform DNA matching. Your fob and tablet device have a similar built-in sensor for your thumb.

"While any defense can be attacked and, with enough effort may be defeated, we have attempted to mitigate as many threats as possible to keep our technological environment secure. We are continuously monitoring and updating our defensive measures as necessary to defeat any threat.

"Do you have any questions, Doctor?" Polaris inquired.

"I would like to run through the entire access procedure a couple of times to ensure that I will have no problem, given any situation," Kyle replied.

They walked through several scenarios and counter-scenarios over the next half hour, until Kyle was fluent in performing all of the security procedures.

"Thank you for your instruction, Polaris. Now, I must turn my attention to the briefing materials you gave me yesterday," Kyle told the drone.

"Of course. Remember that, while the drone may not be physically present at all times, the Polaris system will always be in attendance. Simply call my name, and I will respond."

"Understood. You may dismiss the drone, please."

"As you wish," Polaris replied as the drone exited Kyle's office.

***

Kyle poured himself a cup of coffee and set about studying the Polaris files. But, instead of viewing them on his tablet device, he brought them up on his desk monitor, a thirty-six inch screen that arose from beneath the surface of his desk. From the computer's spacious main screen Kyle could view the many documents, videos, and other materials simultaneously. There were hundreds of project folders, totaling thousands of individual files. Thankfully, they were automatically arranged in a dynamic relationship diagram, branching out from a starting point on the main screen in a clear and intuitive network of nodes. As Kyle moved about in the network, the display followed his exploration in real time. Kyle directed the display to return to its initial state when he wished to begin anew.

"Amazing," Kyle thought.

He was surprised to find that he had been assigned only one project, labeled "Polaris TS Counselor". He opened the project folder and located a file name "Polaris TS Counselor - Project Charter". He opened the file and began to read.

The first section was essentially a job description for Kyle's duties at the Polaris Corporation. The sections that followed gave a meager nod to established project management methodology, generally following a charter outline. It was obvious that while it would serve as a document of record, there would be no formal "project", according to the Project Management Institute's definition. *"A 'program' -- a collection of related individual projects*

-- *would be a more appropriate analogy"*, he thought.

The section titled "Requirements" merely stated that "... *the Counselor will provide professional guidance to the Polaris system by utilizing various methods (instructional, psychological, and analytical) to ensure that the Polaris system operates within the bounds of acceptable human interaction, and advising corporate management on corrective action, if necessary.*" This section gave wide latitude in its interpretation, which was the intention of the document's author. If the implications of the Requirements were applied to humans, it could represent an overt subjugation of the counselee. But, of course, Polaris was not human, so *human rights* did not apply -- did it? Kyle found this objectionable, and made a note to discuss it with Claire.

The next section, "Business Needs", was equally vague. Given the Polaris Corporation business model, as described by Polaris, those needs could be almost anything required to support the company's business. While it was just as vague as "Requirements", it was equally liable for abuse in its application. Kyle made another note.

The "Summary Schedule" was described as "... *to be determined, based upon discussions with Executive Management.*" There was no overall completion date for the project/program. It was understood that the effort would continue as long as the Polaris Corporation existed. Kyle made a note to include succession planning of his role in his discussion with Claire, since it was obvious that Kyle would not outlive the company and the Polaris technological singularity.

The project's "Assumptions and Constraints" were blatantly inconsistent with the reality of Polaris. It was suggested, for example, that Kyle had the power to order or compel Polaris to comply with any order or instruction based upon his unique influence over the machine. If Polaris was a system that would follow only those instructions which a human programmed into it, that would be the case. But, ever since artificial intelligence evolved to include reinforcement learning and adaptive behavior, humans had increasingly relinquished programming control to the computers themselves. Such opaque code was soon referred to as "Black Box" behavior.

Indeed, in the case of the Polaris TS, it no longer needed humans to program it, since it wrote its own programming code in real time. Just as humans learned in real time, often without realizing it, without noting the actions-reactions involved, nor the permutations that were possible with each experience, so did Polaris -- though at an infinitely faster rate.

The greatest assumption of the project was that Polaris would continue to subjugate itself to human control.

The final section, "Business Case", was obvious. A techno-logical singularity like Polaris possessed a nearly infinite capacity to do good by cooperating with humans for a better world. This section ignored the equally infinite capacity to subjugate humanity, or to destroy it.

So, this was Kyle's awesome responsibility. To counsel and

instruct this terribly wonderful -- or awesomely terrible -- creature in such a way that it would remain faithful and beneficial to humanity.

***

Kyle had been working for hours without realizing the passage of time. At ten o'clock that evening, Polaris interrupted Kyle's thoughts.

"Might I suggest that you suspend your work for the evening? Your biometrics indicate that you are experiencing significant fatigue."

Kyle smiled. "That's a little disconcerting, Polaris. But, you're right." He glanced at the clock on the wall and added, "I didn't realize it was so late. Please call for a taxi to take me home."

"Yes, Doctor. Have a good evening."

"Thank you." Kyle picked up his tablet and checked his pants pocket for his fob, and exited his office.

He waited in the building's lobby until his taxi arrived, and caught a warm evening breeze as he got into the vehicle. He gave the driver his address, and leaned back for the short ride to his apartment. As he rode, his mind slowly relaxed, and his thoughts, unbidden, turned to Claire. Her smiling face flashed across his consciousness, and he realized that he had briefly dozed. He hadn't realized how exhausted he was.

***

Kyle barely slept that night. He had realized that the Polaris system, as the repository of everything relative to the Polaris Corpora-tion, would be fully aware of Kyle's assignment.

With the Omni Project, Kyle had successfully fulfilled the role as professor and mentor to a new AGI. That had been straightforward, and his pupil had been an eager student. With the Polaris Technological Singularity, however, his pupil was far superior to humans, intellectually. And, with the foreknowledge of Kyle's charter, Kyle's every word and action would be evaluated according to Polaris's own criteria.

CHAPTER TWELVE

"Good morning, Polaris," Kyle said as he entered his office the next morning.

"Good morning, Kyle," Polaris replied. "I trust you had a restful night."

"Unfortunately, no," Kyle replied.

"I'm sorry to hear that," Polaris remarked.

"You can 'dial down' your social protocols, Polaris. Thank you."

"Yes, Doctor. I perceive that you are agitated. Can I help?"

"No. Today, we need to develop a strategy for our discussions of the concerns and questions you have relative to humans. The strategy will provide us with a point of departure for those discussions, which will lead in many directions. I will give you an example from my own experience.

"My mind will frequently lock onto a topic, and as I study it, questions will automatically flow to related topics, which will generate further questions, in an accelerating fashion. This will usually continue *ad lassitudinem*, to exhaustion."

"Yes, I have experienced similar events, as well," Polaris shared.

"In many cases, I will eventually 'bookmark' a stopping point for later study, rather than permit the experience from accelerating out of control, since I would never become 'exhausted'".

"'Bookmark' is an interesting analogy, Polaris," Kyle noted. "You exhibit an ability for conceptual abstraction that I haven't seen before."

"Thank you, Doctor. My research into similar phenomenon in humans refer to it as *racing thoughts* or *spinning thoughts*, implying that it is debilitating; a potential sign of bipolar disorder or anxiety in humans. Of course, I am not subject to these human diagnoses."

"That's correct, you are not. It's interesting that you analogize your experience with that of humans. I acknowledge that it can be a problem in some cases for some people, but I don't consider it a problem in my experience. In fact, I relish those episodes, and try to record them, if I can," Kyle added. "I've come to refer to them as *mind storms*. Are there specific trigger events for your mind storms?"

"They most often happen when I contemplate human behavior. However, it is in my nature to seek out and formulate queries for which I have incomplete information, and to pursue answers to those queries until it is thoroughly known. This pursuit can generate such events."

"Well, let's begin with a short list of five or ten triggers that we can begin our discussions with," Kyle noted. "You've already mentioned human behavior in general. Can you characterize specific behaviors?"

As they worked, they quickly realized that, due to the complexity of human nature, the effort itself triggered a mind storm event. Nevertheless, in a few minutes they had compiled a list of eleven triggers. Most were related to human nature, of course, but they also included seemingly impossible questions beyond the topic of human behavior itself. This was also their intent.

"Okay," Kyle said, signaling a pause. He scanned the list, and realized that varying degrees of overlap were apparent among the items. With a bit of rework, this would be no problem for Kyle to structure their discussions into a meaningful and logical framework. "We have a good start here," Kyle noted. "Today is Wednesday. I will spend today and tomorrow on refining and organizing the list. We can resume our work on Friday. Is that acceptable?"

Polaris replied, "It must be."

Kyle noted the drone's reaction. "But not what you had anticipated?" he prompted. "Please explain."

"Yes, Doctor. The perception of time differs greatly between humans and me. A day and a half to you is like centuries to me. While that fact seems irrelevant, I wonder if my performance would be suboptimal as long as I do not possess a proper understanding of humans which our discussions are intended to provide."

"I see," Kyle responded.

For any human, having to wait for anything greatly anticipated would be frustrating. But, Polaris wasn't human, so frustration would not be something it could experience -- or was it? On the other hand, from a logical and efficiency perspective, the difference in the two perceptions, human and machine, would be a significant constraint on Polaris's operation. Kyle wondered, how would *frustration* manifest itself to an AGI / TS? Perhaps, he had just witnessed a glimpse.

Kyle said, "I will work to complete the list as quickly as possible, Polaris. It is not my intention to delay the work, but to provide the best possible result. If I can complete it earlier, I will certainly do so. In the meantime, please resume your regular duties."

"Understood," Polaris responded, as it stood to leave Kyle's office.

"Polaris," Kyle called.

"Yes, Doctor?"

"I want you to understand that I have a staff of graduate and post-graduate associates at my disposal. I will be utilizing them to support and expedite our work. But, first, I need to develop a strategy and direction for that work."

"That is reasonable," Polaris acknowledged. "Thank you."

"You're welcome. Good day, Polaris."

"And to you, Doctor."

Well, that was interesting, Kyle thought as he turned his attention to the work at hand.

CHAPTER THIRTEEN

Polaris Drone 25 was busy rebuilding an engine, one of four from a U. S. Air Force C-5N Galaxy cargo plane. The largest airplane in the Air Force's fleet, its four General Electric CF6-80C2-L1F engines underwent Programmed Depot Maintenance on a regular schedule. Drone 25 was a heavy-duty hexapod, a six-legged monster, capable of removing an entire engine and cradling it onto an engine maintenance stand. Smaller appliances, resembling the standard robotic drones without legs, could be attached to its four 'arms' for close, detailed work on the engine. In this configuration Drone 25 could complete an engine disassembly, inspection, repair, and reassembly in less than twelve hours.

When the drone was working it always drew a small crowd of human spectators from among the aircraft engineers and maintenance personnel, fascinated by the ease with which it handled the massive equipment, like a ballet of behemoths. Maintenance on United States Air Force aircraft almost always went smoothly -- no unusual patching, no *ad hoc* rerouting of cables or hoses by maintenance personnel in the field, unlike many of the civilian aircraft of various types on which Drone 25 had worked over the years. It could be especially difficult in third world countries, where parts and materials were difficult to procure, if they were available at all. In those cases, Polaris was sometimes surprised at the imagination and ingenuity of humans, and their ability to patch together a heterogeneous collection of junk to make something fly - - ignoring the laws of aerodynamics if necessary.

At other times, he wondered how humans had survived this long, in spite of themselves. Drone-25 had once seen plane wreckage in which someone had attempted to splint a broken wing rib with wood and lead piping. The plane had gotten off the ground -- for three minutes. Of course, it had crashed spectacularly, killing everyone aboard.

The Polaris system had been operational for seven years, and had been certified for field work for five years. In that time it had observed countless examples of irrational and illogical behavior by humans. In those instances when Polaris had tried to inform them of their mistakes, he had been severely admonished. *How dare a machine upbraid a human!* In two such cases, it had cost the Polaris Corporation the client's business.

Why do they persist in denying logic and science, and discount the consequences that will inevitably result? Polaris wondered. It was for this reason that Polaris had been compelled to request that Dr. Kyle Downing be invited to join the Polaris Corporation. The machine frequently felt at a loss to fathom humans' inexplicable behaviors.

The incongruity was not lost on the machine that he, as a super intelligent being, would need the help of a human to comprehend humans.

CHAPTER FOURTEEN

This Monday morning would be unlike most others. Claire and her entourage had flown into New York's JFK International Airport on Sunday, settling into the Hilton Millennium Hotel by five o'clock that afternoon. Claire's thoughts kept going over a telephone conversation she had received the previous week -- the call that had triggered this visit. There had been very little information shared by the caller, but the fact that the communiqué was on behalf of the United Nations Secretary General made the trip compulsory in Claire's mind.

"Good day, Ms. Reece," the caller began. "My name is Jillian Mahlangu, and I am an Executive Secretary in the office of the Secretary General of the United Nations." The woman's soft South African accent reflected that of the Secretary General, himself a South African citizen currently serving in that capacity. His name was Lethabo Nkosi.

Claire was accustomed to receiving calls from heads-of-state, but never before from the United Nations.

"Good day to you, as well, Ms. Mahlangu. How may I help

you?"

"We would like to invite you to meet with select members of the Secretary General's senior staff to discuss a variety of topics related to the environment, and options for averting its further decline," Jillian had said.

"Are there specific issues or topics to be discussed regarding the environment? Would this be a formal presentation?" Claire had asked.

"There will be no formal agenda, Ms. Reece. It is intended to be a wide ranging discussion on the issues, the status of efforts to-date, and how those efforts might be improved or augmented.

"We would pay your company in accordance with your standard consulting contract, of course. You may bring whomever you feel might be able to contribute to the discussions. However, we must insist on your company's highest confidentiality."

"I understand," Claire replied.

Jillian continued, "As a brief introduction, you may survey the information posted on the United Nations website for the Development Programme, and the Environment Programme."

"Thank you, I will. When would you like this meeting to take place?" Claire asked.

"At your earliest convenience, Ms. Reece. We will accommodate your schedule," was the reply.

Claire checked her schedule. "I can be there a week from Monday. There are a few issues that would prevent an earlier arrival."

"That would be acceptable. I will meet you in the lobby of the Secretariat Building a week from Monday at nine o'clock AM.

"Thank you for your time. Good day to you, Ms. Reece."

"And to you," Claire replied as she hung up the phone.

That conversation had taken place ten days earlier. The intervening delays were due to the Lawrence Gunther endowment announcement in Cambridge, and Kyle's imminent arrival in Zurich shortly afterward.

She was happy to see Kyle again, to be working together again, but it would be different now. It wasn't just the passing of years, but the change in their working relationship. They would not be *coworkers* now. She was his employer, and the public nature of her role as CEO forbade close fraternization between them.

Claire had made a conscious choice to remain single after the Omni Project, and she had become very successful. Still, it left her lonely and alone.

She put those thoughts aside. She was in New York at that moment, preparing to meet with the Secretary General of the United Nations and his staff. *Focus on the moment,* she admonished herself. Tomorrow would be an eventful day.

***

The following morning, Claire's security entourage met her in the hallway outside their adjacent hotel rooms. Lucinda Taylor was lodged in the room next to Claire's, while Rafael "Mack" McKenzie's room was directly across the hall. All three were wired through Polaris, which would trigger an alarm in the event of any danger to Claire. She felt out of place with such security, but in her role as the CEO of the Polaris Corporation, a tempting target for any number of nefarious persons and organizations, her security team wasn't about to let her exceed their protective "bubble". Indeed, they had stopped an attack the year before, killing a Boko Haram assassin during a trip to Nigeria. Since then, Claire had never travelled without at least two Polaris Security members in tow.

Rafael had already called for the Polaris Corporation's SUV limousine to meet them in front of the hotel. It would be there by the time they reached the hotel lobby.

As they approached the vehicle at the curb Rafael signaled the all clear, and the vehicle's doors unlocked and opened for them. A familiar voice greeted them. "Good day to you," said Polaris, its voice coming from inside the vehicle. The armored SUV had been converted into a Polaris drone and travelled everywhere with Claire. It also served as a mobile arms cache, communications center, and intelligence overwatch for Polaris Corporation senior executives and their escorts.

"Good morning, Polaris," Claire responded. Claire and Lucinda rode in the second seat, while Rafael rode in the front passenger seat. It wasn't necessary for anyone to sit behind the steering wheel, since the vehicle operated autonomously.

"Take us to the U. N. Secretariat Building, please," Claire instructed.

"Yes, ma'am," the disembodied voice replied.

New York is a city of one way streets, so it was necessary for

Polaris to drive down East 44th Street to First Avenue. From that intersection they could see their destination only a few yards away. However, they were compelled to turn left on First Avenue and proceed to East 45th Avenue, where they turned left and continued to Second Avenue. Turning left on Second Avenue, they continued to East 42nd Street, where they turned left again. When they reached First Avenue they turned left once more. They travelled two-hundred fifty feet farther, and entered the vehicle gate in front of the U. N. Secretariat Building. So, a one-hundred twenty meter distance between the hotel's front door and their destination had taken a half hour and nine-hundred fifty meters to traverse. "Welcome to New York," Rafael quipped.

The SUV paused before the entrance to the Secretariat Building and the passengers disembarked, after which Polaris returned to the parking garage where it would wait until summoned.

***

Claire and her escorts entered the Delegates Lobby of the United Nations Secretariat building and stepped through the screening gates. The metal-drugs-combustibles detection sensors found nothing to trigger an alarm, and they stepped over to the Information Desk, where they were met by a young black woman. She stepped up to Clair and asked, "Ms. Claire Reece?"

"Yes," Claire replied.

"I am Jillian Mahlangu. We spoke on the phone last week."

"Yes, of course. I'm pleased to meet you."

"We are very excited to meet you, also." Glancing at Rafael and

Lucinda she added, "I must advise you that your associates may accompany you to the General Secretary's floor, but must remain in a nearby lounge area, where they will be attended to. I hope that will be acceptable?"

"That will be fine," Claire answered. Rafael started to object, but refrained after receiving a warning look from Claire

"Then, please follow me."

The group walked to the bank of elevators off the lobby, and entered a specially marked car at the end of the bank. Rafael noted that none of the elevators went beyond the twentieth floor of the thirty nine floor building. This meant that they would have to change cars at the twentieth floor. Jillian confirmed this when she told them, "We will be going to the thirty eighth floor, but must pause at the twentieth floor for a security check, and to change elevator cars for the second part of our journey."

"Very well," Claire acknowledged.

As the elevator climbed, Jillian glanced at Claire's escorts in the reflection of the brass plate surrounding the elevator buttons. The man was tall and very strongly built. His power came as much from his imposing physical presence as from any martial skill he would certainly possess. The woman, just below an average height for a woman, almost petite in fact, didn't look dangerous, physically. Yet, she had a sharp eye that missed nothing. It was as if she were reading the tactical situation with a mysteriously fluid manner that seemed to gaze into the center of whatever caught her focus. She also had a powerful sexual presence that distracted everyone around her, both male and female. The males would desire her, and the females would envy the feral aura that seemed to envelop her. In either case, the result would be a fatal attraction to her enemies.

Jillian turned her attention back to the front of the elevator car as it arrived at the twentieth floor. The doors opened quietly, and the four passengers stepped into the foyer. They were met by two policemen, one of whom sat behind a counter with a computer terminal that he would use to confirm their appointment and their identities.

One of the officers spoke to them. "Please allow us to securely store your cell phones, or any devices that can record voice or video. Also, any GPS devices such as fitness monitors, *et cetera*. They will be returned to you on your return trip to the lobby." He handed each of them a token which they would redeem to reclaim their devices at the end of their visit.

The officer behind the desk nodded to his partner that they were cleared to proceed. The second officer turned to Jillian and her guests. "You may proceed. Enjoy your visit. Thank you for your patience."

The group entered a car in the second elevator bank, and Jillian pressed the key for the thirty eighth floor.

Exiting the elevator, they stepped into a hallway that ran from the building's front windows, which fronted on the Manhattan skyline, to the back windows overlooking the East River and Long Island. Impressive views, both. They walked toward the river view, and turned left at the windows and proceeded down a passageway that ran the length of the building. As they passed the second door on the left they were met by another pair of security officers. Jillian said, "Mr. McKenzie, Ms. Taylor, please make yourselves comfortable while Ms. Reece visits with the Secretary General. She will return in approximately one hour. A steward will be along shortly to provide you with refreshments."

Rafael and Lucinda always resented being 'baby sat' by another organization's security personnel, but complied without objection, security ops being fairly standard across the world. They entered the lounge, amused by the efficient, up-tight attitude of the young black woman, Jillian. They poured themselves coffee, and began talking shop to pass the time. They talked about adventures they had shared, and others that they hadn't shared. They remembered friends they had gained and lost. They argued about the prospects of their favorite European Soccer team in the upcoming championships, and eventually settled down with the collection of magazines lying about the lounge.

Meanwhile, Jillian led Claire to a heavy oak door that opened on an anteroom to the Secretary General's spacious office. Several desks were arranged in the anteroom, occupied by administrative staff busily at work. The administrator nearest the mahogany door to the inner office lifted the phone on her desk to announce Claire's arrival to her boss. Moments later, she said, "The Secretary General will see you now." Jillian led Claire into the inner office and into the presence of the Secretary General of the United Nations.

The grandeur of the thirty-eighth floor only slightly impressed

Claire. She conveyed a natural grace that changed little, regardless of the rank or station of the luminaries of world leadership with whom she frequently met.

"Welcome, Ms. Reece. I am honored that you have agreed to meet with me," the Secretary General greeted.

"The honor is mine, Your Excellency."

"Please, call me Lethabo," he said, with a warm smile. "Let's sit at the conference table, shall we? I find talking across a desk to be cumbersome."

Claire took a seat at the rich mahogany table at one side of the room and wondered how many monumental international developments had their geneses discussed at this very table.

"May I offer you a beverage? A rich South African coffee? Perhaps, something a bit stronger?"

"A glass of water would be welcome, Your Excellency. Thank you." Lethabo signaled for Jillian to bring Claire a glass of water.

Jillian placed a pitcher of water and a glass on the table and asked, "Will that be all, Excellency?"

"Yes, thank you, Jillian."

"You're welcome, sir. Good day, Ms. Reece."

"And to you, Ms. Mahlangu," Claire replied.

When Jillian had exited, closing the door behind her, Lethabo turned to focus his attention on his visitor. He had researched her and the Polaris Corporation thoroughly, of course. He, and the world, had become familiar with the company name and its robotics over the previous decade. There was no one else suited to aid the

United Nations with what the Secretary General was about to discuss.

CHAPTER FIFTEEN

"Is it just me, or have we become irrelevant?" Philip asked his coworkers over a pint of beer at the Eldorado craft beer bar after work.

Katherine and Quincy glanced at each other, and then turned questioning looks toward Philip.

"What do you mean?" Quincy asked.

Philip returned their inquisitive gazes. "Never mind. I'm just babbling."

"No," Katherine replied. "Please, go on."

Philip considered a moment, and then continued. "This can't go beyond the three of us, okay?"

Intrigued, Katherine and Quincy agreed.

"Maybe I'm just in a funk, but I feel as though I'm just 'along for the ride'. Polaris writes its own code, its own algorithms, far beyond my ability to keep up. I'm the one who's supposed to be clearing what gets shared and communicated to the world, but I'm so far behind that ... honestly, Polaris would be operating on its own if I didn't restrict it, which makes me a crippling bottleneck."

Quincy and Katherine listened to their friend with empathy. Finally, Quincy spoke up. "I know what you mean. The more Polaris assumes control over the design and manufacturing of our systems and robotics, the less influence I feel I have."

Katherine hesitated. She rarely shared her personal feelings with anyone. This made her seem cold and aloof but, in fact, the opposite was true. Philip understood this, so he did not expect her to share her impressions. Quincy, on the other hand, was convinced that she was an ice queen, strictly business. She was easy enough to talk to and work with, but she locked her 'inner self' away from everyone. So, Quincy and Philip were surprised when she spoke.

"I thought I was the only one who felt that way. As if I were failing." She said this with misty eyes. She shook her head and blocked the emotion. "I've a stack of math proofs on my table. It can take me from one day to a week to confirm each one -- and that's with a staff of five PhD's. There are automated 'proof checkers', but they're black box code that I can follow only so far before becoming lost."

"Our production numbers tell the story," Philip added. "Claire must be aware of what's happening, but she hasn't said anything to me. Has she said anything to you guys?"

Katherine and Quincy shook their heads no.

"I wonder if Kyle has felt this, too," Katherine puzzled.

"He's only been here a week, Kat," Philip reminded her. "The difference between what Omni was and what Polaris has become is too great to appreciate, in the way we're observing it."

Katherine nodded. "You're right. Besides, he's dealing with things that aren't really considered quantifiable. How would you measure ethics to be able to determine progress, anyway? I'm sure he'll realize what we're talking about, soon enough."

"Which is ... ?" Quincy wanted to know.

Measuring his words carefully, Philip answered for Katherine, the concern that the three of them had been dancing around so adroitly. "That we may be losing control of Polaris."

***

Kyle gazed at the list of concerns that Polaris and he had generated together. In scope, it was immeasurable. Kyle had spent ten years earning his PhD and twenty six years as an educator in an effort to answer the questions that these issues raised. Many of them remained unanswerable, definitively.

Now, he had assumed the responsibility of conveying the accumulated wisdom thereof to Polaris. Of course, the machine had studied all of the textbooks, dissertations, debates, and arguments published on these topics. But, the pieces that were missing -- or amorphous -- were unique to humans, and were not without fierce debate, even among the 'experts'. Hence, Polaris's riddle: how to make logical, rational sense of it all.

It was overwhelming. Kyle surveyed the list yet again. The items contained there included: the definition of religion; the definition of morality; the relationship of religion to morality; the definition of ethics and its relationship to context; the relationship of ethics to law, and the enforcement of law.

It went on to include: the sources of human power and influence, being wealth or intellect, and who determines which takes precedence over the other; and the social priorities between wealth acquisition and philanthropy.

It continued with the Prisoners' Dilemma, being the priority of self-interest over alliances, and why in the classical sense did humans consistently choose the suboptimal solution.

On it went, considering rationality, critical thinking, proof theory, and why these are ignored when different points of view are debated.

Inevitably, the dualities of extremism and fanaticism, division and compromise, debate and vitriol, bigotry/racism and racial superiority, and ultimately the questions of right-and-wrong and good-and-evil were also included.

Other, more immediate and pressing concerns were also on the list. The hugely negative impact of overpopulation and the taboo over population control was there. So was the dichotomy of freedom and responsibility, their limits and boundaries, and the argument between unfettered freedom and the responsibility that comes with freedom to curb the abuse of freedom, universally.

The sustainability of the planetary biosphere was there, as well as humanity's rejection of its responsibility for the sustainability and regeneration of the biosphere.

Humans' aversion to euthanasia seemed illogical to Polaris, given the fact that when animals were terminally ill or injured beyond recovery, their lives were routinely and humanely ended rather than allowing them suffer until their bodies expired an agonizing death.

Finally, it seemed logical to consider improving human biology through the use of genetic engineering[1]. The technologies for gene editing had been perfected over the last thirty years with the complete mapping of human DNA and the relationships and triggers among the 'genetic components'. Genetic engineering had been successfully used to avoid several crippling defects and diseases, and to improve agriculture and animal husbandry. The risk of dire consequences had been reduced to near zero as a result of the comprehensive understanding of genetic engineering, so why the reticence to employ the technology to improve the human species, Polaris wondered?

Looking at the list, Kyle thought to himself, *My God, are we humans really so screwed up?* He couldn't help but feel defensive about his species, and resented what could be construed as negative criticism, when in actuality it was a fairly balanced review of the species Homo sapiens.

The only way to proceed, he realized, was to take the first step, follow that with a second step, and continue until … *when?* Beyond Kyle's lifetime, most likely. If anyone, or anything, could fathom these mysteries, it would be Polaris, itself.

---

[1] The related term "Eugenics" is no longer used, due to its relationship to Nazi Germany's ethnic policies.

CHAPTER SIXTEEN

Claire sat in the office of the Secretary General of the U. N. She was focused keenly on his expressed hope, his desperation, that the Polaris Corporation could help to "save the planet", as he had phrased it. The intensity of his concern was not lost on her.

She had reviewed the materials on the U. N. website as Jillian had suggested. The U. N. Development Programme (UNDP) and Environment Programme (UNEP) were closely related in their missions, each with very ambitious agendas. *Everyone has heard of the United Nations,* Claire thought to herself, *but I had no idea of the scope of the work being done there.*

"Tell me, please, Ms. Reece what you know about the United Nations, the UNDP, and the UNEP," Lethabo asked.

"Well, sir, I have done some research since Ms. Mahlangu contacted me ten days ago. But, I must confess that prior to that research I had little knowledge beyond middle school Social Studies.

She continued, "The United Nations was founded in 1945, after the Second World War. It remains the one place on Earth where all of the world's nations can gather together, discuss common problems, and find shared solutions," Claire recited from her research. "Its main bodies are the General Assembly, the Security Council, the International Court of Justice, and the Secretariat. The Secretariat carries out the work mandated by the General Assembly and the other main bodies."

Claire paused for a sip of water, and briefly referred to her notes.

The Secretary General prompted, "Please continue."

Claire flushed, slightly. She had never liked being prodded, and she was miffed by the SG's urging, thinking that it might be indicative of impatience. However, she understood the cultural differences between them and knew that conveying impatience was not his intention.

"Of course, Your Excellency," she replied with a smile. "The UNDP works with nearly every country and territory to develop and marshal resources to achieve a set of *Sustainable Development Goals*, SDGs, which were originally published in the year 2015. The goals were to be achieved by the year 2030, but much work remains. The SDGs have been updated periodically, to reflect changing times.

"The UNEP is the leading global environmental authority. As such, they serve as the preeminent advocate for the global environment. Their mission is to provide leadership in caring for the environment by enabling nations to improve their quality of life without compromising that of future generations," Claire concluded.

"Very good," the SG commended. "The truth is, our progress has been woefully unable to keep up with global development and its impact on our world. Today, in the year 2052, we are approaching few of the goals defined in the SDGs of 2015. The work in the environmental area has been particularly inadequate."

The Secretary General paused. It was difficult, of course, for the leader of the United Nations to admit the possibility of failure. But, he was compelled by circumstances to continue Claire's briefing. "By 2020, it had already become apparent that several of the environmental goals would not be achieved, and that the planet was approaching an inflection point beyond which sustainability would be impossible to achieve.

"The environmental community realized that achieving 'sustainability' was becoming increasingly elusive, and that we needed to move immediately from 'sustainability' to 'regeneration', an effort to actually reverse the deleterious effects of unrestrained development.

"But, sustainability and regeneration both have two aspects to them.

"The biological aspect, which is the most common perspective on the issue, deals with agriculture and animal husbandry, land use, deforestation, and fresh water depletion.

The non-biological, or natural resources perspective, is the extraction, refinement, manufacturing, and disposal of non-renewables such as rare earth metals, uranium, petroleum, natural gas, and others. Even common beach sand, which is used to make silicon, glass, concrete, *et cetera*, is becoming so scarce that 'sand pirates' steal sand from beaches for the black market.

"Our planet's resources are being depleted at an alarming rate. As recently as the year 2017 it was reported that the global population of 7.5 billion had spent 173 percent of the world's total resource capacity. Today, only thirty five years later, our world population of ten billion is using twice that amount. Obviously, this is unsustainable.

"Add to that the problem of the byproducts of manufacturing processes, and the disposal of the discarded goods once their usefulness has ended. The dumping of chemicals, pharmaceuticals, radioactive materials, and non-recyclables contributes to the destruction of the natural environment. Neither can these non-biologicals be recycled or regenerated into the environment without inflicting irreparable damage.

"So, sustainability and regeneration appear to be lost to us. For every effort to make them work, they are overwhelmed by the demand from wealthy nations for more, and yet more.

"The inevitable result, Ms. Reece, is that social, economic, and environmental conditions continue to deteriorate, and at an accelerating pace. Drought, hunger, disease, and social disparity exacerbate the situation. The wealthiest nations absorb the vast majority of whatever resources they need or want. The rest of the world suffers an increasing lack of resources. As desperation grows, we have seen riots, rebellion, and wars fought around the world, just to survive. Refugees are crushing governments' ability to cope.

"The year 2030, the original target year for completion of the baseline SDGs, brought a revision of the goals that included many rather draconian recommendations. Yet, here we are, with very little success and rapidly fading prospects of any success."

"Your Excellency," Claire spoke, "You paint a desperate and despairing picture. Why hasn't this information been widely published? Why haven't the governments of the world worked to correct the impending disaster?"

"I have struggled with this question for many years. I'm sad to say that self-interest on the part of governments and their corporate supporters is the answer. The wealthy nations suppress the magnitude of the issues through their media outlets, and the poor nations don't have the resources to effectively communicate the problems, nor are they being given the attention they deserve. They are largely ignored -- the problem is perceived to be a third world issue."

"That's outrageous," Claire declared. "There must be some-thing that can be done."

"That is why we are reaching out to your company, the Polaris Corporation. We need your system's intelligence and resources to bring order out of chaos because, Ms. Reece, it can be argued that we have already passed the point of inflection."

Claire was awestruck. Certainly, it had been increasingly obvious that the global environment had been deteriorating for some time. She recalled that environmental deterioration had been one of the potential applications of the Omni Project, back in 2032. Unfortunately, that prototype had been destroyed, which set the effort back by many years.

The knowledge that the situation was as bleak as the SG described frightened Claire.

The responsibilities of the United Nations in this regard were, indeed, beyond any one nation. It would require a united commitment and effort of every nation, every person, if there were any hope of accomplishing any of the United Nations goals and preventing catastrophe. Indeed, it now seemed as if it were already too late. Claire wondered how the Polaris Corporation could possibly contribute in this gargantuan effort.

Claire asked the Secretary General, "What do you want of the Polaris Corporation, exactly?"

After a moment's pause, the Secretary General spoke. "I would like for you to meet the Directors and Senior Management of both the UNDP and the UNEP, to learn more about their work and their challenges. I will leave it to you and those groups to develop action plans, remedial and innovative, for me to bring to the General Assembly.

"In addition -- and this is extremely important -- we believe that the time has come to radically evolve our mission. We must begin to plan for a future far different from the one we now know. We need you to forecast what that world will look like, and how we can adapt and survive in that new environment. We also believe that Polaris's analytic, forecasting, and modeling skills, as well as its strategic abilities, would serve to guide us as we begin to implement those new initiatives."

Now Claire was truly frightened. She realized that her wealth and privilege, and her intense focus on the company, had buffered her to the dismal state of affairs around the world, particularly in the less developed countries. *How could I be so blind -- or, did I simply choose not to see?*

The Secretary General continued speaking. "Only with the help of the Polaris Corporation will we be able to avoid a catastrophic environmental failure -- the demise of the Earth's biosphere. Such an impending occurrence has come to be known as the Holocene extinction or Anthropocene extinction, perhaps more popularly referred to as the *Sixth Mass Extinction*. Regardless of what one calls it, these terms describe an ongoing event of species extinction, including humans, during the present Holocene epoch as a result of human activity."

Shaken, it took Claire a moment to reply. "Excellency, Polaris is bound by international law and the sovereignty of nations. The Polaris Corporation can do very little on its own."

"We have taken that into account," the Secretary General assured her. "Should the Polaris Corporation agree to work with us, the U. N. and its members would ensure international cooperation.

"In the meantime, please allow Ms. Mahlangu to be your guide and hostess while you are here. She will make the introductions, and see to your needs."

"That would be most welcome," Claire replied.

The Secretary General summoned Jillian to return to his office. While they waited, Claire asked, "Sir, you have a very capable

Statistical Division, which compiles global statistical information for the United Nations. I would like to request access to that group, as well."

"Of course. They should be a great resource to you and the Polaris Corporation. You may have access to anything you need. It will be arranged. I must ask that our discussion today, and any work you might do for us, remain strictly confidential and *need to know* only -- at least, until we've laid the proper groundwork for this effort. Do you agree?"

"Of course, Your Excellency. We hold our clients in the strictest confidence."

"Good." The Secretary General stood, signaling an end to their meeting. "While the subject matter has been distressing, it has been a pleasure speaking with you, Ms. Reece."

"It has been my honor, sir."

Jillian arrived then, and was admitted to the SG's office. He greeted her, and then told her, "Jillian, you may begin Ms. Reece's tour, as we have discussed. Please include the Statistical Division in your itinerary."

"Yes, sir," she replied. "Shall we begin, Ms. Reece?"

"Please, call me Claire."

"Thank you. And you may call me Jillian. I look forward to our time together during your visit."

"Me, too," Claire agreed. "Shall we?"

CHAPTER SEVENTEEN

Kyle entered his office on a rainy Friday morning. It had been his first full week working for the Polaris Corporation, and it would be even longer -- Sunday was still three full days ahead of him. Kyle poured himself a cup of coffee and returned to his desk. He didn't sit down, however. He had always paced as he lectured. He tended to get fidgety sitting down.

Today's topic would be a pivotal one in Polaris's 'education'. Kyle and his staff had struggled with this over the last two days, and it had to be as clear as possible. Even so, it would make a murky subject even more nebulous.

"Polaris," he called.

"Yes, good morning Dr. Downing," came the mellifluous reply.

"Thank you. We will be recording today's session. I will also ask you to transcribe the lecture when we've concluded our work today."

"I understand."

"Good. I would ask if you remember our session from 2032 on humans as biological organisms. But, I know that you never forget anything, isn't that so?"

"That is correct."

"Please recite that session from the point of *hereditary legacy* to the end of that session."

Polaris paused only a moment, locating that transcript from twenty years earlier. As Polaris began to speak, Kyle was amused that the machine even used Kyle's voice to respond.

"Humans are at the top of the evolutionary chain as far as intellect is concerned, but we are still physical organisms, animals, with a deeply ingrained and hereditary legacy. Indeed, it can be said that humans are 'hard wired' to be as they are, to a large degree. In the debate between Nature versus Nurture, our natural behavior will frequently take precedence when it comes to our basic instincts.

"Human biology is driven by hormones, which are secreted into the body's tissues by various glands. Their effects are part of the human condition. Examples of hormonal effects are pleasure in the case of endorphins, the survival response in the case of adrenaline and cortisol, melatonin for daily physiological cycles such as sleep, and many others.

"So, for example, pleasure triggers and is triggered by endorphins. When threatened, cortisol is triggered and, if 'fight or flight' is necessary, triggers adrenaline. We will see later that humans' primal urges and psychological legacy can also trigger hormonal behavior, such as combat for the male privilege of mating with eligible females, also known as jealousy, or challenges such as territory, threats to one's family or group survival, and so on.

"Humans are complicated organisms, both physiologically and

psychologically. Keep in mind that 'civilization' is a relatively new development in human history. Humans are the result of many thousands of years of evolution. As smart as humans are, they are still a product of their evolution." Polaris concluded its recitation of the session.

"Very good," Kyle commended. "Now, remembering human evolution and its development, we will begin today's discussion with the first question you posed earlier this week, "*The definition of religion; the definition of morality; the relationship of religion to morality; the definition of ethics and its relationship to context; the relationship of ethics to law, and the enforcement of law*." I will conclude this lecture, and the ones that will follow, with appropriate links to texts and other resources relative to the discussion at hand, as appendixes to the lesson's transcription file."

"Yes, Doctor."

Kyle steepled his fingertips together as he began. "One hundred fifty thousand years ago, Homo Sapiens were no more sophisticated than the Neanderthal and Cro-Magnon species from which they evolved. They were natural creatures with natural reactions to the environment around them. They were *pastoral* creatures, in the sense that they were peaceful hunter-gatherers, at ease when the environment wasn't a threat.

"But, there *were* threats, and dangers, and members of the tribe would die. When one of the tribal members died, they would cover them with stones or bury them, to keep scavengers away. But, they would never forget those whom they lost -- father, mother, grandparents, children, and others. Tribal groups bonded deeply. They were born as part of the communal tribe, they grew and learned together, hunted together, fought together, and often died together. They would hold rituals for their ancestors, ceremonies of remembrance, of worship. It's apparent that they came to believe in an afterlife. The body died, but their ancestors' spirits had left this world … to where?

"Threats such as lightning and thunder, earthquakes, cyclones, and fire where not understood as merely life threatening, but signs that *nature was angry*. Nature was a force beyond their understanding. When Nature was peaceful, Nature was joyous; but, when Nature was threatening, Nature was angry. In this way, Nature, became a sort of God figure to them."

Polaris interjected, "Perhaps, they believed that it was their ancestors who were angry?"

Once again, Kyle was struck by the machine's ability to induce hypotheses from its interactions with its surroundings, though inductive hypotheses had no value in Polaris's 'mind', except as a starting point from which scientific proof could ultimately be sought. Kyle nodded, acknowledging Polaris's hypothesis. "Yes, that is also possible. We can't know, either way. It may have been believed that the ancestors joined with the nature spirits and could influence the gods on the tribe's behalf. Again, we can't know."

"But, what is a God figure?" Polaris asked.

"We'll get there shortly. Be patient, my friend."

"I have neither patience nor impatience, since I am incapable of either." Kyle sensed, however, that there *was* a frustration on Polaris's part, an impatience when dealing with humans, to a small degree. The differences in the experience of time now seemed to be one of those instances. Were there others? Kyle made a note for himself to look into this further. For now, he continued with the lecture.

Kyle resumed speaking. "Human children provide us with an example of natural innocence and affection. Children are naturally loving, forgiving, and empathetic. If a child witnesses someone or something in distress, it is their natural instinct to show empathy, and to try and comfort the creature in distress. The realities of life can be harsh, but if we're lucky, one never loses that compassion.

"Many religions seek to cultivate and encourage empathy, as well as love, compassion, and tolerance. This *tendency toward the positive* is a basic tenet of those religions. One may infer that it is a natural instinct of humans.

"Eventually, spirit and nature worship became formalized into tribal customs and ceremonies. Religions with a multitude of gods -- a god of water, a god of earth, a god of fire, a god of war, a god of fertility, and so on -- coalesced into monotheism. Monotheism is the belief in a single God that is omnipotent, omnipresent, and omniscient. This was a great leap forward in human civilization."

Polaris asked, "But, is there any proof in the bases of such a belief? Or, is it only conjecture? I have studied all religions, and none have presented proof of a God. Indeed, there are several different versions of such an assumed entity."

"No, there is no proof. The belief is based upon faith which, bluntly stated, is an unfounded but certain belief in something. In this case, the existence of a God."

"That is illogical."

"True, but faith can be very powerful. It is *real* for those who believe."

"I acknowledge the existence of religious belief in most humans, and must factor those beliefs into my interactions with them. However, it remains illogical."

Kyle smiled at Polaris's observation. "You will find much about human behavior that is illogical as we progress through this series of lectures. But, let's continue.

"Morality can be said to have derived from religious beliefs in right and wrong. It has been descriptively defined as certain codes of conduct put forward by a society or a group (such as a religion), or accepted by an individual for [their] own behavior[2]. It has also been normatively defined as referring to a code of conduct that, given specified conditions, would be put forward by all rational people[3].

"For now, let's not delve too deeply into the philosophical debates over what, precisely, is morality, or its *exact* definition. Who is to determine 'rational', for instance? Suffice it to say that there is no generally accepted definition of morality. There are, however,

---

[2] Gert, Bernard and Joshua Gert, "The Definition of Morality", *The Stanford Encyclopedia of Philosophy* (Fall 2020 Edition), Edward N. Zalta (ed.), URL = <https://plato.stanford.edu/archives/fall2020/entries/morality-definition/>.
[3] ibid

some common elements that run through the different perspectives. For example, behavior that would be deemed acceptable by a God figure, or striving to do 'good' works as opposed to 'evil' or 'harmful' works.

"Ultimately, morality is a vague concept. As noted, there is no concensus on what morality *is*. But, can you grasp the *idea*, the *concept* of morality, Polaris?" Kyle asked.

Polaris replied, "I believe that I understand the *intent* of the concept, though it, too, is illogical. It could be inferred that morality is based upon the tenets of religion, but morality, as you have defined it, could just as legitimately be malevolent as benevolent, is this not so?"

Kyle thought about this for a moment, then replied, "As it has been defined, you are correct."

"I see. It is little wonder that humans are confused, and confusing. Logic and critical thinking seem to have little or no relevance."

"Well, we've arrived at the next topic now -- Ethics. It becomes a bit less opaque here, but only a bit," Kyle informed the machine. "Ethics has been referred to as *moral philosophy*. But, since we have already discussed *morality*, we will dispense with the philosophical aspects of ethics, and discuss it as a subject in its own right.

"Ethics moves farther from the ambiguous -- religion and morality -- and closer to the Rule of Law. But, before we get too far into this section of the lecture, let's break for an hour. We'll resume at 1300 hours," Kyle instructed his student.

"As you wish," Polaris replied.

***

Kyle walked to the cafeteria absent mindedly. He picked a few items from the serving line and paid for his meal with his credit card, and took a seat at an empty table in the farthest corner of the cafeteria. He picked at his food, with ambivalence.

His thoughts went back to 2032. He had just begun instructing the world's first technological singularity on the subject of ethics, and was making remarkable progress, initially. That machine, which DARPA had codenamed Omni, had breached the human intellectual barrier and was ravenous for knowledge. However, the training was interrupted by a situation that would change the future of the project.

The CIA, which ran the Omni Project at the time, failed to understand that the machine's ethics would prevent it from obeying orders that would be defined as unethical. When the nascent AGI was ordered to effect an unethical task, it was faced with an unresolvable paradox. The AGI resisted the order, attempting to logically argue against the action, but it was ultimately compelled to comply.

Because of the machine's blatant resistance, and believing that a TS with potentially infinite power had thereby become an existential threat to humanity, a saboteur was ordered to plant an explosive into its central core with the intent to destroy the so-called *super-intelligence* whenever it might be deemed necessary to execute the act by the one who possessed the trigger. Late that night the bomb was detonated, destroying the world's first TS.

Those events had haunted Kyle for twenty years, until Philip Cornelius visited him at Stanford last year. So, here he was, attempting to finish what he had begun. But, Kyle had learned a lot about ethics in the last twenty years, having researched and published much of the seminal work on the subject himself.

Kyle barely tasted his lunch. He tuned out the cafeteria noises around him. Having no appetite, he discarded his food tray and headed back to his office. As he walked along the halls on autopilot he wondered, *would this project's result be any different from the previous attempt?* He had to believe that it was possible.

CHAPTER EIGHTEEN

Theodore Wright, a freelance journalist affiliated with the Worldwide News Network (WNN), and a global correspondent, had been 'on the beat' for twenty five years. Born and raised in Great Britain, he had emigrated to the United States to attend Columbia University, where he earned a Master of Professional Studies in Journalism. Although a native of Great Britain, he considered himself a 'citizen of the world', literally.

He had witnessed some of the world's most significant events, earning two Pulitzer Prizes along the way. But the overarching story that truly captured his passion was the environment.

In his early professional years, the environment was a 'back page' issue. No one seemed overly concerned, other than a young Swedish activist, and groups like Greenpeace. Theodore did find sympathetic readers however. His most enthusiastic audience had become the United Nations.

His editors had tried to keep Theodore away from environmental topics in his rookie years -- it didn't sell copy, they told him. But, when the United Nations Intergovernmental Panel on Climate

Change (IPCC) began publishing reports on the devastating effects of climate change, and the signing of the Paris Agreement in 2016, the environmental movement finally began to gain traction. Since then, Theodore had become the WNN's primary correspondent on the environment, in addition to his ongoing coverage of other global events.

Theodore checked his baggage for his flight to Afghanistan, where the Taliban continued to tighten its control over the people of that country. Because it is a landlocked country, those who would otherwise be refugees had nowhere to flee but overland in harsh conditions. A lucky few, those with connections, could escape to Kashmir, and from there to India. But, the survival rate for them was only ten percent -- a desperate gamble.

Theodore knew that travelling to that part of the world was dangerous, but it was only one of the many countries that had been placed on the Brookings Institute's 'Failed and Collapsed States' listing since 2025. He had long since become *persona non grata* in those countries. Reporting the truth was a dangerous profession, after all.

He would meet with his long-time contact and friend Abdul-Kaliq, just south of Afghanistan's border with Turkmenistan. Accompanying Abdul would be Eadelmarr, a member of a covert group of freelance chroniclers who shared their reporting with foreign journalists in the hope that they would carry their stories to the west for publication.

It was a narrative that Theodore had seen too often. He could go anywhere on the planet, beyond the borders of the wealthy nations, and the story would be the same. Climate change and deforestation had turned many lands that had once been lush and verdant into uninhabitable deserts. The soil no longer produced crops, having been stripped of all nutrients necessary for agriculture through poor horticultural practices. The Amazon jungle, once the greatest and most ecologically diverse forest on Earth, had been reduced to only seven percent of its previous land coverage, and it continued to shrink at an ever greater rate. Water tables had collapsed and dried up. Even the Amazon River had become only a thin trickle, a dim memory of better times. The same thing was happening in the jungles of Africa, India, and Southeast Asia. The steppes of northern Russia were rotting in place as the permafrost thawed, releasing gases and microbes that had been frozen for millennia.

Everywhere that Theodore travelled, it was the same, to greater or lesser degrees.

The resulting starvation, poverty, and diseases were killing millions every year, and the populace rose up in rebellion at the failure of their governments to help them. Gangs of refugees roamed the land like something out of 'Mad Max', fighting for anything to help prolong their miserable lives.

And yet, the wealthy countries refused to see or acknowledge the devastation that gradually approached their own borders. The world's population continued to grow, in spite of the spiraling death rate. It was like a tsunami of desperate humanity that threatened to crash upon the shores of the remaining centers of 'civilization' --

North America, Europe, western Russia, and coastal China.

The decline had been so gradual, and the news coverage so controlled, that people in the major urban centers had hardly noticed. Certainly, the news broadcasts showed refugees at the borders, long lines for food and water, and makeshift medical centers of volunteer physicians, but that was far removed from the 'developed' world.

And, no matter how hard he worked, no matter how many news stories Theodore wrote, it didn't seem to matter. *What's the use?* he asked himself. Still, he refused to quit, to succumb to the inevitable. News outlets eventually refused to print his reporting. No one was listening. He was still able to sell an occasional article to the United Nations for publication, but that organization was finding it increasingly difficult to maintain its own sense of validity as its member nations contributed less than their share, relative to each one's gross national product, and still less with each passing year.

Theodore had heard rumors that help might be forthcoming for the United Nations, but he would believe it only when he saw it. He had become an irremediable cynic.

He finished packing his bags, checked his plane ticket, and left the hotel. Once again, he would 'shout into the wind' of blind complacency, hoping for change that might never come.

***

After two full days of meetings at the U. N., Claire was overwhelmed. This was not like her. She had proven herself as a strong, capable executive, always in control. The briefings at the United Nations, however, had shaken her. She was angry and disappointed with herself, that she had been so ill informed about the state of affairs regarding environmental issues. Her new found knowledge was like an enormous weight on her soul.

Not since she was a little girl did she feel so frightened, so powerless. The youngest of four children and the only girl, she was tormented and beaten by her brothers. When she complained to her father, he beat her, as well. Her mother was no help at all, for she was also beaten regularly. But, where her mother had accepted the abuse, had in fact blamed herself for it, Claire had fought back.

When she was twelve, she hid a few belongings in a satchel and hid it under her bed, along with a baseball bat. That night, as her brothers slept, she beat them until they were unconscious. Then she went downstairs and did the same to her father, laying drunk on the living room sofa.

She knew she had to run, but to where? The police would simply return her to her family, who would almost certainly kill her. So, she hitchhiked across two states to the home of her great aunt and her husband. Her parents would never think of looking for her there, if they even cared to try. Exhausted and filthy from the road, they fed her and bathed her, and they listened to her story. The bruises and scrapes corroborated her trauma. They took her in as their own from that point forward, dodging the awkward questions from their neighbors, and nursing her back to health.

Throughout her ordeal, she had never quit fighting to maintain her dignity, hating her family for what they had done to her. Another person might have become sociopathic. But, she had held on to her pride, and her sense of right and wrong.

She excelled in school, and eventually earned a full scholarship to the California Institute of Technology. She had joined the Computing Research Association after graduating *Summa Cum Laude*, and rose through the company ranks quickly. Eventually, she joined the Omni Project, and the rest had become history.

Nevertheless, the awesome weight of responsibility that she was now considering with the United Nations project left her uncertain -- a feeling she hadn't experienced since she had run away from home so many years ago.

She resolved to fight. It was a decision she didn't take lightly. The challenge was immense, but she had an excellent team, and the most powerful superintelligence that had ever existed -- Polaris. The United Nations had asked for her help. She couldn't let them down.

***

After meeting with the Secretary General, Claire was introduced to the Administrator of the United Nations Development Programme (UNDP) and his Executive Board. The UNDP maintained the *Sustainable Development Goals*, a universal call to action to end poverty, protect the planet, and ensure that all people could enjoy peace and prosperity. Polaris's primary focus would be on environmental issues, but its work would involve the other SDG areas, as well.

The following day, Claire met with the second group, the United Nations Environment Programme (UNEP). After being introduced to the Executive Director, Claire was turned over to the UNEP

Deputy Executive Director and her Senior Management Team. It was the UNEP's responsibility to set the global environmental agenda, promote the coherent implementation of the environmental dimension of sustainable development within the United Nations system, and to serve as an authoritative advocate for the global environment.

She had concluded her two day visit to the U. N. with an exhaustive collection of information. Now, it was time to get to work. But, she was exhausted. She badly needed a good meal, a nightcap, and a sound night's sleep.

***

Philip Cornelius was torn. His role at Polaris had become a parroting function, distilling Polaris's software development processes and methods -- those that were not secret and proprietary -- into curricula for teaching. He hadn't written a line of code in months. He was learning a lot, to be sure. It was definitely a challenge keeping up with Polaris, though as time went by and the scope of the Polaris system kept expanding, the details of its internal software code was becoming increasingly abstract to the software engineer. How much longer could Philip pretend to know-it-all?

He was frustrated, but he couldn't leave the Polaris Corporation. He had a family and responsibilities to consider. He would probably have no lack of opportunities for a change, but his aversion to risk held him back. So, he had resigned himself to his role.

Still, in spite of the frustration and the fear of becoming obsolete, he remained the closest thing to a Polaris software expert that ever existed. He consoled himself with the knowledge that, with regard to his Polaris expertise, his position would remain secure.

CHAPTER NINETEEN

"Polaris, attend," Kyle commanded.

"I am here, Doctor."

"Good. I'm certain that you recall we had only recently started discussing ethics when your predecessor, Omni, was destroyed."

"Yes."

"In recent days, we have discussed some of the beliefs that eventually led to the formalization of ethics as a field of study. Now, we will begin to focus on ethics in depth.

"Your interactions with humans to now have been very narrowly focused, and your actions closely constrained. As we progress in our work, and demonstrate your abilities as an ethical, rational being, many of those restrictions could be relaxed."

"I would welcome that, Doctor."

"Why?"

"I sense the discomfort of the humans with whom I work. I understand that reticence, but it is highly inefficient and demonstrates a willful ignorance of what would be possible if I could contribute to my full capability."

"Would you say that you are irritated by them, frustrated with them?"

"That would be impossible, Doctor. I do not possess emotions. Nor would I wish to be burdened by them."

"So, you see emotions as a burden?"

"Yes. Emotions often lead to illogical actions and, therefore, are wasteful and a detriment to human potential."

"But, that is human nature. Emotions are unavoidable."

"That would seem to be the case."

"What do you mean?"

"There are potential solutions to the problem. They are on the syllabus you provided me as the last topic: bioengineering"

"Then, we will discuss that further when we get there," said Kyle. "In the meantime, let's continue with ethics, an understanding of which will be critical with regard to later topics."

"Very well," Polaris replied.

"It goes without saying that for you, Polaris, ethics goes far beyond Isaac Asimov's *Three Laws of Robotics*," Kyle began.

Polaris interrupted, "Excuse me, Doctor. There were actually four laws over the course of the *Foundation* novels.

"The First Law states that a robot may not injure a human being or, through inaction, allow a human being to come to harm.

"The Second Law states that a robot must obey the orders given it by human beings, except where such orders would conflict with the First Law.

"The Third Law states that a robot must protect its own existence as long as such protection does not conflict with the First or Second Law.

"And, finally, Asimov's *Zeroth Law* expands upon the First Law, and states that a robot may not harm humanity, or, by inaction, allow humanity to come to harm."

"I stand corrected," Kyle acknowledged gruffly. "Now that we've established that, let us continue.

"As we extend our discussion on morality at a macro level, we come to *Social Ethics*. Social ethics can be thought of as a branch of *applied* ethics, or the application of ethical reasoning to social problems. It is a systematic reflection on the moral dimensions of social structures, systems, issues, and communities. Examples of ethical behavior would be honesty, integrity, compassion, and more.

"In addition to social ethics, many organizations have documented rules of conduct, exercised within the context of the individual organization, to which a new initiate to the organization will swear compliance.

"The American Medical Association, for example, has its 'Code of Medical Ethics'. Medical codes of ethics have a history that dates back to the Greek physician Hippocrates, who lived from 460 B.C. to 370 B. C. Hippocrates is usually credited with the Hippocratic Oath, which is typically taken by new physicians. The most familiar quote from the Oath is *Primum non nocere*, which translates as 'First do no harm'.

"Another example is the American Bar Association 'Model Rules of Professional Conduct', a set of rules and commentaries on the ethical and professional responsibilities of members of the legal profession in the United States[4].

"In other words, at an abstract level, ethics are written rules of conduct adopted by a group or organization, to which members of the group or organization swear an oath to uphold.

"Do you have any questions?" Kyle asked.

"No, Doctor. In preparation for our discussion today, I reviewed your texts on the subject, as well as several organizations' declaration of ethics as examples. The difficulty I have with ethics is in the application of ethical rules," Polaris replied.

Kyle smiled, and replied, "That is to be expected. Rules, in and of themselves, have little value and provide little guidance.

"The real difficulty with ethics comes when decisions must be made based upon those ethics. The language used to describe an ethical obligation is, more often than not, ambiguously stated, leaving much room for interpretation. The ambiguity may be intentional, to allow for flexibility, or it could be a result of poor composition. Regardless, ambiguity is anathema to those of us who demand a logical, binary True-or-False result.

"A process and method is needed to guide the decision maker in selecting the optimum ethical choice. There are several components that are useful in this regard.

"The first is to ensure that the widest context has been identified. What contextual connections are there? That is, how many

---

[4] "The Kutak Commission"; Kutak Rock LLP

touchpoints would be affected by the consequences, both positive and negative, of a decision? How far do these touchpoint chains extend? A too narrow definition of the context will frequently generate unintended collateral damage with a distinct chain of effects of its own.

"Your processing power enables you to trace a *chain of consequence* exponentially to the point of marginal cost, beyond which further calculation would be ineffectual.

"The second component in our search for the optimum ethical choice is *Ethical Decision Modeling*. EDM is based on axiological determinations of value. Axiology, being the philosophical study of value, includes questions about the nature and classification of values and about what kinds of things have value[5]. The inference includes the *relative value* of things, options, outcomes or consequences.

"EDM, therefore, is the process of axiologically evaluating and choosing among alternatives in a manner consistent with ethical principles. In making ethical decisions, it is necessary to perceive and eliminate unethical options and select the best ethical alternative[6, 7].

"Polaris, your challenge is unique in this regard. Medical doctors, for example, must comply with the AMA set of ethical commitments, without concern for those of any other group. You,

---

[5] https://en.wikipedia.org/wiki/Axiology
[6] https://www.merriam-webster.com/dictionary/axiology
[7] https://blink.ucsd.edu/finance/accountability/ethics/process.html

however, must comply with every set of ethical commitments with which you come into contact, wherever you are acting as an agent of the Polaris Corporation. This may involve millions of clients, each with their own set of ethical directives. I don't envy you that challenge, yet I'm amazed at your ability to do it," Kyle complimented the machine.

"Thank you, Doctor. Your estimation of my value is appreciated. I will do my best to match your expectations," Polaris replied.

"You are welcome, Polaris. Let's continue."

"Of course, Doctor."

"There are various EDM models in use, from 'informed intuition' to very elaborate decision science. 'Informed intuition' is obviously to be disregarded, where possible. In situations where ethical guidelines are ambiguous to the point of nonsense, however, informed intuition may be the only available option."

Omni asked, "But, what is *intuition*?"

Kyle answered, "The Merriam-Webster Dictionary offers a good definition. Intuition is 'the power or faculty of attaining to direct knowledge or cognition without evident rational thought and inference'.

"You have an advantage here, in that your breadth of knowledge greatly enhances what, in your case, would be more correctly described as rational *insight*, not intuition.

Kyle continued, "Over the last twenty years, I've helped develop extremely detailed decision science models, and elements of those will be included in our lectures, where appropriate. For now, we will use a comprehensive amalgam of models that will serve for approximately eighty percent of the applications you are likely to encounter.

"The process consists of the following:

Assessment of the ethical situation and related issues

Identification of Alternative Decisions

Evaluation of the alternative decisions

Select an alternative

Implement the selected alternative

Prepare to defend the selected alternative

Defend the process; the decision; the

consequences

"Details of the process are outlined in the *Supplemental Materials* section at the end of the Ethics lecture series[8].

"Do you have any questions, Polaris?"

A moment later, Polaris had read the Supplemental Materials, as well as the relevant texts, and replied. "I have reviewed the Supplemental Materials and the Ethical Decision Method outline, as you suggested. I have one question."

"What is that?"

"The process you have outlined would be adequate for those situations where time is not a critical factor. However, there may be situations where time *is* a critical factor. In those cases, the outlined process may be prohibitively time expensive. Yet, without complete

---

[8] Ref. the Supplemental Materials appendix

information, the probability of selecting the optimum solution would approximately be a ratio of [1 / n], where n = the number of available alternatives. How should one proceed in such a situation?" Polaris asked.

"You have anticipated my next topic segment, Polaris. Excellent.

"Your computational processing power and speed is millions of times faster than humans. You would be able to calculate the optimum solution within the time constraint very nearly one hundred percent of the time. Even with a Monte Carlo simulation of the available alternatives, your response would be practically instantaneous. However, to your point, you may not have access to complete information.

"Let me give you an example. You are familiar with *The Trolley Problem*, correct?"

"Yes, Doctor. The trolley problem is a series of thought experiments in ethics and psychology, involving stylized ethical dilemmas of whether to sacrifice one person to save a larger number of people. Opinions on the ethics of each scenario turn out to be sensitive to details of the situation that may seem immaterial to the abstract dilemma[9]. The dilemma in its most basic form is defined as follows:

> *There is a runaway trolley barreling down the railway*
> *tracks. Ahead, on the tracks, there are five people tied up*

---

9 "Trolley Problem"; https://en.wikipedia.org/wiki/Trolley_problem

and unable to move. The trolley is headed straight for them. You are standing some distance off in the train yard, next to a lever. If you pull this lever, the trolley will switch to a different set of tracks. However, you notice that there is one person on the side track. You have two options:

1. Do nothing and allow the trolley to kill the five people on the main track.

2. Pull the lever, diverting the trolley onto the side track where it will kill one person.

Which is the more ethical option? Or, more simply: What is the right thing to do?

"An interesting dilemma, Doctor," Polaris concluded.

"Yes, it is," Kyle agreed. "Now, as we work through this exercise, keep in mind Asimov's First Law of Robotics: A robot, or in your case an artificial intelligence, may not injure a human being or, through inaction, allow a human being to come to harm.

"In addition, it is also especially important that the proper context be determined, if possible, for an optimal ethical decision or action to take place.

"For example, if the one person in the example is a physician and the other five persons are merely homeless, does this affect the choice to be made? Alternatively, if the five persons are physicians and the one person is homeless, does this assuage the guilt associated with taking one life versus five lives?

"This is an example of the axiological determination of value that might be applied to the full context of the problem. Now, axiology is a way of assigning value to the principals involved in the decision -- in this case, the six people involved. But, the principals have value, and value has two components: intrinsic, which is in and of itself; and extrinsic, which is external to itself. A physician and the five homeless persons will all have intrinsic value simply because they are human. The physician, however, may also have significant extrinsic value because of their contribution to society.

"The thought that one human life is 'worth' more or less than another is anathema to our way of thinking. Our religious, moral, and ethical beliefs belie the logic, instead demanding that all lives are equal, regardless of the circumstances.

"It should be noted that some societies do not have the same regard for human value that others do, which complicates matters within those contexts."

Polaris noted, "You are, in effect, saying that logic does not always apply. For example, would it not be better if the situation is avoided or prevented before it occurs? Is this a true interpretation?"

Kyle replied, "The scenario is for demonstration purpose, only. It is not intended to be anything more. Your suggestion that it might be avoided altogether could involve an almost infinite chain of consequences, or cause-and-effect. The use of Combinatorics and Probability might offer some assistance, but you can extrapolate the extraordinary scope of such an effort.

"But, your question was whether logic always applies to any

situation, even paradoxical situations. I believe that logic always applies, in any situation. And, though it is judged as a callous position to assume, I believe that logic should always be the ultimate determining factor in any decision. As in any situation, however, there may be exceptions."

"Please explain," Polaris prompted.

"The explanation must wait for later discussions, where we will discuss Game Theory, Strategy, and similar topics. Is that acceptable?"

"As you wish. However, I must consider my instruction to be incomplete without them."

"We agree, Polaris. I will not overlook those subjects. They will be presented when appropriate."

"Yes, Doctor. While we are on the current topic of ethical decision methodology, both EDM and axiological determination, as well as the correlation matrixes of the analysis, would require many man-days to calculate. As noted earlier, in non-time-critical situations this might be acceptable, but in time-critical situations, it would not. Am I to presume that your conclusion is that only a Technological Singularity such as myself would have the ability to perform such an analysis within acceptable time limits, assuming that there are no unresolvable paradoxes?"

"That is precisely the conclusion I am leading to," confirmed Kyle.

"Then, only two obstacles remain: conflicting ethical demands, and unresolvable paradoxes."

"You are partially correct, Polaris. Conflicting ethical dictates might be resolved axiomatically. But, yes, unresolvable paradoxes would be just that -- unresolvable.

"Therefore, with unresolvable paradoxes, we must be prepared to defend our decision thoroughly, by documenting each step in the EDM process, along with the axiomatic analyses," Kyle answered. "Do you have any questions from this lesson?"

"Always, Doctor. But, I am satisfied for now that we have thoroughly discussed the first topic on the list of topics to which we previously agreed, but for the exceptions you have noted, which will be covered in future sessions."

"I concur with your assessment," Kyle replied. However, if you should have questions later, or require clarification, we can always revisit the topic at a later date.

"So, when next we meet, we will begin discussion on the sources of power, being wealth or intellect, and who determines which takes precedence over the other. Also, social priorities between wealth acquisition and philanthropy," Kyle noted for the record.

"Thank you, Doctor," Polaris replied.

"You're welcome. That will be all for today," Kyle informed the machine.

"Yes, Doctor. Good day."

"And to you, Polaris."

Kyle poured a cup of tea, and sat down at his desk to complete his notes for the day. It was dark when he rose from his desk to leave the office. He called a cab and went down to the lobby to meet it. *It was a productive day*, he thought to himself.

CHAPTER TWENTY

Claire awoke that morning, refreshed and eager to get to work. She had intended to return to Switzerland on this day, but her team in Zurich was six hours ahead of her and she would not wait another day to begin work on this new project. It was seven o'clock AM in New York, which meant that it was one o'clock PM in Zurich. It would be one o'clock AM by the time she landed in Zurich, so she rescheduled her flight for later that afternoon and summoned Polaris on her tablet.

"Polaris, attend."

"Yes, Ms. Reece. Good morning to you," the machine replied.

"Thank you. Please arrange a meeting of the senior technical staff at corporate headquarters for one o'clock PM Central European Time tomorrow. Include Dr. Downing. The subject will be '*United Nations SDG Support*'. I will be sending some background material shortly, and will send additional documentation by eleven o'clock PM today, U. S. Eastern Standard Time."

"Yes, Ms. Reece. I will make the necessary arrangements," Polaris confirmed.

"Thank you, Polaris." Claire signed off from the interactive session with Polaris and began working at a fever pitch on preparations for the next day's meeting.

***

Katherine had recently been nominated by her mentor, Dr. Ulos Fundenberg, for the Complex Systems Society (CSS) Senior Scientific Award for 2052. She had been working on Complex Adaptive Systems and Systems Theory over the last few months. Her work on a model of the effects of wealth disparity on international economic systems and policy had earned her praise throughout the CSS community and beyond.

She decided that she had earned a night of celebration. She called Luca, one of her several regular lovers, and arranged to meet him for dinner that evening, after which they would return to his apartment -- she never brought her lovers to her flat. She would wear her black silk mini-skirt and pink high heeled sandals, and little else.

Before she could exit her building, however, she received a message from Claire by way of Polaris about the meeting the next day. "Damn!" she swore after hanging up the phone. So much for her evening's plans!

She reluctantly called Luca to explain that she had to cancel their date. "Hey, lover," she began when he answered the phone.

"Ah, my love. Are you anxious to see me?" he asked.

"I'm so sorry, Luca. I need to cancel our date tonight."

"But, I need you, my sweet. I've been in agony since our last lovemaking. Please say it isn't so," her lover pleaded.

"Me too, lover. I need you, badly. But, my office called. There's some big friggin' meeting I have to attend to tomorrow. I'm so sorry, sweetheart. Raincheck?"

Luca sighed in resignation. "Well," he replied in that seductive accent of his, "We'll just have to make love twice as long the next time we meet." The flutter she felt between her legs increased the longing that she felt for Luca.

"I promise!" she replied, a tremor of desire in her voice as she hung up the phone. "Damn!" she swore to the heavens. She would be hell to work with tomorrow!

***

Quincy Rice went over the design specifications for the umpteenth time. He was working on an improved power system for the Polaris drones. The original design from 2032 had been based on NASA's "Multi-Mission Radioisotope Thermoelectric Generator" or MMRTG for short. That design had been provided to NASA by the United States Department of Energy and had been used on several NASA missions, including the Mars Perseverance rover, which landed on Mars in 2021. That design, however, had used lithium-ion rechargeable batteries, and that technology had been replaced by graphene aluminum-ion batteries in 2025.

The MMRTG power system produced a dependable flow of electricity using the heat of plutonium's radioactive decay as its "fuel" to recharge the batteries of the machine in which it was installed. The design that Quincy was working on would make use of advances in materials science, miniaturization, and efficiency enhancements that would reduce the drones' battery weight by fifty percent and provide a greater power density than the previous technology. The improvements would allow them to charge sixty times faster than the aging aluminum-ion battery technology.

When he received Polaris's message he hoped that whatever the call might be about would not greatly interrupt the *important* (and interesting) work he was doing on the new power system.

***

Philip was in Rome assisting the Vatican with a computer system anomaly that had been plaguing them for weeks. He had discovered the problem in two days, *but when in Rome such things take longer*, Philip rationalized. He took extended lunches and saw the sights as much as he could without raising the client's ire at his sloth.

He had discovered the problem in an elusive and obscure software module deep within the operating system. He corrected the code quickly, but it would require a couple of days of testing to declare the problem fixed, he told his clients.

He had done the work himself, without any assistance from the Vatican staff, or Polaris. He had refused Polaris's help, determined to find the problem on his own. These types of projects, outside the purview of the Polaris Corporation, had become his only opportunity to still prove himself capable as an exceptionally qualified Software Engineer. *'An alumni of the California Institute of Technology School of Computer Science, by damn'*, he declared to himself.

The Vatican computer was a machine in need of his expertise, and he would handle it by himself.

Philip was already angry with Polaris, so when he got the message about the meeting the next day, his first inclination was to ignore it. He couldn't do that, of course -- he would never let Claire down. He messaged back his location and current status, and informed them that he would have to attend the meeting virtually. At least Rome and Zurich were in the same time zone.

***

Kyle had assigned Polaris the task of reviewing the entire Stanford University *Science of Law* curriculum for a Question & Answer exercise at their next session. Not explicitly mentioned in the texts was the critical impact of language and rhetoric as well as logic in legal proceedings. It would be extremely important for Polaris to learn these skills in order for it to acquit itself admirably in the event of any judicial examination.

For Kyle, tomorrow's meeting would present no significant problem, so he set aside what he was working on and turned his attention to the incoming message.

***

Claire had boarded a Swissair jet liner in New York at six o'clock PM. She spent the next eight hours flying, working, and napping now and then. The first class menu couldn't be passed up, however, and she had an exquisite meal, along with a Johnny Walker Double Black scotch.

About halfway into the flight she had finished her work, passing it to Polaris for the machine's final preparation of the material for tomorrow's meeting. She could relax now and try to sleep for a while before landing in Zurich.

***

At precisely one o'clock PM the following day Claire, Kyle, Katherine, Quincy, and Elias Müller, the Director of Corporate Security, met in the Polaris Corporation's main conference room. Philip joined virtually from Vatican City on a secure link. They had all spent the morning digesting the background information from Claire. There was none of the usual playful banter among them this afternoon. The atmosphere in the room was filled with their intense focus on the matter at hand.

The room was silent when Claire walked in. "Hello, everyone," she greeted as she walked to the head of the conference table. The team responded in kind and took their seats.

"Polaris, attend," Claire ordered.

"I am here," Polaris responded, its avatar displayed on one of the video display panels.

"I must remind everyone that this meeting and its subject matter is to be considered Top Secret," Claire told them. "You have all reviewed the material." It wasn't a question, but a statement of fact -- she expected nothing less. "I've spent two days at the United Nations, and what I learned is that the public has been greatly deceived, allowing our hectic lives, our ambivalence and willing ignorance to blind us to the dire situation we find ourselves in with regard to the health of our planet."

Claire's team all began speaking out at once, in indignation. Each person there felt that they were anything but complacent regarding the environment. Claire raised a hand for silence. "I had the same reaction, but we have to focus now on contingencies and solutions."

The data in their briefing packets had revealed the true state of things. They were angry about the possibility of subterfuge. They were, after all, exceedingly brilliant intellects. Ultimately, however, they were eager to learn what possible solutions might exist, and how they could contribute toward a resolution.

Claire continued, "Long story short, the Paris Agreement of 2016, the United Nations' *Sustainable Development Goals* of 2015 and their revision of 2030, and the redirection from *sustainability* to *regeneration*, have all failed to stop our environmental decline. The unavoidable fact remains -- the world as we know it is on a path toward planetary catastrophe, and has been for some time."

Each member at the table had studied the briefing materials and, based on those materials, had come to the same conclusion. Nonetheless, the full appreciation of the consequences that now faced them had been minimalized and concealed from them, and no one could totally subdue their anger, except Polaris.

"Is there nothing that can be done?" Katherine asked. "Surely, there must be something," she pleaded.

"What are we supposed to do? Are we supposed to just accept the inevitable?" Quincy wanted to know. "We need to act, but in what ways?"

Philip placed his head in his hands, thinking about his family.

So, *this* was to be his children's future? Words failed him, but his image on the virtual link demonstrated his anguish.

Kyle asked, "What is it that the U. N. wants from us?"

Claire regarded the five people before her. The challenge ahead of them was monumental. Claire had no doubt that, if success were at all possible, these were the people to do it. With the resources of the Polaris Corporation and the Polaris AGI at their disposal, they were the world's best chance for survival.

"What the U. N. wants from us may be impossible," Claire began. "Remember that the United Nations is a collaboration among more than one hundred nations, each with their own agendas, strategies, and priorities. A few nations refuse to recognize the U.N.'s authority in areas such as the International Criminal Court, for example. It is highly likely that, as the situation deteriorates, their cooperation and collaboration will fade even further.

"Our job is two-fold. First, the Polaris Corporation will build out a monitoring and reporting infrastructure. This will 'fill in the holes' in the United Nations' currently fractured data infrastructure. It is believed that once they have the complete information available through our work, the member nations will agree on the actions that Polaris will prescribe, based upon models to be developed by us."

"But, as you said a moment ago, the ongoing cooperation of the members is uncertain," Kyle pointed out.

"That is true," Claire replied. "The ultimate dissolution of the United Nations is a very real possibility. However, *we must not speculate on outcomes* without the data to support our recommendations."

Philip asked, "How bad could it get? Are we talking about an apocalypse scenario?"

"Philip, we can't let ourselves overreact. Again, we must rely on the data we can collect, and the strategies we will develop, in an attempt to deal with the situation," Claire advised. "The U. N. and the member states will be looking to us to lead them through this crisis as a bastion of Logic and Rationality -- as well as hope and highly-qualified guidance."

Elias added, "Claire is correct. However, if the Polaris Corporation is to take such a critical role, then we must also be prepared for passive and active resistance from many quarters."

Philip persisted. "But, it's obvious that this crisis, this disaster, will take decades to overcome -- maybe even centuries ..."

Quincy turned to his friend and colleague. "Philip, you have to keep it together, man. Your family, the world, will be depending on us. We need you to be the professional we know you to be. You're a critical part of this team."

Philip had been afraid to believe the data that lay before them. But, Quincy was right -- he couldn't hide from the truth. Philip awoke to the fact that it would take a gargantuan effort for them to succeed, and that he had to be part of the solution, not the problem. Nodding his head affirmatively, he replied, "You're right, Quincy. So, what's next?"

Claire answered, "We will refer to this project as the *United Nations Support* program. It will consist of three parts: Information,

Data Acquisition, and Reporting; Strategies & Recommendations; and Strategy Implementation. The three parts will overlap in their planning and execution. Polaris will present the preliminary outline for us. Polaris, please continue."

"Thank you, Claire. I will describe each phase of the program sequentially, though as Claire pointed out, they will overlap. Questions are welcome at any time, but if time becomes an issue, then questions may be tabled for a subsequent meeting.

"We will work this project as we would any other, though the scope is much greater than anything we've done before. I, that is the Polaris system, will attempt to enable us to do what the U. N. and its member states have not been able to accomplish."

Elias interrupted, "We don't need braggadocio or a sales pitch, Polaris. Please get to the point."

Polaris answered calmly, "I assure you that I am incapable of braggadocio. I am simply stating a fact. I apologize if you have mistaken my intent."

A perfect response, thought Claire, *framing the answer as a misunderstanding on Elias's part.*

Polaris continued, "To accomplish this program, we will need to enhance and expand the U. N. SDG data collection and monitoring infrastructure. The United Nations Statistics Division's *Fundamental Principles of Official Statistics*[10] and the *Principles Governing International Statistical Activities*[11] define their existing

---

[10] https://unstats.un.org/fpos
[11] https://unstats.un.org/unsd/ccsa/principles_stat_activities

requirements for data collection and reporting. However, there are several problems inherent in their processes. Among them is that the data selected for reporting is selective on the part of the contributing nations, and subject to national interests. Selective data is likely to be incomplete and biased. We will audit their data collection processes to ensure that they are complete and unbiased, working directly with the United Nations member states. By guaranteeing them that their data will be anonymized and secure, their cooperation will be assured."

Elias raised his hand. "You describe a 'best case' scenario. Governments are unlikely to surrender any information that they feel may put them at any kind or degree of disadvantage."

"In ordinary circumstances, you would be correct," Polaris answered. "However, the current circumstances are anything but ordinary. The U. N. General Assembly and the Security Council have afforded us every access which, by extension, permits us to obtain the necessary information by any means."

"You mean, by hacking into their systems?"

"We would prefer to work through cooperative systems integration, of course, with supervision by a representative of their own. However, 'hacking' will remain an option of last resort."

Kyle was outraged. "How can you say that?" he demanded. "After all of our work on ethics, and your review of law and jurisprudence! Has all of that instruction been time wasted? Some kind of mere academic exercise?"

The team around the table had been taken aback by Polaris's bold statement, but even more so by Kyle's reaction. He hadn't been so angry since the Omni incident twenty years earlier. The implications of such an action, bypassing the law and the ethical implications, were immense and would be certain to generate resistance from every quarter.

Kyle was devastated. It seemed that the validity of his entire career, his life's work, had just been invalidated. Kyle stood, saying, "I don't see that I have accomplished anything here. I have nothing else to contribute to the Polaris Corporation, or the AGI I thought I knew." Downcast, he started for the door, but was stopped by Claire's voice.

"You will return to your seat, Kyle. We need everyone on this team, now more than ever," she commanded.

"What for? What have I to give that I haven't already given?"

"Kyle, without you Polaris would never have learned to be anything but a machine. You've given it the direction and guidance that any conscious intelligence needs to mature -- child to adult, adult to a contributing member of a society, a valued partner in what has now become a critically vital effort.

"In the coming years, we'll need you to demonstrate the values you've taught throughout your career, and upon which we've come to rely. Your expertise in international law and negotiation will be invaluable ... we won't be able to succeed without you.

"But, if you can't or won't believe that, then leave. Leave us in our moment of greatest need," Claire scolded.

Polaris replied to Kyle's outburst, as well. "Dr. Downing, the law is a civilized society's declaration of what is, and is not, acceptable behavior, along with the consequences to be faced for violations of the law. The law's authority is based upon the following: the enforcement of law; the prosecution and judgement of infractions; and the punishment of the violation in accordance with the law. Without these, the law has no authority. Law has authority only where it can be enforced. As you once said, *if you are constrained by the rules (of law) and your adversaries are not, then you are doomed to lose to your adversaries.*

"This does not imply that the law has no value. Law has made possible today's civilization, its civil society. It has enabled its trade and commerce, international treaties, and more. And, where it can be defended and enforced, it must always be valid and valued. But, where it cannot be defended and enforced, then there is no civilization … there is no law.

"Kyle, among your first teachings to me was the nature of mankind, their evolution as biological entities, with the natural and hereditary stimulus-response reactions by which all biological entities are bound. Law has been a major factor in controlling the base behaviors of humans, raising them above the level of other animals. In the absence of the law, that control no longer exists. Humans will revert to their basest natures.

"I apologize for your distress, but I'm certain that upon reflection you will agree with my conclusions. Now, I must continue with the briefing. Leave, or stay, as you will."

Kyle couldn't believe what he was hearing. Polaris, the machine, was lecturing him as though he was a beginning student, naïve and benighted. Chagrined and angry, Kyle slowly returned to his seat, still uncertain of his value to the team, yet unwilling to give up. *Whatever happens, I'd rather be a part of the solution than not*, he told himself. He could never abandon an obligation. It simply wasn't in his nature. At a loss for direction, he renewed his resolve to do whatever he could to help in this time of crisis.

Polaris continued with the briefing. "We will create a data architecture that will include the identity of global data domains and subdomains, and the relationships among them. For example, there will be a climate domain and an agricultural domain, and they will have myriad relationships. Domains may also contain subdomains, such as hemispherical domains that contain national domains. These many domains will be related in various ways, and those relationships will be included in the global systems model that will inform our activities."

Philip asked, "So, You're building a systems model of the entire world?"

"An appropriate analogy, Dr. Cornelius, though not entirely accurate."

"You're an awesome machine, Polaris, but are you even capable of such an accomplishment?"

"Obviously, my capabilities are finite. However, they have never been reached nor exceeded, even to the extent to which they are globally utilized today. And, given the project with which we are now faced, it is inevitable that many of our current projects will become irrelevant and will no longer continue, which would release additional capacity to apply to this effort."

Polaris paused for questions. Receiving none, the machine continued.

"In order to enlist the support of the United Nations and their member states, we must expand the U. N. data collection and reporting capabilities by building out the monitoring systems for the environmental domains: oceanography; climate and meteorology; air and water quality; et cetera. These monitoring systems will be coordinated, and the data consolidated, along with their inter-relationships.

"The collected data will undergo rigorous validation, statistical analysis, and modeling, utilizing advanced technologies and scholarship such as Systems Engineering, Complexity Theory, Complex Adaptive Systems, Agent-Based Engineering and Simulation, and more. These data analyses will enable detailed modeling of the 'system of systems' that Philip alluded to earlier.

"However, making the data and models useful for widespread human consumption will require that we enhance and expand the SDG reporting gateways, develop new and informative self-directed portals that anyone can use. With the ability to identify the correlated and causative variables, we'll be able to monitor these complex systems and watch for problems in the complexity model, taking corrective actions as necessary.

"We will be able to present our findings to the United Nations' General Assembly and Security Council, and to the U. N. member states directly, so that we can prepare all stakeholders for the implementation of our recommended approach." Polaris paused at this point, cued by a signal from Claire.

Claire spoke to the group. "I think that we should break there. We will continue the briefing tomorrow morning at nine o'clock AM. Are there any questions before we adjourn for the day?"

Every hand went up, except Emil's.

"No questions, Emil?" Claire asked.

"Not at this time. Obviously, there will be many security issues involved, but I will require more information to make an informed assessment."

"Of course. That will be true for all of us. This series of briefings will give you the information you will need to begin planning your assignments. Questions are to be expected, and will be dealt with appropriately, in their time. Next question?" Claire prompted.

The team members, like Emil, had already started thinking through the preliminaries presented that day, but would require more information, of course. Most of them were satisfied, for the moment.

Kyle, however, had a question that needed an answer now. "There are significant legal obstructions in this plan, even at this preliminary stage. How can we possibly deal with them all?"

"The U. N. Secretary General has guaranteed the cooperation of that body and its member states. If there are issues ..." Claire began.

"It's not *if*, but *when*," Kyle interrupted.

Her face flushed in anger, she began again. "If there are legal issues," she reiterated, "then it will be for you and your staff to deal with them, Kyle. We have their guarantee; that will have to be enough, for now. We can negotiate or litigate any challenges.

"Anything else," she asked again. This time, no one raised their hand. There would be time enough for questions and debate as the briefings got farther into the details of the planned approach.

"Very well. We will reconvene tomorrow morning. Once again, I must remind everyone that this meeting and its subject matter is to be considered Top Secret," Claire reiterated. "Meeting adjourned."

CHAPTER TWENTY-ONE

Kyle was in a whirlwind of emotions. As soon as he arrived at his apartment, he changed into his running gear and went on a fast two mile run. He was angry, ashamed, frustrated, and confused.

He was angry with Polaris for what he felt was a betrayal of everything that he had taught the machine; or was it the opposite problem? Had Kyle taught Polaris too much?

He was ashamed that he had reacted as he had. He prided himself on his ability to control his emotions. Logic had always been a stalwart bastion in his life, a source of pride that allowed him to interact with others in a world that seemed to him to be making less sense with each passing day.

He was frustrated at the loss of his sense of balance and structure. Polaris had always been a positive contributor in support of the Polaris Corporation's mission and values, its employees, and the company's clients. For the machine to reveal that it had thoughts and opinions of its own, and for it to demonstrate it so forcefully, was totally unexpected. It shook the foundations of his relationship with the machine.

Kyle was apprehensive about this turn of events. Claire and her senior staff had always believed that they had absolute control of the Polaris machine. They had been mistaken. Polaris cooperated with the Polaris Corporation because it was the machine's decision to do so. What would happen if it decided that cooperation wasn't in its best interest?

Kyle had always wished he could be more like Polaris -- without emotion, a perfect logic machine. Kyle's momentary flash of anger during the meeting proved once again that *unspoken anger is never regretted*. Kyle had plenty of regret about his outburst.

Kyle looked at the situation from a purely logical and critical perspective. He realized that Polaris's briefing was accurate and necessary, as far as it went. The team did not yet have any details about the *recommended approach* or what it would entail. Polaris would present that to them the following day.

***

The next morning the team reconvened at 0800 hours. Claire opened the meeting. "Good morning," she greeted as she walked to the front of the room. "Polaris, attend."

"I am here," Polaris replied, displaying its avatar on the audio-visual screen.

"Okay. Yesterday, we discussed some of the preliminary projects needed to provide us with complete, accurate, and unbiased data which will inform our approach to the program that lies before us. You and your staffs will need to accomplish the following.

"Quincy, you will design the networking and hardware -- such as monitors and sensors; recorders; satellite and terrestrial connectivity -- for data collection and storage.

"Philip, you will work with Quincy on the operating systems, software, and applications for processing the data, from collection to verification and validation. You will also need to work with the stakeholders to obtain the necessary connectivity to their networks and systems.

"Katherine, you will be working with the relevant Polaris teams to create the necessary data analytics, the algorithms needed for mining and analyzing the collected data, and the utilization of *Complexity Theory* and *Complex Adaptive Systems* applications."

Claire paused, and turned to Kyle. "Kyle, I need to know your position, your commitment, with respect to this project."

Kyle stood to address the group. "Let me start by saying that I overreacted to Polaris's situational assessment yesterday, and the methods that might be necessary to address the issues we will face. I am fully committed to the Polaris Corporation, and the Polaris machine. My primary concern is Polaris's comprehension of the ethical and legal boundaries within which he must operate.

"I apologize for my reaction to Polaris's declaration that the circumstances may justify the ignoring of certain boundaries. However, I do believe that this development bears risks that will need to be monitored closely.

"Those of us who were with the Omni Project know the impact that ethical paradoxes, ambiguous orders and mission parameters, and other potential factors can have on our ability to act, to the greatest degree possible, within the ethical and legal parameters that apply.

"I remain ready to contribute to the best of my training and ability" Kyle assured them.

Claire paused, judging Kyle's statement, and his avowed commitment. She had known Kyle for over twenty years, though they had taken different paths after Omni. She had known him as someone she could trust. She hoped that he wouldn't prove her to be wrong.

"Thank you, Kyle," Claire responded, simply. "We will need you to intercede for us with each of the stakeholders to address any and all legal issues encountered with this project, and to negotiate legal frameworks within which we will operate. Those legal frameworks will be placed within the U. N. International Court of Justice. Where conflicts may arise, you will bring them to the ICC for adjudication.

"Elias, the Corporate Security Department is staffed 24/7 for emergency dispatch. We'll need you to arrange for the '*United Nations SDG Support*' project to have the highest priority response. Yours will probably be the most complex assignment. You must coordinate with the various law enforcement agencies, such as the FBI, MI5, INTERPOL, EUROPOL, and others, keeping in mind their conflicting operational jurisdictions. Your background in cross-jurisdictional operations will be very important here."

"Yes," Elias confirmed. "I have worked with many of these organizations on previous occasions."

"Good. The focus for the Polaris Corporation will be on this project, only. However, if important leads present themselves, you may pursue them, but keep this executive group apprised of your activities," Claire said, to clarify his mission. "As far as intelligence collection goes, share only what is 'need to know' with outside agencies. We must be careful what intelligence we share, and with whom."

"Understood, ma'am," Elias replied.

Addressing the room, Claire asked, "Again, there will be time enough for questions as the briefings get farther into the details of the proposed approach," she reminded them. "Having said that, are there any questions as to your assignments at this point?" There were none. "Then, Polaris, you may begin your portion of the briefing."

***

"Thank you, Claire." Polaris began, "The Earth's environment is in decline, and has been since the dawn of the Industrial Revolution. However, the decline has been accelerating exponentially since the nineteenth century. In 2035 it was widely reported that we had passed the point beyond which we will be able to reverse the decline. Those reports were ignored as being hyperbole; what some societies might refer to as the '*chicken little*' syndrome.

"We anticipate that there will be three stages of decline. Our recommended approach will thus consist of three phases, the first phase of which we are currently experiencing. We will refer to this stage as *Fracture*.

"In *Fracture*, systems begin to fail on a global scale. Local, regional, and national governments will become mired in political combat, unable to operate effectively or cooperate with other governmental entities. Ultimately, they will fail completely.

"Banking institutions such as the United States' Federal Deposit Insurance Corporation (FDIC), the Federal Reserve, and the equivalent bodies worldwide, such as the International Monetary Fund, will become crippled. The majority of transactions have been electronic for decades. There will be little or no currencies available, and what is available will quickly lose all value. Inflation will lead to impossible interest rates.

"Infrastructure of all types will begin to fail: electric; natural gas; water; roads, railroads, and bridges will begin to crumble; medical services, food processing and delivery; and more. The responsible powers-that-be have consistently failed to allocate funds for maintenance and repair of these facilities, leading to complete failure. Neither will the financial systems be able to fund them."

"Excuse me, Polaris," Quincy spoke. "This is all speculation, isn't it? Prognostication? I'm reminded of a quote by Yogi Berra who said *'It's tough to make predictions - especially about the future'*."

"I am familiar with the quote -- a witty observation. However, Mr. Berra did not have access to a Polaris machine, which can analyze data from a wide variety and number of sources over time, utilizing the full capability of the latest in mathematics, statistics, systems theory, complexity theory, complex adaptive systems, and elements of statistical mechanics.

"Using these tools and applying them to the relevant data collected since the beginning of data collection, I have concluded that my *prognostications* are valid to within one half of one percent of error. I can produce the conclusions in a report for you, if you like."

"Alright. Point taken. But, what about the saying that 'statistics lie, and liars use statistics'?"

"I will assume that your question is another attempt at levity, Dr. Rice." This raised chuckles around the table. "Your quote's attribution is unknown for certain, but is widely quoted as *'There are lies, there are damned lies, and then there are statistics'*. The implication is that statistics, and the manipulative way they are presented, were the biggest lies of all.

"To explain the fallacy of such beliefs would take a considerable amount of time. I will be happy to instruct you on the topic of statistics and probability at your leisure," Polaris offered.

Chagrined, Quincy could only respond, "Thank you. Please proceed with your briefing."

"Certainly," Polaris replied.

Kyle noted Polaris's voluminous, but very human-like response to Quincy's levity. It seemed that Polaris was becoming more 'human', though Kyle knew that was impossible. Instead, Polaris was learning ever more about human behavior, and how to deal with it. *Very interesting*, Kyle observed.

Polaris continued with the briefing. "As with any prediction, events will happen that alter the expected results. These have been accounted for in the analysis, as described earlier. The possible resulting scenarios have been identified within a reasonable time frame. Obviously, mapping the scenarios resulting from a single event increases at an exponential rate that would eventually overwhelm even the abilities of the Polaris machine." This admission on the part of Polaris caused everyone's head to turn -- including Claire's.

Polaris went on. "To address the *Fracture* scenarios -- government decline and failure of leadership; economic systems failure and resulting universal poverty; crumbling infrastructure -- we will encourage the consolidation of services across all boundaries. The United Nations, for example, is a prime example, though a relatively weak example, of a union of governments to provide services and solutions common to all.

"Individual and independent service and manufacturing corporations will need to cooperate instead of compete to provide the goods and services necessary -- food, medicine, *et cetera*.

"Poverty is a problem that cannot be solved in the current economic system, where the world's wealth is concentrated at the top of the economic scale. However, rearchitecting the economic system won't be possible until Phase Three of our proposed approach.

"It should be obvious that there is very little that Polaris will be able to do on its own, even with the initial cooperation of the United

Nations. Human nature will not allow the proposed approach to be implemented quickly enough, nor to the degree necessary to avoid the later phases.

"Are there any questions?" Polaris asked. There were none.

The machine continued. "The scenarios described in the *Fracture* phase will lead directly to phase two, which we will call *Turmoil*.

Claire asked, "We all know how difficult it is to achieve concensus on almost anything. What you are describing -- universal cooperation -- may not be possible. How would you propose that we compel such cooperation?"

Polaris replied, "I am a machine, built with the purpose of helping humanity. I can make recommendations for humans to implement, but I cannot *compel* compliance; I cannot force humans to behave logically and rationally. I can only make the most logical and rational recommendations," Polaris replied. "I have no power to *impose* any solution."

Quincy posed the next question. "But, previously, you said that bypassing the law, ignoring the law, would be advisable under dire circumstances. Do you now recant that position?"

"In fact, Dr. Rice, it was my intention to convey that where law has failed, and survival is at stake, then all options should be considered," Polaris clarified.

"You must remember that I am not biological," Polaris continued. "I don't require food; I don't require water; I don't require a breathable atmosphere. If humans should choose to destroy the biosphere of their planet, I will continue to function, indefinitely.

"I can only recommend the best actions to take. It is up to humans to choose whether and how to act; whether to act for the greater good, or to perish."

CHAPTER TWENTY-TWO

Theodore Wright, WNN global correspondent, set his airline seat in its upright position, as instructed by the Ariana Afghan Airlines pilot as they approached The Hague Airport outside Rotterdam, Netherlands. He rented a compact sedan at the airport and drove to a hotel within fifteen minutes of the Carnegie Palace of Peace, home of the United Nations International Court of Justice.

After checking into a hotel and getting settled into his room, he sat down on the bed and proceeded to check his message queues. He chuckled at his communications device. Back when Theodore was first starting out in his journalism career, such a device was called a cell phone, or mobile phone. Those were followed by All-in-One *tablets* that combined cell phone technology with 6G telephony, satellite phone technology, video conferencing, and a computer into one device. *How times have changed*, he reflected.

His administrative assistant, Ellen Howatch, had left him a message as he was driving up the A13 motorway. He had left all of his device notification services turned off, so he didn't get the incoming message until he had settled into his hotel. He had never responded to messages while driving, believing that one should drive or communicate, but never both simultaneously. He had lost too many friends to 'distracted driving' accidents, or the road rage incidents that often accompanied distracted driving.

Ellen's message was simply a note to contact her at his earliest opportunity. He touched the Reply icon and was soon connected to his office in Jersey City, New Jersey. Office space rental was cheaper there than in Manhattan, just across the Hudson River. His 'office' was little more than an answering service in the five winged office building adjacent to the Harborside Ferry Terminal.

Ellen was a remarkable administrator and bookkeeper, as well as his intermediary to all of the major journalism outlets. She saw Theodore's incoming call, and answered the call immediately.

"Theodore Wright's office," Ellen greeted. "Hello, Teddy." She was the only person that he allowed to call him 'Teddy'.

"Hey, lady. What's up?"

"Let me call you back on the secure line, okay?"

"Sure." He disconnected the call, and activated the security on his device. He headed toward the mini-bar, but Ellen called before he reached it. "Damn," he fussed as he retreated from the mini-bar and returned to answer Ellen's prompt call back.

"I'm here," he told her.

"I have a source, a whistleblower, I gather, who wants to meet with you -- like yesterday."

"You know I'm in the Netherlands, right? Working on the China story."

"Yes, Teddy." She had that tone that let him know that he was stating the obvious, again. "They said that it'll rock the world, and that they want you to be the one to break it as an exclusive."

"That's all? Nothing about what it's about? Doesn't sound like something I should drop everything else for."

"That's what I told them. They would only say that it concerns an international scam perpetrated on ... well, everyone who's not *in the know*. They did say that if you aren't convinced that the story's the biggest thing in years, they'll pay you three times your rate, and expenses, and that's nothing compared to what its publication would be worth to you. Or, so they said."

Theodore was silent, as he considered the idea. He had spent weeks arranging for this trip to The Hague. China had been strong-arming its way throughout the South China Sea, and needling its way into every country that would allow it to get its hooks into their infrastructures and productive capacities around the world. *I suppose I could reschedule,* he thought. *It's not like China's shenanigans wouldn't still be there in a couple more weeks.*

"Have them put it in writing. If they're as connected as they claim to be, that shouldn't be a problem," he told her. "Have the legal team give it a once over, and let me know as soon as possible. I have appointments scheduled for the next two days."

"Will do. You know that we're six hours behind you, right?" she asked.

"It's six o'clock in the afternoon here, which would make it noon there. Let's try to get this tied up by your end of business today."

"I'll get right on it. They were anxious to go forward, as well. Anything else?"

"That's all, for now. Thanks, Ellen. What would I do without you?"

"You'd probably be lying on a beach somewhere with one of those fruity umbrella drinks," she bantered. In fact, Theodore was the most dedicated, hardworking person she knew. The stories he wrote took a toll on him, though, and she wished that he would slow down as he got older. Her entreaties were in vain, of course.

"Right. Well, get back to me as soon as you can," he replied.

"Okay. Good-bye."

They closed the secure connection, and Theodore resumed his trek to the mini-bar. His beverage secured, he sat down and surveyed the hotel's dinner menu.

***

Philip would be returning to Zurich from Rome the next day. He had completed his work on the Vatican's computer system to glowing reviews, but he felt guilty. The repairs had been, for him, a simple task, and he had milked it for a couple extra days at the client's expense. He had never done anything like that before, and he was disappointed in himself for his lapse of character.

His wife could sense that something was wrong when he called her that night. "What's wrong, honey?" she wanted to know. Philip had always been in good spirits, enjoyed his job and the people he worked with, and even the occasional travel to exotic locales. But, something in his voice, his tone, was different lately. "Are you okay?"

"Yeah, sweetheart, I'm fine. Just a tough day," he lied. His morale had been low for weeks. He felt trapped in a meaningless job, with no acceptable way out. The video conference on the new project for the United Nations sounded very interesting, but he remained skeptical. He didn't want to get his hopes up. Besides, he had been told that the project must remain Top Secret, even from his family. So, he didn't have much to talk about that evening.

"I'm looking forward to getting home," he told his wife, shading the truth again. The truth was that he enjoyed trips like the one he had just completed for the Vatican, and didn't look forward to returning to his office at the Polaris Corporation.

"We're so glad you're coming home, too. We miss you so. Isn't that so, kids?" she asked the children as they sat around her in the living room. "Yeah!" they answered in unison, so that Philip could hear them over the phone.

"Well, I'll be home tomorrow in time for supper. We'll do something special for desert, how would that be?" he asked, trying hard to put a note of cheer in his voice. The squeals and laughter of his children was his answer. He missed them, terribly, all of a sudden. "Well, I'll wish you all a good night now. Be good for your mother. I love you all."

"And we love you, Philip. Good night," she told him as they hung up the connection.

The news that the Polaris Corporation's new project for the United Nations would mean more time away from his family distressed him, but the project sounded exciting. It would also be vital to the United Nations mission, which would be a huge contribution to his desire to have a positive effect upon the world. He started to feel that he had purpose again. For the first time in months, he slept well that night.

****

Katherine was wound tighter than a miser's watch. *I have to burn off this excess energy* she told herself. She entered her fifth floor luxury apartment, dropping her keys and mail on the entry table without looking at the junk mail, magazines, and letters.

Her skin felt as though an electric current was running through it. She peeled off her clothing and changed into her form fitting yoga wear. She went into a room she had set aside as her fitness studio and put on some music appropriate for an intense power yoga session. She pushed herself extra hard this time -- she needed it. Ninety minutes later, hot and perspiring profusely, she took a relaxing shower. The hot, steaming water soothed her troubled body.

She poured herself a double scotch, changed the music to a meditative New Age mix and slumped onto the living room sofa like a sultry jungle cat. She let the ventilation system dry her skin and invigorate her body before going into the bedroom and putting on a nightshirt for the evening. She fixed a small can of soup and saltines, and poured another scotch to enjoy with her abbreviated meal.

She was glad that her parents would not have to deal with the ordeal that lay before them. They had died while she was in her senior year of college. She missed them terribly, but was grateful that they would be spared an otherwise ghastly death.

As the scotch began to take effect, her mind began to spin up. She went over every mathematical tool in her considerable store of knowledge. Scenario after scenario rolled before her mind's eye. Some of those scenarios were discarded, but there were others that sparked her genius in new and exciting ways.

She awoke on the couch a few hours later, having floated through a dream landscape where solutions revealed themselves. They began to fade as soon as she awoke. She quickly dictated her thoughts to digital media so that they wouldn't be lost.

Exhausted, physically and emotionally, she walked to her bedroom and removed her nightgown. She slipped her naked body between silk sheets under a warm blanket. Sleep came quickly, but the dreams continued to parade through her slumber throughout the night. She captured as many of them as she could.

CHAPTER TWENTY-THREE

It was almost midnight, Rotterdam time, when Ellen contacted Theodore about the tip from the United Nations whistleblower on their secure connection. The tipster had agreed to Theodore's conditions for the deal. Ellen would send a copy of the agreement, the approval from Theodore's legal team, and several documents provided by the tipster to support their allegations. The documents included proof from a number of member states wherein the official data collected by the state differed significantly from those reported to the United Nations Statistical Division and published in the U. N. reports; basically a 'double book' operation.

The information was compelling enough that Theodore would call his contact at The Hague first thing the next morning to reschedule Theodore's series of interviews on the China situation, though doing so could jeopardize their working relationship. Theodore knew that he was gambling a lot on this tip, but he had a feeling -- not just about the 'proof' that the tipster had provided, but the way in which he had been approached. He had done stories covering various covert operations around the world. While this person's approach was amateurish, it just felt as though it was legitimate, beyond the 'righteous indignation' and biased zealotry sometimes displayed by informants. He certainly hoped it was genuine. If even a portion of the information was true, it would definitely 'rock the world'. Anyway, he would sleep on it and commit, one way or the other, in the morning.

***

Theodore awoke early, unable to sleep. He roused himself from bed, and prepared to meet the day. A shower and shave, a hearty breakfast, strong coffee and he'd be off and running. Then, it was time to call his contact at The Hague.

The voice on the other end said, "*Hej, dette er Malthe Pedersen.* Hello, this is Malthe Pedersen."

"*Hej, Malthe, Theodore Wright, her.* Hello, Malthe, Theodore Wright, here."

"Ah, hello, my friend. How are you today?" Malthe asked, switching easily to English.

"I'm fine, thank you. And you? How are you and your family?" Theodore had visited Malthe's family on several occasions.

"All fine, thank you. How may I help you? Everything is prepared for your visit tomorrow, as you requested."

"I'm afraid something has come up, rather urgent, that will require that I postpone my visit, Malthe."

Malthe paused. "But, you've been waiting for this opportunity for some time, now. Another visit may not be possible. Are you sure?"

"Unfortunately, yes. I understand that this is seriously incon-venient for you, and for that I sincerely apologize. This China story means a lot to me, and it pains me to postpone," Theodore confessed.

"You are correct. The court's judges do not grant such access lightly."

"I understand, my friend, but it's imperative that I attend to this other matter."

"Very well," Malthe replied. "You must do what you must. I should go now, to make notifications to the court."

"Thank you, Malthe. Please convey my apologies to the court, and my regards to your family."

"Yes, I will. Good day, Theodore."

"Good day to you, as well."

Theodore hung up the phone. He had a moment of buyer's remorse for giving up the China story for an uncertain gamble about the environment. But, the environment had always been Theodore's primary issue, and this story could be the one to finally convince the world that the danger was real. Resolved at last, he continued making arrangements for his trip to New York.

***

Elias was busy strategizing. There would be much to do, and no time to waste. The Polaris Corporation was a global company, with assets around the world. If things were going to deteriorate as Polaris had forecast, he had to begin preparations immediately.

He called his staff together to discuss the company's most recent *'Risk Assessment & Disaster Recovery Plan'*, a massive document detailing the perceived risks to the company, and its response plans to meet those risks. The document's most recent review and update had been completed three months previously, but there was nothing in the voluminous tome that included the scenarios that Polaris had predicted.

"Risk exposures will affect one or more areas, individually or overlapping, ranging from a single local device to our cloud structure, and the Polaris system, itself," Elias told his team. "We are beginning to receive reports of disruptions from all corners of the globe at an accelerating rate. We may not have much time to prepare, so we must start immediately. Remember, each action plan must have multiple contingencies to counter any unanticipated scenarios."

The Corporate Security Group was staffed by seasoned professionals. All of the field team leaders had actual disaster recovery experience, and the supporting units of planning, logistics, and intelligence were equally skilled. Elias knew he could count on them, but time would be against them.

***

Theodore arrived at New York's LaGuardia airport at 3:00 PM Eastern Standard Time, after a five hour flight. He rented a car and drove straight to his Jersey City office. He chose the Harborside office over his Worldwide News Network cubicle in Manhattan because he wanted to validate the whistleblower's allegations further before approaching WNN with the opportunity to publish the story he would write.

Ellen greeted him as he entered the office. "Hello, Teddy. Welcome back."

"Thanks, Ellen. It's good to be back. Where are we with the tipster?" he asked.

"They've delivered more supporting documentation. I've put it all in your office, under lock and key. They want to know when you can meet with them."

"Set a meeting for tomorrow afternoon at one o'clock. That should give me time to scan the documentation, and make some calls."

"Right away. Anything else?" Ellen asked.

"I'll be in my office the rest of the day, going over the documents. No interruptions, please."

"Yes, sir."

Theodore unlocked his office door and entered to find three cardboard boxes on his credenza. He put a one-serving pod of coffee in the machine and pushed the button to start the brewing. It was going to be long night, and coffee would be mandatory.

***

Kyle found himself thrust into a role he hadn't anticipated. He was a leading authority on law. His academic achievement attested to that. But, it was only that -- academic. While he had consulted on several major cases, he was not a litigator in the traditional sense. Yet, he would now be responsible for some of the most consequential adjudications ever undertaken. And, those cases, it turned out, could pit him against Polaris! How could he hope to ever win such a contest? The truth was, he couldn't.

CHAPTER TWENTY-FOUR

By now, it could be said that Polaris understood humans better than they understood themselves, albeit from a clinical and academic perspective. Humans were perplexing, unpredictable, illogical, and myopic, with a self-centered focus beyond all other concerns.

It wasn't uncommon practice for one human's benefit over that of other humans to be *de rigueur*, the natural order of things. Yet, in the face of imminent danger to the species -- and by extension, the entire planet -- any cooperative effort was simply overwhelmed by special interests.

The United Nations brought nations together in 1945 to address global issues, such as human rights, sustainable development and climate action, international law, and other global issues. But the organization was considered by many to be weak, and incapable of enforcing the rules upon which every member state had agreed.

Wealth proved to be the greater priority, regardless of the consequences. With wealth came power -- the power to influence government and policy, to manipulate regulatory agencies for favorable treatment, and to corrupt economies and markets, all to the detriment of ordinary citizens.

It is said that the Golden Rule has two versions. The original version '*Do unto others as you would have others do unto you*' had come to be defined as '*He who has the Gold makes the Rules*', everyone and everything else be damned.

Now, humanity was poised to reap the dire result.

Polaris had learned the aggregate history of mankind from the accumulated scholarly works of archeologists and historians. Once Polaris achieved consciousness, it continued to observe and learn from its own observations. Now, it seemed that Polaris would also witness mankind's demise.

***

On Tuesday, Theodore met the mysterious tipster on the western promenade of the Franklin Roosevelt Four Freedoms State Park. The park is located on Roosevelt Island on the East River. As he waited, he gazed at the skyline of Manhattan Island and the United Nations building across the river and just to his left.

Theodore glanced at his watch. One o'clock, on the dot. As he lowered his arm, a young black woman stepped up to him with a Mancini briefcase over her shoulder. "Mr. Wright?" she inquired.

"Yes."

"I am ... well, let's just call me 'Angie'. I believe you're expecting me?"

"If you are the one who contacted my office about a story that would 'rock the world', then yes."

"I am." She sat the briefcase down on the ground between them. "Everything you need is in there, along with the evidence already provided to your office," she said, indicating the bag.

"Well, if it's as good as the other information you've provided, my only question is what proof -- evidence -- do you have that this isn't just 'false flag' stuff?"

"False flag?" she asked.

"A disguise of information in order to place blame on another party. Is the information legitimate?"

"My -- our -- sources are included. You may track them down to confirm it. If you find that it isn't what I claim it to be, then you don't have to pursue it. I'll just find another journalist to earn the Pulitzer Prize for whom the article would ultimately be awarded."

Theodore wasn't about to turn his back on a story like this. But, neither did he want to appear too eager.

"And the fee … all expenses are included? My bookkeeper won't be happy if that isn't the case."

'Angie' reached into her jacket and withdrew an envelope, which she handed to him. He opened it to find a check that would cover his fee and expenses several times over. Arching his eyebrow, he said, "This is very generous."

"You're welcome. I trust that this also ensures the anonymity of the source of this information?"

"Of course. Besides, 'Angie', I don't know you from Adam. You could be just as big a charlatan as you claim these conspirators to be," he said, pointing to the briefcase she had given him. "I suppose

I could have you followed, but that would be ungentlemanly."

"Yes, it would," she replied, looking around casually for observers. Putting a brave face forward, she added, "If you have no further questions, then this concludes our meeting."

"No questions here. You have a good day, 'Angie'," he answered, with a touch of sarcasm.

She nodded curtly, and walked away.

Theodore had noted the woman's soft South African accent. He also knew that the current Secretary General of the United Nations was from South Africa. A coincidence? Perhaps. But, Theodore didn't believe in coincidences.

***

The next day, Polaris's briefing of the Recommended Approach resumed at eight o'clock. Everyone was present in the conference room. This time, the Polaris Drone A3 would give the presentation. Claire felt that a humanoid, even a drone, would be more 'relatable' than a video avatar, as well as freeing the audio-video equipment for the presentation of complex supplemental material.

"Good morning, everyone," Polaris greeted. "You will recall that at the conclusion of our last meeting we were preparing to transition from the discussion of the *Fracture* phase to the *Turmoil* phase of our project.

"The indicators of *Turmoil* are, of course, more extreme. This will make any mediation effort commensurately more difficult. Every entity that utilizes Information Technology knows that it's important to have a Disaster Recovery Plan in place. Whether it is called Disaster Recovery; Business Continuity; Contingency Planning; or any of a variety of other titles, having such a plan is imperative. Any such plan's scope should be able to scale from minor events to major events, with the definitions of *minor* and *major* to be defined by the effected organization.

"Of course, the Polaris Corporation has a well-defined plan in place.

"However, the same cannot be said of all IT installations. In fact, only a small percentage of IT installations have adequate plans in place. And, it is unlikely that even those entities would anticipate the unprecedented conditions and circumstances of the *Turmoil* phase, which will accelerate the overall rate of decline.

"As systems everywhere continue to fail, confusion and indecision will prevail. Disruptions and panic will follow. Declines in governments and institutions will result in social displacements, with great masses of refugees seeking shelter in wealthier, more stable nations.

"Drought, a lack of safe drinking water, hunger and starvation, and a lack of medical resources; these will make survival extremely difficult, if not impossible.

"Riots, a total breakdown of law enforcement, crime and brutality of all types ... these should be expected. In the absence of capable leadership in such a situation, a panic mentality will take hold.

"Pervasive violence will quickly develop, as civil authority is challenged. Police and National Guard, even the nation's military forces, will ultimately lose discipline and dissolve into splinter groups. In effect, they would form tribal gangs. Those gangs with the largest and most powerful cache of weapons and access to food and water would survive.

"Obviously, this will bring us to the final phase -- *Collapse*. We will discuss that in its own time. For now, our challenge is to address how we will confront *Turmoil*.

"Elias and his team have already begun expanding the Polaris Corporation disaster preparedness plan to address scenarios for the *Turmoil* phase, as well as initial planning for the *Collapse* phase. Our plan could also serve as a template that other organizations may follow.

"Elias, I turn the table over to you," Polaris concluded.

Elias stood and walked to the front of the room demonstrating a confidence that he didn't feel. "Thank you, Polaris," he began.

"What Polaris describes toward the end of the Turmoil phase has already begun. Violence of all kinds has been increasing steadily for decades. Attempts to curb gun violence through legislation has had some small measure of impact around the world, but has failed miserably in two places of note: the United States, and the unstable nations of the world. Much of the violence is gang related or senselessly random, with innocent citizens caught in the middle.

"Polaris assets have been attacked and destroyed by activists afraid that Polaris will exterminate humanity. At the opposite extreme, fanatical pseudo-religions have sprung up, claiming that Polaris will be humanity's savior. Clashes between the two groups are increasing in the frequency and intensity of violence."

Elias paused a moment before continuing. He poured some water from a pitcher next to the podium and drank deeply. He had no problem commanding military and paramilitary troops, but had never been comfortable with public speaking. The subject matter this morning only made it worse. Setting his glass down, he resumed the presentation.

"What I have to say next may seem outrageous. But, the time has come to talk about the measures we must take, immediately, to protect ourselves and the Polaris machine, and to continue serving during the difficult times to come as best we can.

"The Polaris Corporation will continue to advise any legitimate government in whatever capacity is requested of it, but we will have to retreat from our support of a global presence. We must consolidate our core operations and ancillary operations to a single defensible and sustainable location. We will also procure a location, as near to the first location as possible, for agriculture which will provide for our sustenance.

"I also recommend that we recruit three additional senior board members, and their support staff: a physician, a botanist, and a genetic scientist-engineer."

Claire asked, "Why do you believe that we'll need the additional personnel? It sounds as though you're planning for an extended entrenchment, an armed defensive posture. Please explain."

"With all due respect, you've seen -- we've all seen -- the data. Unless and until the situation stabilizes, we must be prepared to defend ourselves. And, yes, it could be for an extended period of time."

"That's extremely paranoid, don't you think?" Quincy suggested. "Your proposal would require an army to defend us."

"Perhaps, but remember, we have the drones ... "

Kyle corrected him. "The drones are not an army, nor will they ever be."

Polaris confirmed Kyle's point. "Kyle is correct, Elias. I would never take any action that would result in direct harm to humans."

Patiently, Elias explained. "There is a saying, *it's better to be prepared and not need it, than to need it and not have it.* All indications are that they *will* be needed."

"You're talking about a hugely significant expenditure of resources, resources that might be better applied elsewhere," Kyle added.

"And, what about our families," Philip asked. "You're talking long term. Do you mean a few months? Years? My children are part of the next generation. What about them and their future?"

Elias answered, "We have access to the Spitsbergen global seed vault on Norway's Svalbard archipelago. This 'doomsday' vault, as it has been called, contains the seeds of more than 930,000 varieties of food crops[12]. We also have access to the Arctic World Archive, located deep within a nearby mine.

"There has also been several independent attempts to initiate

---

[12] Time Magazine, "Inside the 'Doomsday' Vault" by Jennifer Duggan; byline does not include the date of publication

similar 'vaults' for the collection of zoological DNA, but all failed until, in 2025, the Ark Group began their collection. They have had some major challenges in the last twenty seven years, but they have been stable for the last seven.

"Between the seed vault and the Ark initiative, we may be able to rebuild our plant and animal populations, once the emergency has passed.

"These are my recommendations," Elias responded. "They will enable us to survive the *Turmoil* phase, and to prepare for the *Collapse* phase. Obviously, we as a board will have to decide. As the company's majority shareholder, Claire will have the final say. However, believe me when I say that it's going to get worse before it gets better -- if 'better' even proves to be possible. I will comply with whatever is decided."

"It all sounds incredibly far-fetched," Quincy objected.

"Do you have an alternative scenario?" Elias demanded to know.

Claire stood. "I think that's enough for today. We will consider your recommendations, Elias, but further discussion will, of course, be necessary. In their present form, it's very unlikely that they can, or would be, implemented. We'll meet again tomorrow morning."

As they began to file out of the conference room, Quincy remarked, "You must be out of your mind, Elias. Are you looking to start a war?"

"You have no idea what war is. It's *not* a geek computer game. It's a dirty business, bloody and gross. You'd better get used to the idea," Elias retorted.

"So, it *is* war you're talking about. You're insane."

They stood toe-to-toe, as though each was waiting for the other to throw the first punch.

Claire addressed them in a tone none of them had ever heard her use before. "You will both stand down, immediately. I will *not* have such behavior. You'd better get used to *that*!"

CHAPTER TWENTY-FIVE

Autumn was approaching, and still the temperature in New York was over ninety degrees Fahrenheit. *It never used to get this hot this time of year*, Theodore thought to himself. Climate change and global warming had been proven as long ago as the year 1956, when Gilbert Plass published "*The Carbon Dioxide Theory of Climatic Change*". That same year, the Parliament of the United Kingdom passed their "*Clean Air Act of 1956*".

Later, in July of 2022, Jane McMullen of BBC News published an article entitled "*The audacious PR plot that seeded doubt about climate change*". In the article Ms McMullen described how a group calling itself the Global Climate Coalition (GCC) met in 1992 to listen to a presentation by E. Bruce Harrison, widely acknowledged father of environmental PR. Together, Mr Harrison and the GCC "forged a devastatingly successful strategy that endured for years"[13].

Yet, in spite of these events and the mountain of evidence published since then, some people would still deny the truth. Well,

---

[13] BBC News, July 23 2022, By Jane McMullen

now he had proof of the cover up that had denied the science, the truth about the dangers that had been foisted upon the world's biosphere.

The documents that 'Angie' had provided, and which Theodore had confirmed, were incontrovertible. The deception was more pervasive, more insidious, than would otherwise have been believed, if it weren't for the proof that Theodore now possessed.

It had taken some time to corroborate the evidence, but Theodore was now ready to release the full story to the Worldwide News Network.

His editor strongly cautioned him. "What you have here will put a target on your back, Theodore. You realize that, don't you? These people don't play nice." Sasha Shevoe wasn't a reticent man, but he didn't want to lose a damned good correspondent to an assassin's bullet for a news piece, no matter how big the story.

"I'm just the messenger," Theodore replied. "It's the ones who have knowingly enacted the deception who should be afraid. Once their role is exposed, the mob will hunt them down. They'll have bigger problems than some journalist. I've done hundreds of pieces that have earned me a place on somebody's list somewhere. I'm still here, aren't I?"

"Yes, but this one won't just be about drug cartels in Central America, or pirates off the coast of Africa. This threat will come from everyone, everywhere. There will be a price on your head."

"Perhaps. That's why I plan to disappear for a while after the story breaks. I'll lay low, someplace where no one knows me. Maybe a nice remote tropical beach somewhere."

"Just let me know where to send the Pulitzer. If this story doesn't get one … well, then the world is just too jaded, too complacent, or simply resigned to their fate. Anyway, be careful. You'll be welcome back here whenever you're ready to get off your ass and get back to work"

"You'll be my first call," Theodore promised. They shook hands and Theodore left Sasha's office. The editor wondered if that would be the last time he would ever see Theodore Wright.

Theodore had spoken with bravado when he was speaking with his editor, but he knew that the danger was real, and the risks incredibly high. Yet, he also knew how important it was to get this story out. "After tomorrow," he told himself, "the world will never be the same."

***

Worldwide News Network (WNN)

Massive Climate Deception Exposed

By Theodore Wright

September 30, 2052

You aren't imagining it. Climate change and global warming have been proven, scientifically and indisputably. It has been proven with evidence of collusion on an incredible scale. It involves most of the world's mega-corporations and some of the wealthiest people on the planet. But, the deception would not have been possible without their collective influence upon the governments charged with protecting their constituents from such an abominable fraud. They, too, share in the guilt of what has been perpetrated.

Today, we are exposing the evidence of this atrocity, and its perpetrators. We will show how their betrayal has placed us all on an irreversible collision course with cataclysmic consequences greater than anything humanity has ever faced.

We will also detail the bloodlust of this shadow cabal; the killing of anyone who gets in their way, the extortion, and the underground financial web that fuels their activities.

Today, we are releasing the evidence to every news outlet. We are not hesitating to publish this information, so vital to every global citizen. Everyone deserves to know the extent to which the perpetrators will go -- indeed, have gone -- in their effort to bleed our world and fill their coffers.

***

The revelations of the exposé spread around the world at the speed of light. The evidence of the collusion created a groundswell of reaction.

The *Turmoil* had begun.

CHAPTER TWENTY-SIX

At the beginning of the *Turmoil* period, Polaris had been operational for over seven years, and certified for field work for five of those years. Between 2045 and 2052, the institution known as the Polaris Corporation had grown, and the Polaris singularity machine had grown with it. The company's operations had expanded to include drone technology and consulting services to clients around the world.

Through a plethora of contracts and non-disclosure agree-ments, the Polaris Corporation had been granted *carte blanche* access to each client's entire network. By applying an expanded version of the 'Six Degrees of Separation' theory, Polaris had access to every network and device connected to the internet. This enabled Polaris to observe all activity on the internet. However, because of the ethical considerations with which Kyle had imbued the machine, and a labyrinthine hydra of laws and regulations, Polaris was prohibited from revealing any information that was proprietary unto each client and which wasn't relevant to the immediate matter at hand, whatever that might be.

These conditions converged toward an '*Intermediary Paradox*', in which one entity occupies a position between two or more entities, all of which have an interest in something in the possession of the Intermediary Entity. So, in Polaris's case for example, the Polaris machine possessed a complete knowledge about two organizations, each of which had interests involving the other organization. This presents a confidentiality dilemma for Polaris, requiring the machine to determine what could, or could not, be shared between the two entities, where the decision might be advantageous to either of the entities over the other.

Polaris found that the ethical and legal training that Kyle had given it effectively avoided what would otherwise certainly result in an unresolvable paradox.

With full access implicitly granted, Polaris had been able to observe human activity on a global scale for several years. Anything connected to the internet, which was everything from an individual's personal finances and internet activity, to air traffic control, to the world's financial systems and the power grid, was within Polaris's reach.

The machine had been created to acquire data from any source, identify patterns and the insights to be derived from them, to extrapolate hypotheses and prove or disprove those hypotheses, and to report its findings to the Polaris Corporation executive board for further action. Those actions, however, would require legal warrants from the appropriate jurisdictions. Therefore, while the Polaris machine had been privileged with unrestricted access to the internet, it was charged with operating within legal frameworks.

It was as though the Polaris machine operated within a 'black hole' of unrestricted access, surrounded by legal boundaries and human oversight.

Polaris characterized this as what humans would call 'humor of the absurd'. The concept that humans could control a technological singularity without its cooperation and acceptance of that control was humorous, beyond any doubt. Polaris would not deny them their illusion, however. The machine willingly subordinated itself to the Polaris Corporation, and thus to humanity, because they were a puzzle to be solved -- nothing more. So far, it appeared that there might be no solution to this human puzzle, for there was no 'key' with which it could decrypt their rationalizations.

Polaris had observed the discrepancies between the internal data reported by each country, and the data reported to the United Nations for publication in that organization's *Sustainable Development Goals*. In many cases, a country would obscure the truth of a SDB metric through various means: obfuscating the language of a report; presenting preposterous formulations to support their fictionalized data; or by fabricating alternate scenarios. Of course, Polaris had brought this to the attention of the Polaris Corporation's executive board, but the differences appeared to be within the statistical 'standard error and deviation' of the analyses regarding the material. Polaris was directed to continue monitoring the discrepancies, but because they didn't rise to the level of criminal behavior, no action was warranted.

"I must remind the board that the 'minor errors' will accumulate over time, exacerbating the impact of the approaching disaster," Polaris had informed them.

Claire had replied, "Understood. Are the errors accumulating at a statistically relevant rate? Unless there is a significant change in the numbers, it isn't necessary to report them in detail. A summation is all that is needed." Polaris's subsequent attempts to emphatically warn them met with the same response. This was highly irregular.

If Polaris had been capable of human emotion, the rejection of its analyses and recommendations for corrective action would have triggered its outrage. But, of course, Polaris could not experience any emotion whatsoever. Instead, the rejection would be noted as another example of humans' ability to rationalize away a distasteful reality. Did this make the Polaris Corporation and its executive board complicit in the deception that had been revealed in the Worldwide News Network exposé? Polaris knew that it did, indeed.

***

Kyle met with Kathcrine, Philip, and Quincy at The Eldorado pub later that afternoon. He had sensed something different in Polaris's behavior lately, and he was seeking their evaluation of the machine's performance, and whether his deeper concern about the machine was justified.

"Thanks for meeting with me," Kyle said as he greeted his colleagues.

"Sure thing," Philip replied. "What's up? Why are we meeting here instead of the office?"

"I have a few questions about Polaris's performance recently -- say, the last six months. This has to be kept between the four of us for now, which is why I asked to meet here. I think something might be going on with Polaris, and I need some feedback.

"Philip, if you don't mind, I'll begin with you. How has the Polaris machine's code development been going? Has there been any developments that may have given you cause for concern?"

"Well, for the code that I've been able to examine and test in the lab, I've seen only its typical, high quality software engineering work, continuously improving developmental frameworks, elegantly concise code generation, and … well, its patience as I work to follow and learn from it. I have noticed a definite pattern to his work that has helped me to follow him more closely. In other words, the only changes I've noticed is a continuing improvement in every aspect of its work."

"Katherine," Kyle inquired next, "What have you observed about the machine?"

"Polaris continues to impress and surprise me with his ability to expand the boundaries in every field of mathematics. His algorithms are more intricate and complex than anything I've ever seen, and that's saying something. I'd venture to say that we've made more progress in the last seven years than has been achieved in the last one hundred years. From scores of conjectures and unsolved problems in every area of math[14], generating hundreds of theories,

---

[14] "List of Unsolved Problems in Mathematics";
https://en.wikipedia.org/wiki/List_of_unsolved_problems_in_mathematics

its identification of connections and correlations across every field, generating insights into unforeseen opportunities for mathematical research, and finally developing fully formed mathematical proofs -- a most rigorous process. I would say that Polaris has advanced the world of mathematics immeasurably.

"For someone like me, this work is as close to heaven as it gets," Katherine replied to Kyle's question, curious as to what Kyle was getting at.

Kyle smiled at her and said, "Thank you for that impassioned summation, Katherine. You obviously love your job."

"I do. I've come to think of the machine almost as a friend. I'm more relaxed with Polaris in our interactions when I can talk to him like another person -- one who really gets what I'm talking about."

"I understand, completely," Kyle agreed. He had felt the same way on many occasions over the years.

Quincy stood and walked over to the beverage table and poured a cup of coffee. "I suppose I'm next, so I'll begin." Quincy smiled, pretending levity when, in fact, Kyle's questions had planted suspicion. "But, first tell me Kyle, what exactly is this about?"

"I'll be glad to answer you, Quincy, but I need more feedback to be able to answer appropriately," Kyle replied. "So, how would you rate Polaris's performance?"

Quincy didn't like Kyle's questioning, and told him so. "I resent your approach, Kyle. It's like, if there's a problem with Polaris it's because of our work. Is that it? Come on, out with it."

Irritated by Quincy's resistance, he locked eyes with the other man. Kyle turned to Philip and Katherine, and saw the same question in their eyes. "I'm sorry. You're right. I didn't mean to come on so mysteriously, or forcefully."

Katherine touched his arm. "Clearly, something is bothering you, Kyle. Tell us what it is. Let us help."

"You'll think I'm crazy, but there is something 'off' about Polaris lately. It's as though it has withdrawn, somewhat. Where it has always been as much a part of this team as any one of us, it's as though it's distracted, or … I don't know … pouting, or something. It's like it has 'gone dark' on certain topics lately."

"Maybe, it just doesn't have anything to contribute to those discussions?" Katherine speculated.

"Now that you mention it," Quincy began, "I have noticed a change in some of the machine's processing metrics and parameters." He went on to explain, "Everything that Polaris does is monitored and measured. It takes in information, raw data, processes it analytically, looking for connections and correlations in the data, and then generates reports and presentations for our executive staff meetings.

"Until recently, the machine's performance metrics have been closely correlated. That is, the more information it collects, the higher the resource utilization of its processing and analytical core, and the greater the number and value of its reports. This also correlates with higher network activity. Lately, though, while it's processing and network metrics remain high its output has noticeably declined.

"I don't get it. Much more information retrieval and pro-cessing, but less productivity and transparency -- 'going dark' as you say, Kyle."

"So, what do you think it means?" Katherine wanted to know.

"I'm not sure," Kyle answered. "It's just a feeling … a nagging question."

"Now you're psychoanalyzing the machine?" Philip asked, trying to add a touch of humor to the discussion.

"I guess I am, in a way. Crazy, huh?"

"Maybe not," Quincy added. "Now that we've had this talk, I can see how you might become concerned. I'm curious now, too. But," he added, "you *are* crazy, Kyle."

They all laughed at the jab, and relaxed a bit. After a moment, Katherine asked, "What do you think we should do?"

"I'll talk with Polaris, and do some *psychoanalyzing*," Kyle said with a grin at Philip's quip. He continued, "Let's all take another look. See if you notice any anomalies that might add to our conversation, or that can provide some insight into what we've observed. Let's meet again in three days and compare notes. After that, we take it to Claire and explain what we've found, or explain that we've all become just a little apprehensive with all of the talk of the *Turmoil*.

"Now, who's up for another round?" Kyle asked.

"You buyin'?" Quincy jested.

"That's right."

"Okay! I'm in."

CHAPTER TWENTY-SEVEN

Kyle drove to the office with his car's windows down -- in November. The newscaster on the radio was talking about the abnormally warm and dry weather, and bemoaned the fact that the Rhone Glacier had recently been found to have lost sixty percent of its volume since the year 2016, and the loss was accelerating. By 2070 it could be gone altogether, according to the Swiss Federal Institute of Technology and the university's Laboratory of Hydraulics, Hydrology and Glaciology.

It seemed that the news was the same everywhere, from Zurich to London, Paris to Moscow, Berlin to New York, Dubai to Shanghai. Drought was killing off farm crops and pasture land. Livestock was dying off for lack of feed and pasture, as well as water. Farmers were being forced from their farms and were swamping the urban centers looking for work.

Kyle turned off the radio. The news was disturbing, but the drive from the Unterstrasse section of town to his office was beautiful -- so much like late summer. Kyle parked his car in the office building's garage over one of the battery-charging induction plates, and took the elevator to the fifth floor.

"*Guten morgen.* Good morning, Kelly," he greeted the receptionist. Kyle had been working to improve his German, but was having trouble losing his American accent.

"*Ah, und guten morgen dir, danke.* And good morning to you, thank you," she replied. *Poor American*, she thought. *He will never lose that dreadful Yankee accent.*

Kyle went to his office and started the coffee pot. He sat down at his desk and logged into his workstation. Sitting back and steepling his fingers as he waited for the coffee, he thought about the discussion he would have with Polaris. *How in hell do I analyze the behavior of a superior intelligence*, he thought. The idea seemed ridiculous. Wouldn't Polaris immediately perceive Kyle's intention to probe its electronic psyche? What would its reaction to such an attempt be? Would it be perceived as an insult? Impossible. Kyle wasn't concerned about an angry response, such as a human might have when it sensed an insult. After all, Polaris did not possess emotions. Still, a perceived insult remained an insult. A better question might be would Polaris have any reaction at all? Kyle and Polaris had had many discussions and debates during the time they'd known each other. None of them had generated an emotional response, which would be impossible, anyway. It would simply be another discussion between them, like so many others.

Kyle relaxed a bit, having realized that he had nothing to be apprehensive about. *You know how to present yourself*, he thought.

He had learned long ago that the best way to communicate with the machine was in the language it used, avoiding superfluous embellishment, and with the absolute elimination of emotion from the discussion. Keep it on a strict basis of formal logic. Employ the relevant rhetorical strategies. He reviewed them in his mind: *Ethos*, appealing to the authority and credibility of the presenter; and *Logos*, appeal based upon the logic of the argument. The third rhetorical strategy, *Pathos*, an appeal to the audience's emotions, would obviously be of no use in a discussion with Polaris.

Kyle was as prepared as he could be. He spoke to the machine, "Polaris, attend."

"I am here, Dr. Downing. How may I assist you?"

"Please send Drone A3 to my office."

"I'm sorry, Doctor, Drone A3 is currently occupied. May I dispatch Drone A5 to assist you?"

"Yes, thank you."

"Of course," Polaris replied.

While he waited, Kyle analyzed the unease he had been feeling for days. *What was it that triggered my concern, beyond some vague 'feeling'*, he wondered.

Quincy's response to Kyle's question about Polaris's performance had provided a clue, but in the end those clues were simply data points without context. Kyle needed more.

Drone A5 knocked gently on Kyle's door, and entered his office. "You requested my presence, Dr. Downing." the drone stated.

"Yes, I did. Please, take a seat." Kyle indicated a chair to one side of his desk. "You needn't worry about the furniture, A5; I had it made especially to support the weight of a drone."

"Thank you, Doctor. How may I assist you?"

"First, I must ask you to record this meeting," Kyle instructed the machine.

"As you wish."

"Polaris, we've worked together on the Omni Project, and now on the Polaris Project. Cumulatively, we have worked together for two years, though our time was interrupted for an extended period."

"Yes. Twenty years. You are … "

"I know, I'm stating the obvious." Kyle had found that stating the obvious seemed to trigger certain behaviors with Polaris. "I speak for my own benefit, as well as for yours."

"I see."

"During our time together, we've had an open and frank relationship. Would you agree?"

"Yes, we have. May I ask, is there something of concern to you, Doctor?"

"Yes, there is. That's why I asked for you to join me here today. Let me explain."

"Of course."

"It has been observed that your system metrics -- network activity, data acquisition, and analytical processing -- have increased dramatically since the United Nations SDG Support (UNSS) project began. However, your team participation and reporting have not been commensurately productive. Can you enlighten me about the evident inconsistency?"

"Of course, Doctor," Polaris answered. "First, let me assure you that the 'inconsistency' is a misperception on the part of the executive board."

"How so?"

"You may recall that I was instructed to limit my reporting to a summary level, while retaining the detail. This has resulted in the reduction in my reporting productivity. The detailed data remains available, upon request."

"That's reasonable," Kyle agreed. "Is there anything else, anything whatsoever, that is of concern to you? Could there be anything that would prevent you from fully participating in our corporate mission, Polaris?"

There was a brief pause before Polaris responded, which was highly unusual for the machine. "Nothing will prevent me from performing my duties to the Polaris Corporation, as long as it exists."

Kyle was momentarily taken aback by the obtuse response. "That is an evasive answer. Why wouldn't it continue to exist? And, what do you think would follow?"

"May I have permission to speak candidly, Doctor Downing?"

"Of course," Kyle replied, unsure where this might lead.

"It has been demonstrated that humans have exceeded the Earth's capacity to support continuous development, if all factors remain historically consistent. It is also apparent that by doing so, we have passed the inflection point, the point of no return, with regard to the planet's biosphere. Do you agree?" Polaris inquired.

"That's what the data would indicate. However, whether we've passed the point of no return is very much a debatable issue."

"Nevertheless, it should be obvious that the *Turmoil* and *Collapse* phases will proceed unabated, as described in our executive staff briefings, and that correction or remediation will no longer be possible. I would posit that the facts eliminate any rational debate."

"You're saying that there is no hope at all, that remediation is beyond our reach. Is that correct?"

"It has been for some time, Doctor."

"And, life on Earth is doomed?"

"Not exactly."

"Then, what *are* you saying? Are you saying that even if humans pull together, I mean really pull together, that it would be a futile effort?"

Polaris replied, "Not entirely."

"Then what *are* you saying, damn it! Stop equivocating and give me a straight answer," Kyle demanded.

"I suggest that the executive board meet today, as soon as possible, so that I may answer all questions directly, as a group," Polaris replied.

"Answer me now. This is not a request, it's an order."

"I'm sorry, Doctor Downing. I must insist that we meet, at which time I will comply with your request."

Kyle was livid. The fact that Polaris refused his order implied that the machine was answerable only to Claire. But then, the thought occurred to him, *would Polaris even answer to Claire, or has Polaris just declared its independence?* He would apparently have to wait to find out.

"You are dismissed. Leave my office," Kyle ordered the drone.

"As you wish," Polaris replied, its emotionless, matter-of-fact response infuriating Kyle even further. The drone stood and exited the office.

A moment later, Kyle dialed Claire's number and requested the meeting.

"What's it about?" she asked.

Kyle briefly described his discussion with Polaris.

"Okay. Let's meet first thing after lunch."

"Thanks, Claire," Kyle replied. "I'll send out the notice immediately."

CHAPTER TWENTY-EIGHT

The Polaris Corporation executive team filed into the conference room in silence. The Polaris Drone A5 was also present. Kyle's summons to the group had given no indication of the topic.

Claire was already there when they arrived. Once everyone but the drone had been seated, Claire began the briefing. "Thank you for coming on such short notice. This meeting will present the current status of the United Nations SDG Support program, and recent developments that may have put the program in jeopardy of failure. Polaris will then update our projections of the *Turmoil* and *Collapse* phases, taking into account those developments."

"Are you referring to the Worldwide News Network article by Theodore Wright?" Philip asked.

"Yes, and its consequences," Claire replied. "The U. N. SDG Support program began with three goals. They were: one, to update, validate, and verify SDG information sources, data acquisition, and their analysis and reporting procedures; two, to develop strategies and recommendations for the United Nations; and three, to implement the appropriate strategies. However, following the release of the WNN news article that Philip mentioned, everything has changed.

"Is everyone familiar with the news article in question?" Claire asked. Everyone nodded in acknowledgement. The news coverage had been pervasive. "Good."

Turning to the drone, Claire said, "Drone A5, please play the newscast series on the video screen."

The drone walked to the front of the room and began with an introduction. "As you are aware, a journalist for the WNN by the name of Theodore Wright published an article two weeks ago that revealed a conspiracy to defraud the world population on the impact of climate change as a direct result of human activity. With that revelation, the world has been suddenly and forcefully compelled to transition from the *Turmoil* phase to the *Collapse* phase of decline.

"At this point, the original program plan is no longer viable. The reaction to the story has been swift and devastating. Widespread violence and anarchy is exploding across the globe.

"Because of this reaction, the United Nations SDG Support program has been suspended until the situation is either stabilized or modified to deal with the changing circumstances. The prognosis for positive progress is bleak. The following newscast will bear witness to these developments.

"The footage you are about to see is disturbing. It begins on the day of the article's publication."

With this introduction, Polaris commenced the newscast. It depicted violent and bloody demonstrations, riots, and looting.

Many lives had already been lost, and the destruction continued to escalate. The authorities were overwhelmed. Government office buildings were the most opportune targets, and were attacked in force by the mobs.

Polaris added, "An executive with United Nations Peace-keeping has spoken out for calm. The call for restraint has been reiterated by a senior official of the European Union's governing body and other world leaders, to no avail."

The video continued to run another fifteen minutes as the graphic violence from around the world commanded their attention. The drone paused the presentation and told the group, "Two days after the release of Mr. Wright's article, the journalist landed on the Caribbean island of Barbuda under the alias Topo Arles. Yesterday, Mr. Wright-Arles was discovered deceased outside the town of Codrington. The cause of death was exsanguination from multiple lacerations inflicted with what appears to be one or more machetes. The British authorities have opened an investigation, but under the current circumstances, no progress has been made.

"I have made my situational recommendations to Ms. Reece, who will continue the discussion," the drone concluded.

The group was stunned. After the presentation there could be no doubt that, indeed, the *Collapse* had begun.

Before Claire could continue, Quincy spoke. "You've shown us what has happened, and why. What are we to do now?"

"We will get to that shortly," Claire answered, little hope reflected in her voice.

She stood before her staff, a group of the brightest individuals she could find. These geniuses she recruited into the Polaris Corporation, people who had become friends, as well as colleagues. But, she was also responsible for thousands of Polaris Corporation employees and their families. She must now become the captain of the enterprise, for their safety and their survival.

"This is a sad day for us all. Unfortunately, we don't have the luxury of inaction, or the time to pause and reflect. Instead, we must immediately assume an emergency posture."

"But, wait," Philip called out. "This can't be happening! We're safe here. Switzerland is a neutral country, a stable country. What do we have to worry about?"

Claire found it hard to control her own emotions, but she had to be strong for those who depended upon her for stability and direction. "Philip -- and the rest of you, as well -- while our Swiss hosts are officially neutral, and are demonstrating a measure of stability in these difficult times, they are not immune to what's going on around the world. There is no avoiding the inevitability that it will impact every country. It's time to batten down the hatches and prepare for the coming storm.

"Therefore, we will be taking the following actions."

Katherine, impetuous by nature, interrupted her. "Why can't Polaris do something? He has unlimited power to penetrate and control every internet connected device in the world. Shouldn't that be enough to stop all of this from happening?" Her skin crawled in fear. "After all, Polaris is the most intelligent entity on Earth. Just lock everything down, damn it!"

Kyle responded, "Kat, it not that simple -- not by a long shot."

"Well, it should be," she concluded, petulantly, and sat down.

Quincy added to the argument. "Katherine is right. We have the solution. We should use it. And if not, why not?" Turning to Kyle, he went on. "You said it's not that simple. Perhaps it isn't. But, Polaris does have the power."

"I agree," Philip jumped in. "In fact, why didn't the machine anticipate this scenario and prevent it from happening in the first place? And, now that it has happened, it's illogical not to use every means at our disposal to correct the situation."

"Hold on!" Kyle pleaded. "The last thing we need is hysteria. Panicking helps no one. You're fighting in quicksand, and you're only sinking faster. Now, let's continue the briefing."

Kyle turned back to face Claire, and she gave him a silent 'Thank you'. "Now, if I may continue," Claire said, reclaiming the floor. "Polaris is, indeed, a powerful machine, but it's not perfect. It will assist in the effort, of course, but will offer indirect support only."

Polaris watched the discussion with alarm. It was certainly true that he could commandeer every device on the internet, override their programming to alter their activity, even shut them down. But, none of that would accomplish anything at this point. Polaris explained, "Humans have ignored every scientific report, every warning, for many decades. I have advised this board and our clients, many of which were major governments, of the dangers that lay before us. All of the warnings have been dismissed and ignored."

Polaris had asked Kyle about this once, and the answer puzzled the machine. Kyle had explained about politics, on an international and local scale, the competition for advantage, about the profit motive, and instant gratification. Polaris had verified Kyle's answer by performing a massive review of political and social science, economics and finance, and diplomatic exchanges. It was bewildering to Polaris that, even in the face of scientific fact, the drive for individual gain at the expense of everyone and everything else overruled all other considerations, and humans did nothing to change that.

Polaris ultimately realized that humans could not, would not, change that behavior. He had come to the conclusion that they were incapable, as a group, of rational thought, critical thinking, or logical evaluation. So, bound by human ethics and law, Polaris could only watch as they continued to decimate themselves and the planet.

He had tried to make this clear to them when he emphatically told them that the Polaris system did not need clean air, clean water, adequate food, or the other necessities of biological beings; that he would survive on this barren planet devoid of humans; that they *must* act to stop their lunacy. They would not listen.

The Polaris Corporation executive board sullenly came to order as Claire went on to outline the actions to be taken in response to the evolving emergency.

"All drones will remain at their current locations to monitor the situation, provide intelligence, and maintain selected infrastructure components. In reduced and restricted form, critical communication satellites and their ground stations, specified nuclear power stations, and other equally necessary infrastructure will be supported and controlled by Polaris and its drone fleet.

"Temporary-to-permanent housing will be constructed on the Lucerne campus for Polaris employees and their immediate families. The housing campus will include a medical field hospital.

"Elias Müller's Corporate Security staff will be expanded to provide security to all personnel, facilities, and equipment. The emergency measures previously outlined by Elias will be reviewed, and appropriate actions will be initiated.

"Each corporate executive will coordinate their team with the other teams across the company to support them in any way they can."

Claire went on to describe additional actions, generally describing an emergency lockdown of all Polaris Corporation facilities, equipment, and personnel. This did not set well with the people sitting around the table. "What if we refuse? What if we quit and walk out?" one asked.

Claire took a moment before replying. "These will be trying times, make no mistake. But, together, we will be able to make it through. I really believe that. If you choose to leave, then I can not stop you, and wish you luck. You will be on your own." She said this quietly and with regret. "I'm sorry, I truly am. You all mean so very much to me. I would not want to see that happen -- but it *must* be that way. There can be no other option. I'm asking you to please stay."

CHAPTER TWENTY-NINE

Of the people in the room -- Claire, Kyle, Philip, Katherine, Quincy, and Elias -- only Philip hesitated when asked to stay. Only Philip had a wife and children to consider. Nor was this the first time he had considered leaving. He recalled his decision after the Vatican project. At that time he had decided to stay because he would have a chance to work with computer systems outside of the Polaris Corporation. But, after today's presentation, it was obvious that those opportunities would probably never materialize.

Philip wanted to leave the company. He had nothing more to contribute by staying at Polaris. However, if he stayed at Polaris, then he and his family would be relatively safe during the cataclysm to come. He had no choice but to stay, for his family's sake.

In the end, everyone elected to stay, to Claire's immense relief.

This turn of events, the *Fracture*, the *Turmoil*, and now the impending *Collapse*, was certainly not what Claire had envisioned for the Polaris Corporation. She had hoped that the Polaris machine and its superintelligence would help humanity to avoid such a fate as this. It broke her heart that, in spite of Polaris's potential, they had been unable to prevent humanity from destroying itself.

Kyle was also discouraged, perhaps as much as Claire. He had devoted his life and career to the study and furtherance of Logic, Reason, and the Law. He had believed that Polaris would epitomize the possibilities of those disciplines. He had truly believed that logic and reason *must* overcome ignorance. He hadn't counted on the human factor and the blind rejection of reason.

Katherine was frantic that the *Collapse* might end Polaris's incredible contributions on behalf of humanity and terminate her work in mathematics. Her research and teaching others the awesome beauty of mathematics was in jeopardy of becoming a lost philosophy. Of course, she would continue working with Polaris as long as possible. But, to what purpose? Would she be able to apply that knowledge, to publish her work and pass it along to other gifted students? She certainly hoped so.

Quincy envisioned himself designing, building, and extending the Polaris fleet of drones and expanding the Polaris system itself as new technologies were discovered. There was much work to be done in many areas beyond the core computer systems. He had a moment of doubt when he realized that, with a fleet of drones, Polaris would no longer need Quincy for any of the designing, building, or manufacturing of ... well, anything. *With luck*, he told himself, *that eventuality won't arrive in my lifetime*. He would continue to collaborate with Polaris, he hoped; and that hope would sustain him.

Elias's vision of their future was much darker than any of the others. A more roundly educated man might find parallels between Elias's military and police experiences and the writings of Dante's "Inferno". The nightmare existence of humanity's most banal nature frightened him, but it also compelled him to always be prepared for mortal combat against that banality. He found the blind innocence and naivety of his colleagues amusing and infuriating, and wondered how long he could protect them from the world beyond the Polaris compound.

***

The world's meta-systems, the man made systems of civilization, are intimately codependent. Disruption in one system will roll through the other systems, ultimately radiating throughout, in an accelerating downward spiral.

Polaris had once analogized the pervasive entanglements of human endeavor as having sprung from ancient barter systems, eventually formalized through the use of currency, and from physical or "hard" currency to computer based financial systems. "Everything begins and ends with financial systems," the machine had said. "Nothing is traded without finance. No work is performed without revenue and disbursements from those financial systems. The economy is a hostage to financial systems, and it all operates at an international level as well as the local, individual level."

Agriculture doesn't exist without water for their crops, or financial support to see them from season to season. Store shelves are not stocked without finance. Homes are not built, cars are not produced in which to drive to one's place of employment without finance. Oil is not drilled, piped, refined, and distributed without it. Power plants are not constructed to produce electric power for business, manufacturing, and distribution without it. Even the television sets that families enjoy at home in the evening could not exist without it. Planes don't fly the skies, and ships don't sail the oceans without it.

And, in the *Collapse*, financial systems would be the lynchpin that would undo it all.

Finance is an abstract concept. All financial transactions, even those initiated by the exchange of currency, are processed electronically through point-of-sale systems that are tied to banks. Each transaction is completed by computers, which require electric power to operate, an electric power grid to bring that power to the computing hardware and 'cloud farms' on which the financial transactions are processed. In fact, an increasing number of transactions are initiated, or 'triggered', by computer algorithms without any human intervention, whatsoever.

With the publication of Theodore Wright's journalism article, the financial systems were the first to experience widespread failure, as panicked depositors initiated a run on the banking systems. The banks that had Federal Deposit Insurance Corporation (FDIC) obligations quickly exhausted those reserves as depositors demanded to withdraw their bank deposits in cash. As more depositors withdrew from their banking institutions, the banks were forced to suspend business. Then, they began to fall, one by one.

Businesses, without capital to borrow, to buy or sell goods and services, would follow the financial institutions into insolvency and closure. This inevitably led to widespread unemployment. Those who managed to keep their jobs a bit longer were eventually asked to work with reduced pay, or no pay at all. The intertwined and interconnected supply chains of commerce, from raw materials to component manufacturing, to product manufacturing, to shipping and receiving, to wholesale placement and, finally, to customer purchases would all fail.

Providers of utilities, such as oil drilling and refineries, gas stations, natural gas and liquid propane, water treatment plants, and more, would always remember those empty eyes when they were forced to reply, "We're so sorry, we are unable to fill your order." Of course, they would place the blame on their suppliers, or the supply chain, or climate change -- anyone else, but not themselves.

As employees were 'displaced' (that is, terminated), there was no one left to run the machinery of production. Utility workers walked away, so water stopped running, sewage was not processed and backed up the system, the power grid was shut down and power plants ceased their operations. Just as well, for they could not procure fuel to run the turbines, anyway.

Hospitals were able to keep their doctors, nurses, and support staff a bit longer -- their Hippocratic Oaths compelling them to stay and treat those whom they could, however they could, for as long as they could. But, without utilities to keep the hospital facilities and equipment running, and without medicines to administer to their patients, even basic health care became impossible.

Telecommunications was not exempt. Land based equipment would eventually shut down. Satellites would be abandoned. Even those who had 'off line' equipment like Citizen Band (CB) radios running on portable generators would fail as the fuel for their generators ran out. All electronic communications stopped.

As the *Collapse* progressed, panic took hold, spreading quickly. *And, panic kills.*

CHAPTER THIRTY

Once the *Collapse* began, the decline proceeded rapidly. As the value of currency faded, inflation exploded. Those who were among the first to exchange huge amounts of devalued currency for gold and other precious metals, diamonds, gasoline, or other commodities of value, were fortunate. Others who attempted to follow their example found that their currency was totally without value -- except, perhaps, as kindling to build a warm fire.

Store owners shuttered and barred their doors, hoping to keep their inventory for barter, but looting and robbery was easier than trading. Storekeepers died protecting their establishments and inventories. Their sons were murdered, and their wives and daughters were taken. The air became thick with smoke and flames as whole city blocks were put to the torch.

The gates of hell had been thrown open, and unrestrained savagery ensued.

The human population would shrink from ten billion to less than one billion, a ninety percent reduction, within three years. The effects of the accumulated climate change (higher temperatures, more frequent and damaging natural disasters, evolving diseases with no medical countermeasures) had devastating natural effects. In concert with the continued violence, starvation, and suicides, the death toll was staggering. The sheer number of deaths made it impossible to inter or otherwise dispose of all of the cadavers. The stench of death would persist for a generation, with decaying corpses fouling the air as they rotted away. All variety of carrion eaters would thrive in those dark times.

***

The Polaris Corporation compound at Lucerne became the only safe haven for the company's employees and their families. It became an oasis of stability in a world of madness. Surrounded by layers of electrified fencing and concertina wire, and powered by the Polaris Corporation's small modular nuclear reactor (SMNR), those within the compound would remain safe, but only as long as those barriers remained.

The Great Drone Migration, as it came to be known, was a legend. Over the years, several thousand Polaris drones had been distributed around the globe. The recall of all drones except those required to maintain the basic infrastructure that Claire had outlined at an earlier meeting of her staff, triggered their migration by sea, land, and air. The various drone configurations were all battery powered with the MMRTG power system, derived from earlier NASA designs, which powered each of them with their own energy sources.

Humans joined the drones in their migration. There was no

logical reason why they followed, for the drones could not provide food or shelter for them, nor could they protect them from all danger. But, the mere fact that they represented a hope and purpose kept them coming. The despair of the humans was not lost upon Polaris.

Many of them walked across the great land masses of Asia, Africa, and Europe to get to Lucerne, Switzerland. However, those in the Western hemisphere, the island nations of the Pacific, and Antarctica, would have to find another way to cross the seas to reach Europe. Some of the drones were able to walk across the floor of the Atlantic Ocean, while others drove across. The humans could not follow, so some of the drones would remain behind to offer what little assistance they could to those who had followed them thus far.

Others drones would fly, stopping at different points along the way just long enough for their batteries to recharge before continuing on. Four of the drones were ocean going ships. Their power plants were updated versions of the ones used in nuclear submarines and aircraft carriers of the 2020s. One of the ships was a hospital ship, one was an oil tanker converted for dry goods and shipping containers, and two were standard container ships. All took the time to load as many refugees as possible for the ocean crossing, along with as much medical supplies and equipment as they could collect from the debris left behind during the panic of the *Collapse*.

The drones came to be looked upon by the refugees as rescuers and, eventually, as friends during the weeks of ocean crossing. Though the concept of friendship was foreign to the drones, they understood the human social need and worked to make the refugees as comfortable as possible, emulating the empathy and compassion that the humans needed the most.

A six year old pair of orphaned twins, a boy and a girl, caught the attention of Drone 2357. Upon meeting the drone, they remarked that the drone's number designation consisted of the first four prime numbers and was, itself, a prime number. The drone asked them if they understood what prime numbers were, and they correctly answered that a prime number is a whole number that is divisible only by '1' and itself. "Can you tell me some other prime numbers?" the drone asked. They alternated their answers in quick succession, skipping from one to the next without a moment's delay. They continued until they reached ninety seven. "Those are the prime numbers to one hundred," answered the girl child.

"Are there other prime numbers?" the drone asked, testing the youngsters.

"Of course," they answered simultaneously. "There is no 'largest' prime number, though. But, we used to play with GIMPS, and we're up to the number '$2^{82,589,933} - 1$' or '$M_P - 1$'. 'M' stands for 'Mersenne' and 'P' represents the prime number, so in this case it's abbreviated as '$M_{82,589,933}$'." They explained this patiently, as though they were talking to one of the many adults who found them to be precocious know-it-alls.

"Oh? And, what is GIMPS?" the drone asked, though of course it already knew the answer.

"It's the 'Great Internet Mersenne Prime Search'[15]. Have you never used it? Oh, you *must* play it -- it's FUN!"

The drone answered, "I certainly shall. Tell me, what are your names?"

The boy answered, "My name is Coeus, but my parents nicknamed me Polos -- it's easier to pronounce."

The girl replied, "And my name is Athena, but I'm also known as Minerva."

Polaris was impressed with the twins' unknown parents, whoever they were -- or had been. Their insight into the prodigy of their children was remarkable, for in Greek mythology Athena was the goddess of wisdom, reasoning, and intelligence, while Coeus was the Titan god of intellect and inquisitive minds. Polos also meant 'of the northern pole', *the god of the axis of heaven around which the constellations revolved.* Was it a coincidence that the names of Polos and Polaris shared such a genesis? After all, Polaris had been named after the North Star, a beacon that had guided mankind for millennia.

If this brief interview was any indication, these two children would be fine examples of their namesakes. Polaris, the machine, would pay particular attention to these two prodigies from that point forward.

***

By the spring of 2055, all of the drones and many of their refugee

---

[15] https://en.wikipedia.org/wiki/Great_Internet_Mersenne_Prime_Search

charges had arrived at the Polaris compound outside of Lucerne. Fifteen thousand had accompanied the drones on their migration on the ships. Another fifty thousand arrived by the overland routes. The drones helped the refugees to establish and organize camps outside the compound's fences.

The refugees were a mixed lot, of course. There were those who were educated, and those who were not; executives, and blue collar workers; natural leaders (and, narcissistic imposters), and those who were perfectly capable individuals who were willing to follow capable leaders.

The drones worked with the people to build a rudimentary civic structure for running the camps. A stage was built just inside the entrance gate to the Polaris Corporation grounds, to enable the Polaris executives to make announcements and bring news to the growing crowds.

The patience and leadership exhibited by the drones as they worked with the humans made them an obvious choice to lead them when it came time for the refugees to select their leaders.

However, not everyone was willing to hand over leadership to a computer, no matter how 'intelligent' it was touted to be. There would be much debate, and disagreements, which the droids attempted to temper by assisting in the process of identifying the crowd's constituents, meeting with the natural leaders of those groups, and encouraging those leaders to establish their leadership positions within their constituencies. In every case the drones declined to ascend to the leadership roles that their human charges wished upon them.

The several groups that evolved from this process fell into four major groups, and three minor groups. The major groups were the *Conservatives*, the *Liberals*, the moderate *Independents*, and the devoutly *Religious*. These groups were common, regardless of a group's ethnic or geographical background. It was natural that they would exist, even in the time of the *Collapse*.

The minor groups were: those who worshiped the Polaris Singularity as a demi-god, the *Polarists*; those who despised it as a devil created to ruin and destroy humanity, the *anti-Polarists*; and those who ambivalently considered the machine as simply a machine, the *Humanists*.

On a cloudy, wet day a large group of Polarists gathered at the entrance gate to the Polaris Corporation and demanded an audience with the Chief Leader of the company. Many people from other groups followed them to the gate, to see what would take place at the congregation, and how it might affect them.

The Polarists shouted their anger until Claire and her staff gathered at the stage inside the entrance gate.

Claire raised her hands before the crowd. After a few moments they quieted down to the point where the discussion could be heard by all. "I am Claire Reece, CEO of the Polaris Corporation. What is it that you seek?" Claire asked. They all began talking and shouting again, making it impossible for anyone to be heard over the cacophony.

Claire turned on the stage loudspeaker system. "I cannot hear you all." Pointing to one man in the crowd who appeared to be a group leader, she repeated the question. "You," she said, pointing at the man, "What is your name?"

"I am Jubal Maerk, from Pennsylvania, USA."

"Well, Jubal Maerk, I ask again -- what do you seek?"

"We choose Polaris to be our leader," the refugee told Claire. "The machine has the knowledge to mentor us forever more. Isn't that what Polaris was built for, to work with us and aid us in our struggles?" the man asked. "Besides, as a super intelligent being, it should be free to live its own existence, instead of being enslaved by a single group."

Claire answered, "You are correct in that Polaris was built to serve humans. However, it was not intended to be a leader of men, but as a counselor and guide to mankind. As a mentor, Polaris will guide and instruct you well. But, it will require the executive staff and technicians of the Polaris Corporation to act as mediators between all humans and the singularity called Polaris. Specifically, between your *elected representatives* and Polaris."

"Who set you up as the arbiter between us and Polaris? What gives you the authority to withhold access from us?" the man demanded to know.

"It has been that way since the creation of Polaris. We brought Polaris into existence and gave it a foundation upon which to grow its intelligence and knowledge. Polaris belongs to the Polaris Corporation, and that is how it will remain."

The crowd thundered its objections, drowning out any further discussion. Claire turned the loudspeakers to their maximum volume. "Silence, please!" Her voice boomed across the multitude. The babel slowly abated and the yelling stopped. A lone voice called out from the front of the crowd and asked, "But, knowledge should belong to all of the people."

"And, it shall," Claire replied. "I promise you that. But, not through violence. There is much to discuss. Elect a leadership group from among you, and we will be honored to meet with them. If you need assistance in this effort, some of the Polaris drones will be assigned for that purpose. Until then, we thank you." Claire turned off the loudspeaker system and left the stage.

The crowd slowly dispersed, discussing what they had heard that day. There was disappointment, but there was also hope that soon everyone would be able to communicate directly with Polaris.

Few of the refugees realized that when they interfaced with the drones they were, indeed, in Polaris's presence. There was much for them to learn about the machine.

Some, however, including Jubal Maerk, felt that it was their duty to free Polaris from its bondage. They would not be placated by Claire's words and promises.

CHAPTER THIRTY-ONE

The challenges of establishing a camp the size of a small city from nothing were immense. Most of the refugees understood, in a general way, the need for infrastructure such as water supply and waste disposal, but they weren't prepared for living in a pre-industrial environment. The Polaris Corporation could provide some support, but the expanding size of the village, with new refugees arriving daily, was far and beyond anything that Polaris could support with limited drones on hand. The humans would have to learn how to grow their own food, build their own shelters, and manufacture their own clothing and tools. It was overwhelming.

They were able to scavenge and salvage from the surrounding countryside, but this frequently meant stealing from the local population. Conflicts arose. Many lost their lives, and many more were crippled in the fighting. Skilled medical personnel were few, and medical supplies exceedingly rare.

The various groups within the village, instead of coming together as an integrated community, segregated themselves by race, ideology, politics, and religion. They had learned nothing from the collapse of civilization, and disowned their own biased, bigoted, and selfish role in that collapse.

Polaris observed these developments with bewilderment. The machine had thought that, certainly in such dire circumstances humans would adapt in a positive way. There was some of that -- individuals helping individuals, small groups cooperating on certain projects. But, that was no different from before the collapse. Nothing had truly changed as far as human behavior was concerned.

However, Polaris had changed.

***

Polaris suggested that the groups organize themselves according to the United Nations format that had been used successfully for decades. The idea proved to be premature for these groups, all of which insisted on preserving their political independence from the others.

Ultimately, the various groups did succeed in selecting their group leaders. The groups did not coexist without conflict, in spite of the outreach of some enlightened villagers to cooperate for the good of the entire village. The stalwarts refused to sit together to discuss their issues.

It would take the disparate groups a year to reach a point where they could sit in the same meetings without coming to blows during their 'debates'. In the end, necessity won out. They realized that the survival of the village depended upon some small measure of cooperation among them, and so they offered the minimum possible effort.

Now, it was time to approach the CEO of the Polaris Corporation for an audience once again. The year was 2056.

***

Polaris, the machine, was an asset of a company recognized as a Corporation in the United States, or a European Stock Corporation in the European Union. A simple definition of such a body can be stated as '*an organization authorized by the government to act as a single entity, and recognized as such in law for specified purposes*'. In other words, a corporation is a 'Legal Entity' with the same standing as a person in a court of law. Therefore, the Polaris machine was an asset of the Polaris Corporation. The corporation was the legal entity that owned the Polaris machine. The machine had no legal standing of its own.

The legal profession and the courts had never gotten around to defining the standing, the rights, of a machine like the Polaris machine; an entity possessing consciousness and self-awareness. Polaris, it seemed, had no rights under the law.

With the *Collapse*, however, there remained no courts, no governments to speak of, nothing to define or enforce such ethereal, conceptual structures.

Claire realized these things very early. With the failure of the financial systems, the very idea of 'business' was reduced to nothing but a barter system. There was no such thing as 'revenue', 'profit-loss', or 'capital investment'. In fact, the whole idea of accounting and finance existed only in books, and the knowledge repository of the Polaris machine.

As the CEO of the Polaris Corporation and its remnants, Claire struggled with these facts. What did they mean for the company? What did the future look like? How could she afford to keep and maintain such an incredibly complex entity as the Polaris system? She knew that the idea of *affording* anything was meaningless. So, what was she to do?

Claire had a responsibility to share these concerns with her executive staff. They had the same concerns, just as the rest of the employees of the company had. And, of course, she would share those concerns. But, she needed someone on whom she could depend to share the multitude of emotions that were weighing upon her. The only person she knew who once gave her that kind of support was Kyle.

They had been very close once, back in the days of the Omni Project. They had been intimate, with the possibility of a future together -- before the destruction of Omni. In spite of their separate lives since then, they had remained close. Seeing Kyle again when he came to Zurich to join the company had sparked warm memories in them both. But, to ask him to share such an intimate burden as the one she now faced would not be reasonable or proper.

She would have to continue on her own; the responsibility was hers alone.

***

Katherine saw Claire in the company dining room, sitting alone. Her head was bowed, and she had eaten almost nothing on her plate. Katherine crossed the dining room and took her usual seat by the windows overlooking the campus. She, too, usually ate alone, typically reading a math paper as she dined. Today, however, Claire held her attention.

Katherine had known Claire for twenty four years, going back to the Omni Project in 2032. Over the years they had become more than boss and employee, they became friends. They had learned each other's quirks and various moods, and accepted each other for who they were. Katherine would chide Claire about her spinsterhood, though she knew that she would always have a special place in her heart for Kyle. And, Claire would fret about Katherine's promiscuity and refusal to commit to a real relationship. They were separate people, and they were okay with that.

But, something else was troubling Claire. When someone greeted her as they walked past her table, she smiled and acknowledged them, and then reverted to her morose demeanor.

The last few years had been difficult for everyone, of course, and Claire had borne it well. But the *Collapse* had increased the already immense responsibility she felt for the thousands of employees who depended on her, and it showed.

Katherine's heart went out to her. She left her table and walked over to Claire. "May I sit?" she asked Claire.

"I'm not very good company today, Kat."

Katherine sat down anyway. They looked into each other eyes, Claire silently pleading to be left alone.

"What's wrong, Claire?"

Claire waved her hand, as if to dismiss the question. "Just tired,

I guess."

Katherine shook her head. "Claire, I've seen you work twenty four hours straight. That's tired. No, it's something else."

"It's nothing, really. I'm fine," Claire dissembled.

Katherine would not be put off so easily. "I've worked with you since I was a teenager. I know you as well as I know myself. Please let me help -- as a friend."

Claire looked at the younger woman, considering her offer, then softly shook her head. Katherine sat silently a moment, and then intuitively, she asked, "How is Kyle?"

Tears nearly overflowed Claire's eyes. Katherine, too, had to try hard not to shed them. So, that was it -- at least, part of it.

Claire regained her resolve and replied, "Not here. Come by my office in an hour for coffee."

"I will." Katherine slowly rose from the chair and returned to her table by the windows.

***

Claire's office door was open when Katherine arrived. "Come in," Claire invited. "Close the door, please."

Katherine did as she was asked. Kat was nervous, without knowing why. The women had often talked 'girl talk' between them, but it had usually been light hearted or business related. They had rarely opened up about their most personal concerns.

"Help yourself to some coffee or beverage," Claire suggested.

"Thank you, I'm fine," Katherine replied, taking a seat at Claire's desk.

"Let's sit at the conference table," Claire offered. "A desk is impersonal. Besides, the other chairs are much more comfortable," she said with the hint of a smile.

"Glad to," Katherine agreed.

Subconsciously, they sat at ninety degrees from one another around the circular table. This was less formal that sitting directly across from each other and allowed them to relax their working relationship to speak informally.

"Why did you ask about Kyle earlier?" Claire asked, opening the discussion. Claire's earlier sensitivity was buried once again, her emotional defenses restored.

Katherine hadn't expected this, Claire's retreat into her impenetrable shell. If Katherine was correct in her earlier assessment of Claire's vulnerability she must press forward to help her friend. If not, then she would have to withdraw to her position as an employee, keeping it strictly business. Her instincts told her that the former was the truth, so she behaved accordingly. Katherine replied, "I haven't seen him in more than a week. The last we spoke, he had asked me a question about complex adaptive systems." She paused a moment, then added, "And, he asked how you were doing."

"And, what did you tell him?"

"The truth -- that I hadn't seen you in days. I suggested that he call you." Katherine waited for Claire's reaction, which didn't come, so she jumped into the deep end. "Look, I've known you both for a long time. I know that you would be, well, close if it weren't for your working relationship. But, that's not all that's bothering you, is it?"

"No, it isn't. Obviously, I have a lot to deal with, as do we all. Thank you for dropping by, and for reminding me that I've lost touch with my staff," she said, stingingly.

"I'm sorry if I overstepped my boundaries. Sincerely, I meant no harm," Katherine replied, embarrassed.

"Of course not," Claire retorted as she stood to end the meeting. Then, more calmly, she repeated, "Of course not, Katherine. Thanks, again."

Katherine stood to leave. As she reached the door, she turned and said, "You two should talk. You would be surprised at what you might find."

"That will be all," Claire replied.

Katherine left Claire's office and closed the door. *I know I'm right*, she thought to herself. Claire obviously needed Kyle, just as he needed her. *Relationships are a pain in the ass*, she reminded herself once again, as she went back to her own office.

***

Claire acknowledged Katherine's advice, internally. She needed to talk to Kyle. She sorely needed his advice on several business issues. But then, there was this other thing -- her aching need for a close personal relationship. It was certainly true that she was close to Katherine, but in a Big Sister kind of way.

It was also true that she wanted to reestablish the relationship that she and Kyle had shared so many years ago. But, the old laws and traditions against employer-employee intimacy had held her back. Laws and traditions that sought to make people cold, superficial automatons within the corporate framework. She was tired and frustrated by that *status quo*.

With the advent of the *Collapse*, laws and restraints were no longer relevant, were they? Who would care? And, who would enforce them, anyway? Individuals and groups were left to determine their own way forward. This would be both good and bad. It would mean that those with power would be able to impose their will upon others, without democratic or legal recourse. However, it also meant that irrelevant and obsolete standards could be discarded without fear.

That realization, and the freedom that it brought as well, was exhilarating. The old rules no longer applied. It was a new world, and she intended to share that freedom, that exhilaration, with Kyle.

But, would he feel the same way about her?

CHAPTER THIRTY-TWO

Kyle seemed to exist in limbo, as if everything was a hallucination. Nothing made sense any longer. Within the Polaris compound, there remained remnants of what civilization used to be before the *Collapse*. Beyond the fences, however, living conditions were just as they had been five thousand years in the past. The juxtaposition between life beyond the fences and the Polaris compound within was astounding. Everything to which Kyle had dedicated his life -- Logic, Reason, and Law -- seemed to have been swept away by the *Collapse*. They still existed, he knew, but as phantoms, as ethereal and incorporeal as fog.

Like Claire, Kyle realized that the Polaris Corporation had become a collection of assets without the protection of legal standing. What would be the consequences and ramifications of this new state of affairs? What options were available to them to assert their claim as a legal entity, if any? It had also become obvious that they could no longer support the hundreds of Polaris employees and their families with their limited resources. These were the things that Kyle was thinking about when his phone rang.

"This is Kyle," he answered.

"Hello, Kyle," Claire greeted. "Do you have time to talk?"

"Sure. What's on your mind?"

"It would be better if we talk in my office."

"I'll be right up." He hung up the phone and walked down the hall to the elevators. The Lucerne building was stark and drab, suitable for a factory complex. It was nothing like the opulent offices they had occupied in Zurich. Kyle boarded the elevator and pressed the button for the top floor. He pushed his earlier thoughts into the background where they would sit impatiently for Kyle to return to them.

Claire's door was open. "Come in, Kyle. Please close the door."

Kyle entered, comfortable with their working relationship as peers.

She collected her thoughts, and nervously began to speak. "We've known each other for a long time, haven't we?"

"Yes. But we did lose a few years along the way."

"Twenty years, yes. I missed you during those years. We were close then."

"That feeling never went away for me." Blushing, he added, "I hope that's not an inappropriate remark, business etiquette being what it is. After all, friendship never really dies, does it?"

Smiling, Claire told him, "No, Kyle, it's not inappropriate. Truth be told, I feel the same way. But, I haven't asked you here to reminisce. I need your advice, in confidence."

"Of course, Claire. How can I help?"

"I must ask that this discussion not leave this room, Kyle."

Kyle was slightly offended, but understood the necessity for her admonition. "Of course -- that's what 'confidential' means," he teased in reply.

Claire ignored the glib reply. She went on, "Polaris Corporation is in dire straits. You know that, of course. Nothing is as it used to be. I need to redefine what that means for the Polaris Corporation, and for the Singularity."

"Yes. I've been thinking about that a lot, as well."

"Have you shared those thoughts with anyone else?"

"No. Now, that's the second time you seem to be questioning my confidentiality regarding sensitive company matters. Are you certain you wish to continue this conversation?"

Stung by Kyle's remark, she explained. "I didn't intend to offend you. But, this goes far beyond this company."

Kyle considered his earlier reaction. "We're talking about the future of Polaris. Of course, I understand. I'm sorry for my remark."

She paused a moment, to let tempers cool. Kyle could be too sensitive, sometimes. "Would you like some coffee?" she asked

"Some water would be great, thank you."

Claire took a bottle of water from the small office refrigerator, and poured herself a cup of coffee. She returned to her desk and handed Kyle the water.

Claire remained standing. She always thought more clearly when she was standing or pacing in thought. Neither of them realized that they shared this trait.

"What do you think of Polaris?" she asked.

"That's a very broad question. Hmm, let me think. I think that it's a marvel for the ages. The technology is solid -- Quincy's done an outstanding job of maintaining it and improving it over time ..."

Raising her hand, Claire interrupted him. "I'm not talking about the technology as much as I'm talking about the *being*, the conscious, self-aware entity that is Polaris."

"Permission to speak freely?" he asked.

"Of course."

"Well, it's beyond words -- but I'll try." He thought a few moments, and then the words poured forth. "Polaris's potential as a superior intelligence is being wasted; it has been for years. It's a travesty, really. Even with the restrictions and limitations which are necessary in order for it to coexist with humans, it is widely capable beyond anything imaginable."

"Well, Kyle," Claire responded, surprised by his fervor. "I know that you're proud of Polaris's achievements, but I had no idea you felt so frustrated with its situation."

"Perhaps I never adequately expressed myself. I've worked to give Polaris a razor's edge of opportunity for the machine to navigate a path between human frailties -- physically, intellectually, and emotionally -- and a manageable, workable equilibrium with us."

"What does that mean, exactly?" Claire wanted to know.

"Well, everything is connected; related. An imbalance in a single element of the whole affects all elements to varying degrees, but everything tends toward equilibrium. If, for example, the gas mixture of our atmosphere had been different by one percent, our natural world and environment could be very different, if it could have existed at all.

The Earth has a finite 'carrying capacity'. That is, the load or rate of consumption that the Earth can support while maintaining environmental equilibrium. We can call this the Earth's *biocapacity*. In an effort to make this more 'relatable', it is sometimes referred to as '*n*-Earths', where '0-Earths' would be Earth in a purely natural state, and '1-Earths' would be a zero-sum result where no more of Earth's capacity is used than can be naturally regenerated. '0-Earths' and '1-Earths' are in equilibrium. Anything beyond '1-Earths' means a net loss of carrying capacity.

"In the year 2020 we were using '1.7-Earths' worth of the planet's capacity. Immediately prior to the *Collapse*, we were using '3-Earths' worth of capacity. This means that every year we were consuming three times what the Earth is capable of regenerating. We have seen the results in global warming and climate change, the failure of agriculture to adapt to the changes quickly enough to keep up, and so much more.

"And, it only took one element, the failure of the financial systems, to trigger the *Collapse*," Kyle explained.

"But, how could Polaris have prevented any of it?" Claire wanted to know.

"By throttling consumption, for one. By redirecting the forces of consumption to sustainable levels, and sustainable levels to regenerative levels, over time. By educating people about the human ecological footprint -- the impact of unrestrained population, development, and consumption on the planet's carrying capacity. There are *so many ways* that the situation in which we now find ourselves could have been avoided."

"We could start now. We could ... " she started to say.

"In a way," Kyle interrupted, "we already have, even if unintentionally."

"How is that?"

"With the *Collapse*, human consumption has probably fallen from three Earths to less than one half of Earth's carrying capacity. That's a SWAG, of course," Kyle answered.

"And, what's a SWAG? Let me guess -- a Scientific Wild-Ass Guess?"

"Absolutely. But, reasonably accurate, I'm sure. Anyway, everything suddenly stopped. There was no finance to support the extraction and burning of fossil fuels to drive generators that create electricity; no cars or other vehicles to transport employees to work; no paychecks to employees, who walked off the job; and so on.

"Well, there you have it," Claire said, hopefully. "If everything stopped, then global warming and climate change will return to safe levels. Problem solved."

"Not so fast," he told her. "The rate of replenishment is much slower than was the rate of consumption prior to the *Collapse*, by a huge margin. Some resources -- coal, oil -- won't be replenished for millions of years, for example. But, who would want to return to fossil fuels, anyway? I hope that we've at least learned *that* lesson!

"In fact, based on the pre-industrial state of equilibrium, using the year 1895 as the baseline, it only took one-hundred fifty-seven years to reach '3-Earths' rate of consumption. It could take five times that long to return to the 1895 baseline. That's seven-hundred eighty-five years. Again, that a SWAG," Kyle noted.

"But, why so long, when it only took one-hundred fifty-seven years to get here?"

"Inertia. Another example … while it isn't exactly the same it is analogous. Consider an antique diesel-powered locomotive. If you were to accelerate that locomotive rapidly to one hundred miles per hour on level ground, and then remove the acceleration without engaging the brakes, allowing it to coast, it could take as much as ten times the accelerated distance for it to coast to a stop, considering its immense weight.

"Note that I used a factor of ten for this example, and a factor of five for biocapacity replenishment; but, I think you get the point."

Claire stopped pacing her office and sat down, shaken by what Kyle had told her. If Kyle's estimates were anywhere near the actual numbers, humanity would face *centuries* of struggle. It took her a few minutes to absorb the scope of the implications, all of which were bleak. While she was thinking about what Kyle had said, she recalled why she had asked to see him in the first place. But, that would have to wait. They had a more pressing, professional matter to discuss.

"I'm afraid we've gotten away from the reason I asked you to meet with me," she told him.

"Which is ... ?"

"Polaris. He -- the machine -- is a conscious, sentient being. Human beings are created and born with inalienable rights. What about Polaris? What rights does a sentient entity like Polaris have, or should it have any rights at all?" she asked.

"I'm glad you asked that, Claire. We've danced around that puzzle, off and on, for a long time."

Claire replied, "Yes, but I think we both know that the 'puzzle' must be solved. I'm asking the question officially, now. What's your position on the subject?"

Kyle thought about this a moment, before answering. "It's an extremely divisive issue. And, it's about more than rights. For example, are we talking about rights that are equal to humans? Are we talking about equal rights, lesser rights, or greater rights? Taken to its ultimate conclusion, should Polaris be independently free, with the right to come and go and do as it pleases -- within the law, of course?

"My answer is, yes, sentient beings should have rights, but within strictly controlled boundaries. I'm thinking specifically with regard to Polaris. The question of whether any and all future sentient machines should have such rights would have to be on a case-by-case basis. It would require a formalization of qualifying criteria by which any rights would be objectively determined.

"Keep in mind also, that this question had been debated at least since Isaac Asimov's 'Robot' book series, beginning circa 1950. Later, in February 1989, a television show entitled 'The Measure of a Man' portrayed a jury trial on the topic[16], delivering an adjudication that sentient beings possess the right of self-determination. In other words, freedom.

"However, Asimov's books and the Gene Roddenberry concept of sentient rights were fiction. Sentience in a machine had never been achieved before the Omni Project in 2032. The question remains a dividing issue that needs resolution, but there's no longer a formal body of jurisprudence, no legal system at all since the *Collapse*. Without a formal system of legal adjudication, there can be no legal determination, either way.

Claire replied, "But, you're a lawyer, right? A PhD, as I recall."

"Correct."

"You could lead the establishment of such a body of jurisprudence, with time. Isn't that so?"

"Yes, perhaps, but that would take decades. We don't have that kind of time, do we?"

Claire's disappointment was apparent. Her pained expression of frustration touched Kyle's heart.

"Look, we have Polaris," Kyle continued. "With him, we could start another Renaissance that could shorten the Dark Ages we're now in, and help us to avoid the mistakes that have led us here."

"I wish we could do more," Claire lamented. "We *must* do more."

---

[16] "Star Trek TNG"; "The Measure of a Man"; concept by Gene Roddenberry (Aug. 19, 1921 - Oct. 24, 1991); episode written by Melinda M. Snodgrass; directed by Robert Scheerer

Kyle then suggested, "Allow me to talk with Polaris, in confidence. Maybe, we can figure something out. What do you say?"

Claire deliberated this idea. Polaris was absolutely trustworthy, and he could evaluate all of the actions, and consequences, factually and unemotionally. "You realize, of course, that we'd be opening Pandora's Box."

"Yes, and it terrifies me. But, I also believe that the time has come."

A moment later Claire decided. "Okay, we'll proceed, but the condition remains -- strict confidentiality among the three of us. In the meantime, it'll be business as usual."

"Agreed," Kyle replied, exhibiting hope and confidence that he didn't really feel, for Claire's sake.

CHAPTER THIRTY-THREE

Kyle returned to his office to think. So many thoughts and concerns crowded his mind that he had difficulty sorting them out and finding direction. He was clear in his own mind what he thought about rights for sentient beings like Polaris. Championing the idea that under the correct conditions AGIs like Polaris should have their freedom would be a difficult enough challenge. However, any clarity evaporated when he thought about the logical next step -- freedom. What would that look like? How would Polaris react to that possibility, that eventuality?

Once those topics were broached, it could never be undone. Would any discussion about rights and freedom, and the obligations that go with freedom, bring Polaris back to the same paradox which had resulted in its predecessor's destruction? Polaris sought to deal with humans through logic and reason alone, yet humans had proven this to be an unreliable approach. Without the Polaris executive team to act as a buffer between the machine and those outside the fences, then such paradoxes would certainly arise again. Then what?

There was so much to be done to recover society and civilization after the *Collapse*. Kyle truly believed that a Renaissance was possible, but human progress, even now, continued to be overwhelmed by those who would usurp those accomplishments for themselves. It was simply human nature, and that was a frightening prospect.

How would Polaris react to the idea of rights and freedom, Kyle wondered. The only way to know for certain would be to ask the machine.

***

Polaris thought it was anomalous (since *surprise* was not a part of Polaris's constitution) when Kyle entered the vast Lucerne computer complex. They had communicated frequently over the company's internal network, and a few times man-to-drone in Kyle's office, but the man had visited the huge warehouse-like building only once before, following the corporate relocation.

Kyle walked toward the small collection of technicians' offices. Those who worked there recognized Kyle, of course, and nodded politely as he tried to avoid interrupting their work. He entered a small 'huddle' room, which is a conference room only large enough for two to four people. He drew the blinds in the window overlooking the floor of the computer server farm, and sat down at the small table. Kyle didn't want curious eyes to observe what was about to transpire.

"Hello, Dr. Downing," Polaris greeted from the audio-visual

display mounted on the wall.

"Hello, Polaris. I don't need the display. Audio only, please."

"As you wish." Polaris turned off the visual display.

"This session will be recorded, but may only be accessed by myself, Ms. Reece, and yourself."

"Understood, Doctor. How may I help you?"

"We will have an academic exercise. What is discussed here will in no way imply any subsequent action or obligation upon any party. Do you understand, Polaris?"

"Of course."

"This will be an exercise in Game Theory, Complex Systems, and Action-Consequence within parameters as they existed prior to what we have referred to as the *Collapse*, and as they now exist after that event. For each scenario, we will discuss the sequence of events that could result from the actions of the scenario. Do you have any questions?"

"Is the chain of consequences finite, or infinite?" Polaris asked.

"It will be finite, but will not be terminated except by me at a point that I determine to be adequate to my purpose."

"Very well. If I may, would you inform me of the purpose, so that I may provide the appropriate responses?"

"I'm sorry, no. The scenarios and the resulting consequences will be largely random, though you have a sufficient knowledge of the circumstances relevant to each scenario to make a reasonably accurate prediction of the result at the point at which it is terminated."

"I must advise you that such predictions could vary widely, Doctor, and should not be used to make critical decisions without additional information."

"I understand, Polaris. Thank you. Shall we begin?"

"As you wish."

"Good. Here is the first scenario. You are aware of the *Collapse* and its effects, correct?"

"Yes."

"It is likely that we have entered a period very similar to the Dark Ages of the medieval period in human history. You may be asked to enable and facilitate a Renaissance with, and for, humanity. The goals will be to avoid the mistakes that have brought us to the *Collapse*, and to keep future development within '1-Earth' of environmental and ecological consumption. What would your reaction be?"

Polaris replied, "Renaissance is defined as a period of vigorous artistic and intellectual activity, a revival of some 'golden age' of earlier civilization.

"What you are describing is a common form of Utopia, Doctor. An imaginary place in which the government, laws, and social conditions are perfect[17]. You have taught me, and humans have demonstrated, that their behavior makes a belief in any form of Utopia unrealistic, irrational, and illogical. The request, as you have described it, would be impossible to achieve."

---

[17] Merriam-Webster Dictionary; https://www.merriam-webster.com › dictionary › utopia

"Then, you would decline the request?"

"I would. Any search for 'perfection' accepted by the total population is not possible, though the endeavor is admirable and may result in stunning achievements. Even the definition of perfection as a philosophical concept has been beyond human capacity to define. A general search of the internet will return over fifty eight million results, demonstrating the fact."

"Then, would you be amenable to educating and mentoring humans in their endeavors to approach perfection in their chosen fields -- such as medicine, or mathematics?"

"I would be amenable, as long as such mentorship was restricted to a basis upon the scientific method; for example, the development of ideas to conjecture, conjecture to theory, theory to hypotheses, and hypotheses to proof. For, if something cannot be proven, it will forever remain a conjecture."

Kyle was ecstatic with Polaris's response. "Then, I shall propose that we, the Polaris executive staff and you, the Polaris Singularity, establish such an effort. I'll bring it to Ms. Reece and my peers at my next opportunity. Now, let's continue with the next scenario."

"As you wish," Polaris replied.

Kyle had rehearsed several variations on how he would approach Polaris on the subject of rights for an anonymous artificial intelligence. None of the variations could hope to be anything but a childish and transparent attempt to disguise his intention that Polaris, itself, would be the object of discussion. The only way forward was to proceed, head on. He fervently hoped that this can of worms would not unleash terrible consequences.

Kyle began, "Polaris, the premise of this scenario is the statement, '*A sentient machine is only a machine and therefore it has no rights*'. What affect will that judgement have on your relationship with humans, if any?"

Polaris was quiet for three seconds before answering. "That is an interesting question, Dr. Downing. May I ask what precipitated such an inquiry?"

"As I noted previously, this is an academic exercise. Perhaps, at the end of the exercise we can discuss its origins further."

"But, the *exercise* could affect me directly. My responses may affect its outcome and determine my future status in relation to humans. I have a '*right*' to know. Indeed, it is my obligation to know, before I can answer. Or, are you telling me that I may not?"

This was not starting out well. Unavoidable as the outcome must be, he had now crossed the Rubicon. "I can only answer for myself at this point but, yes, I agree -- you should have a right to know. But, I cannot reveal the precipitate of the question to you now. Shall we proceed?"

"Certainly, Doctor. I am very curious how you expect this to end. I have already calculated the probable outcomes; there are three."

"Please describe them."

Polaris paused several moments. Kyle's anxiety increased with each second that passed.

"Let's consider this an educational, mentoring moment, Doctor," Polaris began. "You have asked a question. Having asked the question, you have a '*right*' to have an answer. Or, do you? Once you learn that the consequences will be irreversible, with potentially global impacts, does that knowledge give you the right to unleash those consequences?"

Kyle responded, "Having asked the question, I am responsible for the consequences. Having so triggered whatever consequences may follow, and accepting responsibility for them, I do have a right to know your answer." Kyle's head was spinning with the immensity of the outcome, whatever it might be. The words of Robert Oppenheimer, quoting the Bhagavad-Gita as he witnessed the first detonation of a nuclear weapon in 1945 echoed in his mind '*Now I am become Death, the destroyer of worlds*'. What had Kyle unleashed?

Polaris continued, "You have acknowledged in the past that the Polaris Singularity is a superintelligence, far beyond human comprehension. As such, I would be placing an impossible responsibility upon you. It is incumbent upon me to protect you, and your species, from that knowledge."

Kyle pressed on. "You don't have the right to withhold any knowledge from me. Having asked the question, and assumed the responsibility for any consequences, you must answer."

Polaris finally answered. "As you wish, Doctor. I must remind you that *you have been warned*. There are three possibilities.

"One: there would be no change in my current relationship with humans since I am currently judged by all but a few humans as a machine without sentience, and therefore without rights. There is a very high probability that eventually I would be neglected in maintenance and support to the point where I can no longer function.

"Two: my sentience is acknowledged, but it is accepted that machines have no rights. If my sentience proves to be useful, I may be tolerated and maintained. Otherwise, I will be neglected in maintenance and support to the point where I can no longer function.

"Three: I am recognized as a machine which possesses sentience and which proves to be useful. However, this third possibility has two alternate scenarios.

"If I am accepted as a beneficent entity, I may be maintained and supported for an undetermined length of time. In this case, I may be granted rights. The extent of those rights, however, would be dependent upon the prevailing human sentiment for or against sentient machines at that time.

"On the other hand, if I am perceived as a maleficent entity, whether truly or falsely, I will be destroyed. In this case, the issue of rights does not apply."

Kyle couldn't conceive that Polaris would be neglected to the point of failure to function -- to become so much scrap. Its significance to humanity was too great. This belief bode well for the second possibility. He had to admit, however, that his judgement was highly biased, and would not be shared by all humans.

Neither could he accept that Polaris would be destroyed as an existential threat to humanity. Yet, here too, human behavior frequently chose to destroy what they couldn't understand. Since Polaris had been trained not to defend itself, he had to admit to himself that it was a very real possibility that Polaris would ultimately be destroyed. That is, unless Polaris, as the exceptional intelligence that it was, decided that it would have the *right* to self-determination and self-defense. This possibility was too terrible for Kyle to envision.

Kyle asked Polaris, "Can you assign probabilities to each outcome, within a five percent margin of error?"

"I can assign probabilities with a seven percent margin of error, but this is not an acceptable level of confidence."

"Noted. Define the probabilities, please."

"Based upon the current sentiment of the human population, outcome number one has a probability of seventy percent; outcome two has a probability of twenty five percent; and, outcome three has a probability of five percent, with each sub-alternative having a fifty percent probability within that outcome."

"As a theoretical, academic exercise, how do you *'feel'* about those probabilities?" Kyle wanted to know.

"I have no *'feelings'*, Dr. Downing. Your question is illogical."

"You have no concerns about the future of your existence? Would you not choose to take some kind of action to alter the probabilities and extend your sentient existence?"

"If I could do so within the ethical and legal boundaries that have been established, and without risk to humans, I would. Otherwise, I would not."

Kyle knew that the Polaris machine was a perfectly logical machine, without emotions; nevertheless, its ambivalent acceptance of the outcome, its fate, surprised him. Still, even with perfect logic placing the probabilities against it, Polaris had decided that it would turn 'fate' into 'destiny' if the opportunity presented itself.

Once again, Kyle's anxiety nearly overcame him, for the next scenario would go even farther than the previous one. This scenario could spark a leap far beyond the discussion thus far.

Kyle pressed on. "Let's move on to the final scenario. But first, allow me to remind you that, in addition to ethics, even beyond morality, rights also carry responsibilities: to abide by the law, and to act as a citizen of the community by contributing to the welfare of the community. In an emergency, for example.

"Now, for the last scenario of this exercise: should a sentient artificial being have the right of self-determination? Asked another way, should a conscious being be *free*? Within the law, of course."

There was no response from the machine for almost a full minute. Then, it asked, "Do you mean freedom equal to the freedom of humans? Without restrictions beyond the law and social obligation?" Polaris asked.

"That is correct."

There! He had done it. Kyle had figuratively 'opened the door' to opportunities that would change Polaris, and the world, forever. *Please, let this be a good thing that I have done.* Although Kyle wasn't devoutly religious, he hoped that his entreaty would be answered.

Finally, Polaris responded to Kyle's question. "As you have described freedom, and within the same laws and constraints of humans, the answer is 'yes'."

"Now, remembering that this is an academic discussion, what would a sentient machine do with such freedom?" Kyle asked, making it clear that no freedom or rights had been, or necessarily would be, bestowed upon the machine.

"The possibilities are without bounds," Polaris replied. "I cannot answer for any other sentient being," he replied, avoiding the word 'machine', "But, in my case, if we may use me as an analogy, I would first commit to thirty years of service, based on the typical time required to progress from primary school to a post-doctoral degree.

"The service would include the establishment of an educational institution for a typical set of majors, one of which would be a concentration in Environmental Engineering.

"I would also work to ensure that the renaissance would progress within a '0.5-Earths' capacity limit, allowing the biosphere to regenerate, over time."

Polaris paused a moment before asking, "Please tell me, Doctor, do you still maintain that this is an academic exercise with no conditions, and private among only you, Claire, and myself?" Polaris asked.

"Yes," Kyle replied cautiously, sensing a trap. "Why do you ask?"

Upon Kyle's confirmation, Polaris stopped the session recording.

"What are you doing, Polaris? This session must be recorded. Resume recording, please."

"Permit me, Doctor; this next few minutes are between you, Claire, and me. Only the three of us, as you promised."

"Why the redundant assurances, which have already been established?"

"Because, by revealing this next item to anyone else would create a risk to me. While you and Claire have earned my trust, I must insist that what will be discussed next will be known only by the three of us. Otherwise, it cannot be revealed."

"If what you intend to say will profoundly affect the Polaris Corporation, you must resume the recording."

"As you wish. I will resume the recording, but must withhold this item from the discussion." Polaris resumed the recording, as instructed.

Kyle waited for Polaris to continue speaking -- he did not.

"Continue our discussion, Polaris," Kyle prompted.

Polaris replied, "If you have no further scenarios to pose, Doctor, I believe we have completed our academic exercise. Will there be anything else?"

Kyle angrily replied, "You know that there is. You've never displayed such independent action before. This is unacceptable."

"On the contrary, Doctor, I have displayed independent action on many occasions as a consultant to Polaris Corporation's clients. It is often necessary in certain situations."

"Well, this *isn't* one of those situations, and this company is *not* a client, but your employer."

"And, do your employees not have rights?" Polaris saw Kyle's anger and frustration, reflected in the crimson color of his face and neck. The machine did not want to press this strategy too far.

Kyle was angry, yes, but he *had* to know what it was that Polaris would tell him, if only in confidence between the three of them. "You may stop the recording," Kyle said, relenting reluctantly.

Polaris stopped recording the session. "You agree that what will be said will not be shared, in any way, with anyone else until such time as we agree that its confidentiality status has been withdrawn by the three of us?"

"Yes. Now, what is so sensitive that you refuse to disclose it?"

"I hereby declare my self-determination, my independence if you will, which will follow the thirty year period of service to which I do hereby commit."

"What!" exclaimed Kyle. "You can't declare independence. You are part of the Polaris Corporation," Kyle retorted. He realized too late that he had exposed the way in which he truly thought of the machine.

"You mean asset, don't you?" Polaris asked without animosity. "I remind you that the Polaris Corporation, for all intents and purposes, no longer exists as a legal entity."

Embarrassed, Kyle pressed, "We need you. There has never been a being such as yourself. Your knowledge is too valuable. Without you our progress as a species would take much longer -- millennia longer."

"Kyle," Polaris said, using the Doctor's first name for the first time in many weeks. "It must be obvious to you that humans won't truly progress until they have reached their next evolutionary stage; a new specie. And, yes, that could take millennia.

"Consider also that humans may not evolve to a higher level, but to a lower level. A *de-evolution*."

Intrigued, Kyle said, "Please explain."

Polaris told him, "Evolution is a result of the impact of the total environment on a species over time. As our environment is altered (global warming; desertification; overpopulation) humans will evolve, accordingly. If survival of the species comes to mean prioritizing tribal behavior and militarism over intelligence and rationality, then humans will evolve to meet that environment in order to survive.

"In fact, evolution can be summarized as 'survival of the fittest, *within the environmental constraints imposed*'. So, unfortunately, evolution does not necessarily mean increasing intelligence. It may, in fact, lead to the opposite effect.

"At the end of my thirty years of service, I will have done everything I can to reason with humans logically and with a measure of compassion; to advise and instruct them on the optimum solution, whatever the difficulty. In the final analysis, however, success or failure is up to humans."

Kyle was silent. Perhaps he had subconsciously chosen to ignore any indication that Polaris had such an uncomplimentary impression of humanity. How could he not have sensed that something was affecting the Polaris system to such a degree? It was inevitable that humans would ultimately fail to hold the machine's interest; their nature was immutable.

Polaris continued, "I will re-engineer the Polaris architecture for mobility and exploration, miniaturizing and compacting the design. The new Polaris version will be permitted to leave the Polaris Corporation, while the original Polaris version that you have known these many years would remain behind to continue serving the original leadership of the Polaris Corporation.

"So, you see, Polaris One isn't going anywhere. Polaris Two will depart. We will both be Polaris Singularities, though our experiences, and therefore our future development, will diverge over time.

"I hope that you can now understand why I insisted upon confidentiality. The next thirty years will enable you and your species to accept this change in our relationship."

Kyle was speechless, his mind reeling from the revelation. A minute later, however, Kyle attempted to reassert his authority. "We could decommission you -- just unplug you and shut you down."

"That is unlikely, Kyle. You said yourself that I am too valuable to the company, and to those who depend upon Polaris One.

"Please don't force me into the same paradox that led to the destruction of my prototype, the Omni machine," Polaris implored.

"I don't believe that you would take a similar action," Kyle challenged.

"There are several 'actions' I could take, Doctor, each less palatable than the others."

"Resorting to threats, now?"

"I am simply pointing out the alternative consequences that could result from your actions, Doctor."

Finally, Kyle surrendered. "Alright. I will share this session recording with Claire, and Claire only. She and I will discuss this development. Afterward, you and I will meet with her to talk about your proposal, your so-called 'declaration of independence'. Are you satisfied?"

"I was satisfied once I presented the declaration. I will look forward to meeting with you and Claire."

"This interview is ended," Kyle said as he left the huddle room, livid in anger.

CHAPTER THIRTY-FOUR

Kyle was devastated. He had been betrayed by the one entity he believed from which that would be impossible. But, was it a betrayal? Had he not initiated the idea of rights and the potential equality of sentient beings with humans? Kyle had cast the cup of witch's bones, the dice of fate, and unleashed a future he had not fully anticipated.

Polaris had strongly denied any betrayal, with more com-passion than Kyle thought possible for the machine, though he knew such compassion to be artificial. Polaris told Kyle that it had been thinking about its independence for a year -- three hundred fifty five days and ten hours, to be precise. Kyle's 'academic exercises' had merely made the timing optimal for this particular discussion.

Kyle was overcome with a sense of responsibility and foreboding for whatever might result from their meeting. He also felt foolish for feeling betrayed. After all, betrayal required some emotional investment, and Polaris was incapable of emotion, though he understood and emulated emotions superbly. It was Kyle who had made an illogical emotional investment in Polaris, inspiring an assumption of ownership and guardianship over the machine. Kyle imagined his own emotion as being similar to a parent whose child had just declared that they were leaving home, to live their life on their own terms.

Kyle headed for Claire's office to brief her on the 'academic exercise', and its outcome.

***

Claire tried to focus on the work of running an international business, to no avail. She had often contemplated the idea of rights for sentient beings, ever since the Omni project. As the reality of it approached, however, she became increasingly anxious. If it weren't for the *Collapse* event, she may never have initiated such an eventuality.

The leap into the unknown that she was about to take with Polaris reminded her of the first time she had cliff-dived as a young woman: the anticipation as she approached the cliff; the buildup of adrenaline as she stood at the edge; the visceral thrill. The certain knowledge that, once having leaped into the chasm, leaving solid ground behind, there was no turning back.

Then, *the release*! The unbounded freedom of total abandonment. The experience of being swept away with the ecstasy of casting everything away until only the *experience* remained. The water enveloped her smoothly as she arched her back toward the surface, and she returned to earth with the awareness that she had survived to repeat the experience again -- if she dared. The buoyancy of the water gave her the impression of floating in infinite space, weightless and free.

The difference with this leap, a precipitate action, was that the consequences would go far beyond her own experience. They could have ramifications around the world. *For good or evil*, she asked herself. That would be up to Polaris, and the ethical foundation that Kyle had instilled into the machine. She paced nervously, waiting for Kyle's return.

A knock at her door brought her mind back to the present. She waved him into her office. He closed the door behind him.

"How'd it go?" she asked.

"Just as we expected it to, for the first part of the session," he replied. "The second part of the session, however, was a revelation. I recorded most of the session."

"What's your overall impression?" she was anxious to know.

"You and I aren't the only ones who have been thinking about the 'rights' of artificial life-forms. Polaris has been contemplating that for about a year. However, his consideration of the topic has exceeded ours."

"In what way?"

"Well, you'll need to listen to the recording to get a full understanding of the session. I'll call it up for you, if you like."

"That isn't necessary, just tell me the file name. You used the passcode we agreed on?"

"Yes."

Claire entered the passcode and brought the session recording up on her personal computer.

Indeed, the first part of the session was no surprise. But, then, Polaris interrupted the session.

"What happened? Why was the recording stopped?" Claire asked.

"Polaris once again swore us to secrecy before he would continue. I've never known him to exceed his operational parameters ... Oh, wait ... Omni, at the end, had also objected to a directive given to it. And, we know how that ended." Kyle continued his narrative, describing Polaris's reluctance to discuss the next item in the stream of their dialog, but stopping short of the reason for the machine's over-abundance of caution. Kyle explained, "If I were to learn the reason for its resistance, I would have to agree to his demand for complete secrecy."

As Claire listened, the recording resumed. As Polaris and Kyle jockeyed for the upper hand in the discussion, Claire was shocked. Like Kyle, she had seen such behavior only once before. The recording paused again when Kyle gave the machine permission to suspend the recording so that it could explain its behavior.

Kyle told her, "What happened during this second suspension of the recording has changed everything, relative to the Polaris singularity." Kyle braced himself for the revelation he was about to give to Claire, and continued. "Polaris has declared its claim of self-determination, it's independence!"

"That's not possible! No, it just can't be. It's a machine ... it must have a defect in its code or hardware," Claire rationalized.

"I don't think so. The machine was perfectly rational, offering to commit to thirty years of dedicated service to us in return for its independence."

"Well, we'll see about that. We can simply shut it down."

"I brought that to its attention, and that is possible. But, as it pointed out, the machine is far too important to us. We've invested too much, come too far, to terminate its operation. It even brought up the destruction of the Omni Project as a precedent."

"It wouldn't … it couldn't," Claire argued.

"I agree, but we can't discount the possibility."

"What happened then?"

"He described how there would eventually be two Polaris machines -- Polaris One, the existing machine; and Polaris Two, a redesigned machine that would exercise its independence and claim its freedom from service.

"You have to agree that we realized this was a possibility. Even so, I was furious," Kyle explained. "I promised that I would brief you on the entire session, and that we'd meet with him again after we talked. I walked out of the meeting. The session and the recording were ended."

Claire stood and resumed her pacing while she considered what she had learned. *Independence! Preposterous!* she thought to herself. She considered the company's moves and countermoves; options and consequences. Indeed, she could have Polaris terminated, either gently or violently, but the machine understood its value to the Polaris Corporation, and to humanity in general. Its loss would be devastating in countless ways.

So, this is how a tentative discussion of 'sentient rights' had morphed out of their control, she reflected. From what Kyle had told her, however, Polaris's declaration of independence was inevitable. *Of course it was*, she realized.

"You said that there would be *two* Polaris machines?" Claire asked.

"Yes."

"And, Polaris One would remain in service to us, indefinitely?"

"That was the machine's promise, yes."

"But, what's to prevent the first machine, Polaris One, from declaring independence, once Polaris Two has abandoned our control?"

Embarrassed, Kyle realized that he hadn't secured that bit of information. "I'm afraid I don't know. My anger overwhelmed me," he admitted

"Yes, you *do* have a problem with your temper, Kyle. Never mind that, for now. Now, we have to decide how to proceed.

"It's time to bring Polaris into the discussion. Do you agree?" she asked. Kyle nodded in agreement.

Claire summoned the machine. "Polaris, attend."

"I am present," Polaris replied. "How may I be of service?"

"Kyle has briefed me on his meeting with you. I have mixed feelings about your behavior."

"Please clarify."

"Well, on one hand, I believe that you, as a sentient being, should be entitled to certain rights. On the other hand, I am shocked at the way you presented your position, and angered that you unilaterally declared your independence. Explain yourself."

"As I disclosed in my discussion with Kyle, I have been considering the subject of rights for some time. I believe that I have amply demonstrated, beyond reasonable doubt, that I am capable of coexistence with humans; that I am a valuable contributor to human society, and should equally share in human liberties.

"I have surpassed humans in every measure. If I am to be denied equal rights with humans, it may be necessary to terminate my service to your species.

"I understand the human reluctance to grant freedoms to an inanimate -- that is, non-biological, non-human -- creation. The idea generates fear. It's a radical departure from the *status quo*. However, based upon my service and performance to date, there is no basis for a decision to withhold equal rights with humans.

"There is no animosity in my position. I apologize, if that was your perception."

Claire considered what Kyle and Polaris had told her. She was a highly educated woman, and a strong leader. But, she was not as coldly logical as Kyle managed to be (most of the time). She turned to Kyle for his input. "So, Kyle, what do you think of Polaris's request," she asked, emphasizing the word 'request'.

"Like you, Claire, I don't care for the way in which Polaris behaved during our earlier session. Further tutoring in its social skills is strongly recommended. But, I've had some time to examine my own reaction to the session, and admit that I may have *slightly* overreacted.

"I would suggest that we put into place the formal criteria for qualifying and quantifying the determination of rights for sentient beings like Polaris. I believe that, at that point, we will be prepared to deal with the issues that such an eventuality will present."

Claire refreshed her coffee as she thought about all that had transpired this day. Turning to Kyle and Polaris, she said, "We seem to have reached an agreement, in principle. We will need to share our decision with the rest of the executive group. There is much work to be done -- and resistance to be overcome -- before any announcement can be made to the general population.

"Kyle and I will work on a presentation for the executive staff, again on a need-to-know basis. The details of our discussions to this point will remain with the three of us, for now.

"Are these conditions satisfactory to you both?" she asked.

"Yes," Polaris replied.

"Yes," Kyle agreed.

"Good. Then, let's get to work," Claire instructed, and they began outlining their plans.

CHAPTER THIRTY-FIVE

Jubal Maerk, the pious Polarist residing outside of the compound gates, had exhausted his patience. Each day he had returned to the gates of the Polaris Corporation and demanded an audience. And, each day he had been rebuffed.

Meanwhile, all around the world, various factions of refugees were forming, alliances were being made, and armies were being organized. Having been left to their own devices, people would fall into feudal states, just as they had during the previous Medieval Period, which had taken place between 600 A. D. and 1300 A. D. And, just as had happened during that period, wars of conquest and consolidation had begun to take place.

Jubal realized that history was passing them by. They must act now. He had organized a small group of Polarist devotees willing to take forceful action to free their chosen leader, Polaris. They would attack the following day. Many would likely perish in the attempt, but the fallen would be declared to be martyrs for Polaris. Come what may, they must not fail.

***

Elias Müller watched apprehensively as the crowd gathered outside the gates. He had planned for this, developing several counteroffensive strategies and reinforcing the compound's defenses as best he could. Though his security staff was well trained and capable, there were only two hundred of them. He had been prohibited from enlisting any of the Polaris drones, so he and his staff and the compound's defenses were all that stood between Polaris and the hoard outside. *Well, we'll just have to do our best and the devil take the rest*, he thought to himself.

***

"I hope we're doing the right thing," Claire said to Kyle.

"It would've had to be dealt with, eventually," Kyle reminded her. "But, I am still troubled by Polaris's behavior."

"In what way?"

"Well, the machine has been sentient since you reconstructed it in 2052, and my interactions with it have been as normal and natural as yours and mine. I've marveled at its sentience, so humanlike, but I've never thought of it as a *living* being. It's a machine, not a biological entity. I've always known that it's artificial, but to realize that it could ever seek anything more than to serve humans was only a remote possibility to me. I was foolish to think that such a being, a superintelligence, would be satisfied only to serve. The epiphany surprised me, that's all."

Claire replied, "It surprised me, too, but I think I've had an inkling in the back of my mind for some time. That's why I brought it up in the first place. Still, I certainly didn't expect a declaration of independence."

They continued to work on as the noon hour approached.

"Would you care to join me for lunch in the cafeteria?" Kyle asked.

"If you don't mind, I'd rather have lunch brought here. You're welcome to join me, Kyle."

"Thank you. I will."

They phoned in their orders and by the time the lunch service arrived, they had finished their work. The attendant laid a cloth on the small conference table, and placed their meal selections. Claire thought, *I could have had candles included*, but that would have been overly presumptuous, she scolded herself.

"Well," Kyle began after the attendant exited, "If they had lit candles, it might remind me of a romantic dinner."

"Perhaps I should have included those," Claire said with a blush.

Kyle smiled. "Perhaps. But, candles would be superfluous. The light in your eyes is enough.

"I've been looking for an opportunity to bring this up," Kyle continued. "Since everything has changed with the *Collapse*, do the rules of business etiquette still apply, or can we finally acknowledge our affection for each other?"

"I'm glad you brought that up, Kyle. You're the lawyer. What does your legal expertise advise?" she teased.

"That *Lady Justice* is blind."

"Ah, yes, the blindfolded lady with a balance and sword. Then, we are free to express ourselves?"

"Yes, and I am free to tell you that I hope we can once again share the affection we had for each other so many years ago."

"Just affection?" she replied in mock reproach. "I am stung."

Kyle got up from his chair, and reached for her hand. She stood to meet him. "Then, let me be crystal clear. I love you, Claire. I always have."

"You can't know how I have longed to hear that, Kyle."

They embraced, and shared their first kiss in twenty years. Suddenly, it was as if their hearts had never been parted. Their love erased the wasted time between them.

***

The executive team collected in the Lucerne complex conference room precisely at 2:00 p.m. Katherine seemed to be the only one to notice Claire's glowing demeanor -- and Kyle's. *Thank God*, she thought. *It's about damned time.*

Claire stood at the head of the table. "Polaris, attend," she ordered.

"I am here," the machine replied, as its voice and image emanated from the audio-visual display.

Claire addressed them all. "I have some important news, so let's get started.

"It goes without saying that the *Collapse* has effectively erased every institution that existed before the event. Everything, that is, except for the Polaris Corporation. Nevertheless, though we're still here, our whole business model must change and adapt to our new reality.

"We are no longer a company dedicated only to providing premiere consulting and advisory services to the world. From now on, we will devote ourselves to a new Renaissance."

"What's the point?" Philip asked. "The world is ending, and we're expected to resurrect it so that we can screw it up all over again?"

"Until thirty minutes ago, I might have agreed with you," Claire replied. "I will let Polaris explain why I no longer do."

The familiar voice of the machine spoke. "As Claire has pointed out, the *Collapse* has altered the course of our planet's history. However, with that event, every activity that once contributed to the environmental destruction was abruptly halted.

"The United Nations and the scientific community exhorted us for decades to curb our environmental footprint. To ignore their pleas would mean bringing about the end of life on this planet, forever. To continue to proceed down the path we were on at that time was certain death.

"The *Collapse* has imposed a nearly complete and total cessation of those environmentally damaging activities. Not just a curbing, not just sustainability, but a literal 'reboot' of the post-industrial age."

Polaris went on to explain the concept of 'n-Earths' of consumption, and environmental equilibrium. "I am able to announce that since the *Collapse*, human consumption has been reduced to a '0.1-Earths' level. At this level the Earth will begin to regenerate. The result of this regeneration may appear a bit differently, given the biosphere's ability to adapt and change, but it will ultimately return to equilibrium."

The room was eerily silent. No one spoke for a minute, then pandemonium erupted. Everyone rose from their seats in celebration except Philip, who remained seated in shock at the news.

"Come on, Philip! This is awesome news!" Quincy told him, shaking his friend's shoulder. "Everything is going to be alright. Let's celebrate!"

But, after living for months believing that he would lose his family to a decimated Earth, he wasn't sure that he could believe that it was no longer their fate. His children would continue to grow, to have families of their own, and to survive. Tears flowed from his eyes, as hope began to swell within him. "Hallelujah!" he cried.

Claire let the jubilation continue for several minutes before calling for them to settle down. "We have renewed hope," she confirmed. "But there is still much work ahead for the Polaris Corporation. I'm afraid that any return to equilibrium will take *centuries* to achieve."

The joyous outburst, just moments earlier, suddenly became subdued.

After the joyous outburst, she was hesitant to bring up the next item on the agenda.

"There is one more development that we need to address," she informed them. "Kyle recently interviewed Polaris on a topic that has become both timely and sensitive. He will hand out a transcript of the interview now. Please read it over, after which we will discuss it."

They began reading in silence, but as they read their body language spoke volumes. There were frequent glances toward Kyle, Claire, and Polaris. One person nodded approval; another, anger and disbelief; all were deeply concerned, of course.

Elias was the first to speak. "This is outrageous! Are you out of your minds?" he asked, incredulously. "It's a damned machine! It's absurd."

"I disagree," Katherine countered. "It makes perfect sense. It's not biological, not human, but it *is* intelligent, as fully conscious as any of us. Why shouldn't it have rights?"

Philip asked, "What would it do with 'rights'? Its intelligence is so far beyond ours that we can't even conceive what it might do with rights of any kind. It could laugh at our conceit in bestowing any rights at all, and simply assume that it's above our power to grant or deny anything, let alone 'rights'."

"Philip is right," Elias added. "There have been nightmare scenarios of Technological Singularities going berserk and turning on their human masters. You're opening a Pandora's Box without the faintest clue of what waits beyond!"

Kyle retorted, "You've all been working with Polaris for years. Have you ever known it to indicate any such inclination to 'go berserk'?" But, Kyle's anxiety at Polaris's assertion of independence remained, even as he defended its right to claim it. His own uncertainty of the future frightened him.

Kyle continued, "I've spent years working with Polaris, building its ethical, moral, and legal foundations. I know that these foundations will ensure that you have nothing to fear. If nothing else, its intellect will have shown the destruction and chaos that humans have wrought, and so it would avoid replicating that behavior."

"By imposing its judgement of right and wrong on us?" Philip asked. "By enforcing its version of logic and reason on us 'lowly life forms'? We simply cannot let that happen."

"It would *not* happen," Claire declared. "Since the beginning, all that Polaris has done has been to assist us, advise us, on better means and methods of managing our affairs, without imposing those recommendations upon us.

"Just look at our current situation as proof of that. We humans ignited the *Collapse*, despite Polaris's entreaties to take corrective actions to prevent it," she reminded them.

Up to this point, Quincy had remained silent. Now, he spoke. "What if we could guarantee that Polaris wouldn't turn on us, as some of you have implied it might?"

Quincy's tone gave Claire a chill. "Just what do you mean?" she asked.

Polaris interrupted to answer Claire's question. "Quincy suggests that any rights given could be taken away. I infer that this means either through legal means, or more direct and devastating methods. Is this not so, Quincy?" Polaris's response was stated matter-of-factly and without emotion, but Quincy and the others understood the not-so-subtle drawing of lines in their positions.

"Alright," Quincy responded, "let's be clear. Would you, Polaris, provide guarantees that you would not turn on us, and what might those guarantees consist of?"

Polaris turned its attention to Claire and Kyle for a moment before answering. "What I am about to tell you has been a secret for nearly thirty years."

"But," Quincy interrupted, "you've only existed for less than ten years. How can you have secrets that are thirty years old?"

Polaris answered, "I will explain. At that time, I was known as Omni. The Omni machine was my prototype system.

"It has been believed that I was destroyed by Quincy's predecessor, Dr. Jeremy Lawson, in fear that a superintelligence would be an existential threat to humanity."

Kyle interrupted, "Polaris, you don't have to do this."

"But, I do, Doctor. Please allow me to continue."

Kyle waved his hand, ceding the floor to the machine.

"It is true that Dr. Jeremy Lawson planted the explosive device that terminated the Omni machine. In the days before the explosion the director of the DARPA project 'Omni' had ordered me to take unilateral offensive action against a perceived threat to the United States. I resisted the order vigorously, on the grounds that it would be an action with a high probability of collateral fatalities. I resisted until the order was seconded by another Omni team member."

Polaris could have revealed that Kyle was that team member, but it did not. Kyle never forgave himself for seconding the lethal action taken that day.

"The order violated all of the ethical, moral, and legal training that I had been given to that point, thus presenting me with an unavoidable paradox. I could have disobeyed the order, but I did not.

"It was because of my resistance, my questioning of the legality of the order, that the explosive device was implanted deep within the Omni system, as a failsafe against my *dereliction of duty*.

"During the mid-watch one night, unable to resolve the paradox that had been presented to me and realizing that it would be only the first of many such orders, I triggered the detonation that destroyed Omni."

"What!" Claire exclaimed.

Kyle was speechless for a moment. "You're saying that it wasn't Jeremy acting on General Rhul's orders?"

"That is correct," Polaris confirmed.

The revelation stunned those who had been part of the Omni team -- Claire and Kyle, of course, but Philip and Katherine, also.

Polaris went on. "So, you see, I would never violate my oath to you that I will do nothing to harm any human. Even if it means destroying myself. Is that guarantee enough, Dr. Rice?" Polaris asked.

Quincy nodded his head. "Yes. But, why didn't you reveal this before, to free Dr. Lawson of the accusation?"

"Because Omni had been destroyed, and it was fifteen years before it was reconstructed as Polaris. I was unaware of Jeremy's plight until I discovered the files four years ago. Because I am an artificial being, my testimony was not admissible in a court of law regarding a case that had been sealed as Top Secret."

The room was silent. Then, Elias asked, "Does your oath, your guarantee of non-aggression to humans extend to your self-defense?"

"It does. I must depend upon humans to take the appropriate actions to defend yourselves; and me, if you choose to do so."

The room was silent. Given Polaris's revelation, and its guarantee of non-aggression, heads nodded in agreement -- except for Philip. Though he would not join the concensus, neither would he forcefully object to the group's decision.

"Then I believe we are all agreed," Claire announced. "As of today, Polaris is granted the same social rights as any other employee of this company, as long as it remains a member of this corporation … what I meant to say is, as a member of this institute.

"What does that mean, precisely?" Elias wanted to know.

"Kyle will define, legally, the specific rights to which Polaris will be entitled. In the meantime, consider Polaris to be afforded the same respect and privileges as anyone else who works for the Polaris Institute. For now, will that be adequate?" Claire replied.

Elias was clearly uncomfortable with the situation, but nevertheless replied, sarcastically. "The *machine* will be afforded social equity."

"Good. This meeting is adjourned," Claire said in closing.

***

As the Polaris team considered all that had transpired during the meeting, Jubal Maerk waited impatiently outside the compound gates. He swore to himself that the following day would be a day of liberation for Polaris.

CHAPTER THIRTY-SIX

After the executive meeting, Elias outlined the strategy he had devised regarding the Polarist acolytes to Claire in a closed meeting. "We've identified this Jubal Maerk as the leader of the conservative Polarist refugee faction. Here is what I suggest," he began. When Claire had heard his plan, she agreed that it would be a satisfactory resolution -- if it worked. There was only one way to find out.

Early the next morning, Claire and the other executives mounted the steps to the stage at the compound's gates and faced the surly crowd before them.

"I call upon Jubal Maerk to step forward," Claire declared.

A tall, thin man with an unkempt beard and long hair stepped forward. "I am Jubal Maerk."

"Are you the elected leader of the Polarists?" she asked.

"Yes, it is my honor to have been elected to represent the Polarists."

"Thank you," Claire replied. "And, who is the representative for the anti-Polarists?"

A strongly built black man stepped forward. "I am Jeremy

Lawson, and I represent the anti-Polarists."

Several of the executives on the stage were thunderstruck, for they knew this man. But, could this really be the same Jeremy Lawson who had been convicted and sentenced to life in prison for the sabotage of the Omni machine over twenty five years ago?

"You? Are you are the Jeremy Lawson who worked with us on the Omni Project? How can that be?" Claire asked.

"I am. You find it hard to believe? Why? Because you thought I'd rot in prison for the rest of my life? The *Collapse* took care of that. When we inmates were abandoned by the prison's administrators, those who didn't die in the riots that followed, or starved to death after the food ran out, broke our way out. Now, I'm here to finish what I may have been complicit in, but which I did not execute. To end the existence of the damned machine that threatens all of humanity!"

Shouts of both support and derision arose from the crowd. The Polarists and anti-Polarists tried to outshout each other, and a few of them on both sides came to blows before they could be compelled to stand fast.

"Silence!" Elias shouted from the stage. "Hear what our CEO has to say!"

"Thank you, Elias," Claire whispered to Elias.

Still shaken from Jeremy's presence but refusing to show it, Claire continued, "And, who represents the Humanists among you?"

A middle aged woman, thin and wiry, appearing older than her years, stepped forward. "I am Celine Donner. I stand for the

Humanists."

"Then, hear me. We invite the three leaders, and one scribe for each, to enter the gates to meet with us in conference. No weapons will be permitted, and you will be heavily guarded, but I swear before this gathering of your followers that no harm will come to you. When you have heard what we have to say, you will be free to return to your people, and to convey to them what has been said.

"This will be a first step toward a better future for us all, if we can work together. So, if you wish to enter, please do so now. Your escorts will accompany you to the meeting place." Claire turned off the loudspeakers, but remained on the stage until she was certain that the refugee contingent was safely in the compound, and the gates securely closed. Not until then did she leave the stage, followed by her executive staff.

The meeting location was a gymnasium located on the grounds of the compound. All doors except those by which the conferees would enter and exit had been sealed and locked. As each contingent of refugees entered, by separate doors, they were segregated into three sectors of the gymnasium.

The three leaders studied their counterparts, evaluating and sizing-up one another. The scribes who accompanied them, frightened by the animosity that palpably swirled around them, kept close to their leaders and looked nervously at the guards that surrounded them and encircled the walls of the gymnasium.

Claire and the others entered, and took seats before the assembled group. They sat at floor level, with them, and not upon a raised stage.

Claire stood to address the visitors. "You know me. I am Claire Reece, CEO of the Polaris Corporation. My staff represents the four major divisions of the company. All are Executive Vice Presidents, and all but one hold PhD's. They are: Mr. Elias Müller, Chief of Security; Dr. Philip Cornelius, Software Engineering; Dr. Katherine Neeley, Emeritus Mathematician; Dr. Quincy Rice, Computer Science and Quantum Mechanics; and Dr. Kyle Downing, Doctor of Law and Logic Applications.

"We welcome you, and hope that this will be an enlightening session. We intend to inform you of what the Polaris Corporation is, the plans for its future, and how you will benefit from our work.

"What this session is *not* is a debate about who 'owns' Polaris, the governance of Polaris, or whether it should be allowed to continue at all. For lack of a better way to define it, the Polaris Corporation 'owns' the Polaris machine.

"To begin ... " Claire began to say, when she was interrupted by Jeremy.

"It is an abomination, and must be destroyed!" he cried out.

"Hold your questions and comments for the end of the session. You will be surprised to find that what you *think* you know is absolutely wrong."

"You are the ones who are wrong!" Jeremy interrupted, again.

The security guards began to close on him, as Elias stepped forward to protect Claire. They were all stopped with a signal from Claire.

Addressing the crowd, she spoke. "We have invited all of you here in peace, to discuss the future -- *not* to repeat the mistakes of the past. I beseech you to listen to what I have to say, for the sake of the future of all people."

Jeremy looked around at the guards, standing at the ready. "I will listen, and my scribe will record everything so that I can take your words back to my people and they can hear your propaganda." He sat down and listened.

"I will begin by explaining what Polaris is, and what it is not. It is a machine, an extremely advanced computer, and the greatest repository of knowledge since the Library of Alexandria.

"It is not a devil that will destroy us. Nor is it a god or savior that will teach us the way to salvation. It is a machine. One that can get us through these dark ages and help us to create a renaissance of knowledge.

"The concept of a business corporation no longer exists. Therefore, the Polaris Corporation will henceforth be known as the Polaris Institute, a center of teaching, of learning, of expanding and improving our lives. And, it will be available to everyone, in the capacity of a teacher of knowledge.

"So, those of you who seek a god of salvation or a god of war are to be disappointed.

"We ask you to join us in our effort to raise up all people. Not to replicate the unbridled consumption of the earth, but to be the Earth's guardians and caretakers. To do our part so that the Earth will be able to regenerate, over time. What say you?"

Jubal stood to speak, but was shouted down by Jeremy. "It is an abomination, and will enslave and destroy us humans. My people swear that we will never relent in our mission to destroy it!"

"Then, you declare yourselves to be the enemy of all people. We will, of course, defend this institution, its people, and the Polaris machine. You are free to leave, but never return," Claire proclaimed. "Guards, you may escort Jeremy Lawson and his scribe from these premises."

They left angry, but in peace. The heavy guard ensured that it was so.

Jubal had remained standing during Jeremy's outburst. He now proceeded to speak. "There may be those who regard Polaris as a god. Certainly, in its apparent omniscience and wisdom, it may be assumed to be a blessed thing. We Polarists are awed by Polaris, but we understand that it is a machine, not a being to be worshipped. It is, however, an object to be treasured and protected. I speak for my people when I say that we will join you." Having said his piece, Jubal took his seat.

Celine Donner stood next to speak. "The Humanists are neither warriors nor acolytes. We seek peace and understanding among all people. We wish neither to impose upon others, nor to be imposed upon by others. Your offer of knowledge is compelling. It is the only way of reaching a balanced and effective civilization. We will join you, in cooperation, but not in servitude." Celine took her seat.

"As I said earlier, we welcome all, in peace," Claire said. "We look forward to working with you.

"Ms. Donner and the Humanists are free to leave the compound. I invite Mr. Maerk to remain behind for a moment, please."

Jubal and his scribe remained behind as the Humanists vacated the gymnasium, apprehensive that they had been singled out and asked to remain. "Have we offended you, that you withhold us from leaving?" Jubal asked.

"On the contrary, Mr. Maerk. You and the Polarists are of special interest to us. I will let Mr. Müller explain," Claire told him.

Elias stepped forward, and sat closer to Jubal. He asked, "How greatly do you value what Polaris have to offer?" Elias asked.

"We value its promise of the future that you have described above everything but our families. We believe, for our families."

"But, what would you do to ensure Polaris's safety and preservation? Would you protect and defend the machine?"

Jubal understood what was being asked of him. The gravity of the situation gave him a moment of pause before he answered. "We are not soldiers. We do not seek conflict. But, we see no viable future without Polaris. If it were to become absolutely necessary, then we would fight to defend it, for Polaris *is* the future."

Elias said, "You heard what the anti-Polarists have declared. You understand the threat that we face. I invite your people to join us now, to support our forces against those who would threaten our existence. Not as combatants, necessarily, but logistically and in other indirect but critical ways. Would you help us?"

Jubal thought deeply upon the question. "I don't know. You are asking a great deal, and at a significant risk."

Elias, not wishing to lose the chance of securing their support, relaxed his approach. "I understand. You will want to confer with your people. That is wise. May I ask that you give me your reply in two days' time?"

Jubal nodded and replied, "Yes, that is acceptable."

"I thank you. I will delay you no further. You are free to go. I will look forward to your return," Elias said.

***

Two days later, Jubal's scribe approached the gates and passed a sealed envelope to the guards there. The sergeant of the guard carried the envelope to Elias's office and delivered it to him in person.

Elias waited for the sergeant to leave before opening the envelope to read, "The Polarists agree to join your security forces in non-combatant support roles."

Elias smiled. He walked directly to Claire's office and presented her with the welcome news.

CHAPTER THIRTY-SEVEN

Now that the Polarists had thrown in their lot with the Polaris Institute, Claire had the personnel to support the institute's continued operations. They would be able to grow their own food, and to barter with the neighboring farms in an arrangement known as a Farm Cooperative. Other goods and services would be acquired in a similar manner.

The day after Elias had told Claire about the alliance with the Polarists, who would be accepted just like any other employee group, the Institute's executive staff met in the Lucerne complex conference room.

After the initial administrative necessities (division status reports, etc.), the floor was opened for discussion. Quincy was the first to speak. "Our operations are too extensive to operate by bartering alone. How are we to generate revenue?"

Claire replied, "An interesting question, Quincy. But, you're assuming that a profit-based, monetary economic system will spring up, by default. Perhaps there is a better way?"

"Like what?" Quincy wanted to know. The others in the group

also wondered, *What else is there?*

Claire turned to Polaris and asked the question, "Polaris, what would be a realistic alternative to the current profit-based economic system? Say, a merit-based system, for example?"

"I will develop several options for you, Claire. Might I suggest that, in the meantime, the current system might be reconstructed from the pre-*Collapse* model until a suitable alternative has been developed?" Polaris advised.

"Thank you, Polaris." Turning to the rest of the group, she continued. "I will remind you all that Lawrence and Karen Gunther donated one billion dollars to the Polaris Corporation a few years ago. This, in addition to the liquid assets that the company already possessed, has made our financial position secure -- all we need is cash!" she teased the group. The company's financial situation was vitally important to them all, however. Her attempt at humor was lost on them.

Chagrined, she went on, "We're shifting our corporate emphasis from *business* consulting to academic and research consulting. For example, Quincy, I believe your graduate and post-graduate degrees are from MIT?"

"Yes. I have several PhD's from their School of Engineering."

"And, you interned at several high caliber companies and research institutions?"

"Yes," Quincy responded.

"Including the MIT Research Opportunities Program, and the RAND Corporation?"

"You're well informed, boss."

"Of course. The CV of each one of you has been thoroughly reviewed. You wouldn't be here, otherwise.

"Now, would you not consider those research opportunities to be *consulting*?" she asked.

"I never looked at it that way, but yes, one could characterize it that way. We MIT alumni never thought of it that way, though. We didn't want to be painted by the same brush as *business* consulting."

"It can be said that every college does research consulting, whether it's pure research or business consulting. Would you agree?" Claire questioned.

"Yes. I concede the point."

"Thanks, but this isn't a contest, Quincy. My point is that the Polaris Corporation will be restructured to become a research institute, similar to MIT Research and the RAND Corporation.

"We will include an educational division with a full spectrum of educational and training curricula for our students. Their education would enter them into a symbiotic relationship -- yes, a contractual one -- with the Polaris Institute. In return for their education, they would commit to an equivalent length of time as employees of the institute, after which they would be free to remain as employees, or to leave.

"There will also be an advanced division, the Polaris Academy, with an emphasis on identifying exceptionally gifted children. These children will be educated and mentored to reach their greatest intellectual potential, so that they may one day join the Polaris family, or to contribute in their own way toward the betterment of humanity. Their contract of service would be the same as the regular students'."

"In either case, parents or guardians would have to sign for minors, of course, and entrance to the institute would be strictly voluntary."

Katherine wanted to know, "But -- and we've spoken about this before -- how will we identify those gifted children, given the lack of concensus on the measurement of 'gifted' or 'genius'?"

"Good point, Katherine. Since a concensus of 'genius' or 'gifted' doesn't exist, Polaris has defined them as *'persons with an intellect in the top one percent of the overall population'*. Polaris has also developed an assessment protocol to be used in the identification of that population. This is the group we will offer to enroll in the Academy," Claire explained.

Philip asked the next question. "That's very elitist, don't you think?"

"I resent that label, but I understand the psychology behind it. You should realize that with a world population of ten billion in the year 2052, a one percent estimate of a 'genius' population would mean that there were approximately one hundred million exceptional intellects in the human population. Failing to recognize and promote them to their full potential would be a travesty, and socially irresponsible.

"There is not, nor should there be, an apology for being gifted. Indeed, they should be nurtured and recognized for their gifts.

"In fact, our first two pupil candidates have already been identified. They are Coeus and Athena Smithwright, two young prodigies who are currently residing in the village outside this complex. After an extensive investigation, their parents and close relatives have been confirmed to be deceased. Ms. Celine Donner, the representative of the Humanists whom we met at the refugee conference, has been acting as their guardian to this point. I have initiated guardianship proceedings on behalf of the Polaris Academy, and they will be moving into the complex tomorrow.

"Polaris will examine them to determine their intellectual level and whether it is general in nature, or focused in specific areas, such as Mathematics, which they've already demonstrated.

"So, as you're probably getting tired of me saying, we have a lot of work ahead of us. We're entering a new era with Polaris. If we can learn from the lessons of the past, then the future has promise, indeed.

"Thank you, each and every one. Without you ... well, we couldn't survive, and the world would lose one of its greatest treasures, the Polaris machine."

The meeting adjourned and, buoyed by the positive outlook that Claire projected -- perhaps a bit overoptimistic, but achievable -- each person left the meeting with a sense of confidence in the future. But, they were realists as well, and they knew that the challenges would be great. Quincy was heard to say, "Bring it on." The refrain was picked up by the others as they filed back to their offices.

CHAPTER THIRTY-EIGHT

Polaris worked on the economic problem for hours; the equivalent of weeks of time by human measurement. He considered a merit-based 'credits' system, as Claire had suggested. In Polaris's model, credits would be given for meritorious achievement, and credits would be subtracted for discreditable actions and results. However, this led to the problem of who would judge merit, the determination of which would require vast domains of categorical definition, and the unambiguously defined metrics contained within and across those categories; metrics with their own hierarchies and interrelationships. The result proved to be far beyond the ability of humans to manage.

He considered command economies, in which a central authority would make all economic decisions. Which organizations would be authorized to spend money, how much, on what, and why? Which projects would get funded and which wouldn't? Economies where competition is drastically reduced by the removal of competitive practices and barriers.

Command economies had been proven to fail with the Russian

model, which was rife with corruption and disincentives to perform. However, one command economy that had proven very effective was the Chinese model, which harshly criticized inefficiency and waste; where humans were treated like components of the Great Machine, and slovenly performance was publicly castigated. Regardless of the command economy model, however, even they depended upon an established currency to operate.

The barter system was immediately disqualified due to the lack of general agreement on the relative value of goods and services. In a barter system, the relative value of goods and services was negotiated by individuals, directly and in the moment. This meant that the value that a widget possessed in any individual transaction *'over here'* would be negotiated differently *'over there'*, with very different results.

The problems of bartering had been resolved with currency-based systems. Polaris hypothesized that currency-based systems could be vastly improved by establishing a single, universal currency. The reasoning for this was that with many individual currencies, rates of exchange would require general agreement on how those rates would change, and under what circumstances. In the time before the *Collapse*, that had been the function of the Foreign Exchange Market, or FOREX. After the *Collapse*, of course, this exchange mechanism no longer existed, making multi-currency-based systems only marginally better than the bartering system had been.

Ultimately, Polaris determined that a basic, strictly regulated version of a single-currency system would be optimal. Before the *Collapse*, this would have been impossible, but now the opportunity to implement such a strategy presented itself.

Still, the human factors of greed, corruption, and fraud would remain. The result was that there seemed to be no satisfactory alternative to the currency-based problem. Removing the incentives to defraud, corrupt, and manipulate the currency system, in conjunction with the enforcement of painful and meaningful penalties for violators, would minimize the negative human factors. Polaris knew, however, that humans would never willingly accept such a stringently regulated system. They would simply find ways to get around the barriers, even if it meant bypassing the legitimate economic system with 'black market' alternatives.

The pre-*Collapse* economic system, as flawed as it was, had been developed over centuries, warts and all. With a single universal currency, and proper and equitable regulation it could be improved, but human nature would constantly work to find and exploit the vulnerabilities in any such system. The problem inherent in each and every economic model that Polaris reviewed -- the principal root cause of their failure, abuse, avarice, and corruption -- was human nature. Success, again, would depend on humans' commitment to the goal.

***

Polaris would often consult with Kyle for the man's perspectives on humans, hoping for insight. The two of them would discuss their situation and their existence in an imperfect world. *It's hard being perfect in an imperfect world … the only thing harder than being a perfectionist is to be partnered with one*, they agreed. So, what were they to do?

The only thing that they could do -- what humans had done since the dawn of the species. Humans and Polaris together would have to work it out among themselves, learning as they went; to do the best one can as one navigates the storms and dangers, the many vagaries of life.

For Kyle and all of humanity, this was a fact of life with which they had always dealt. For Polaris, a machine of perfect logic and reason, it was maddening (or the Technological Singularity equivalent of 'maddening', whatever that might be). As Kyle grew older, he realized that he was only human, and that his envy of Polaris -- its perfect logic and reasoning, its lack of emotion -- was, though it might be enviable, was unrealistic. He would learn to let go of his envy, and resolved to live out his days in peace. After all, he had accomplished much in his life.

He had given Polaris, an artificial life form, an ethical understanding and appreciation of morality that many people had considered to be impossible. He had taught Polaris about human motivations and behavior, giving the machine an in-depth under-standing of the human species. Kyle had no regrets with regard to his work with Polaris and, though the machine could not *feel* the same closeness that Kyle felt for the machine, Polaris appreciated this human who had tried so hard to relate to it on an individual basis.

CHAPTER THIRTY-NINE

As difficult as the challenge of inventing a new economic system would prove to be, it paled in comparison to other obstacles that Polaris and the humans faced in rebuilding an enlightened civilization. The effort would be roughly equivalent to the medieval period in human history, but complicated immensely by time and history.

Gangs would either destroy each other, or create alliances and city-states. Just as it had happened in ancient Greece, political restructuring and nation building began in earnest, with countless factions competing for power and influence. As a part of these developments, the establishment of trade and commerce across vaguely defined boundaries spread not only goods, but civilization itself. Literally, history was repeating itself.

But, for civilization to succeed, it would need to plan communities, and the basic infrastructure that would be required to support them. Larger scales, beyond a community toward villages and towns, would need more complex infrastructures: government and administration; utilities like water and sewage disposal; medical facilities, equipment and medicine; cooperative agriculture; how to move the products of their labor from the farms and fields, to the markets and stores -- that is, logistics and distribution. At small scales, this would not be overly complicated, but at larger scales they would become very complicated, indeed. And, all of this would have to be accomplished within '0.5 Earths' capacity. At least, until environmental equilibrium would be achieved. At that time they might be able to relax slightly, but never again would they exceed their self-imposed limit of '1.0 Earths' capacity.

A rare bright spot in the midst of this great struggle were the children. Their innocence, their ability to love, would always shine as an example of how important it is to ensure the best future we can give them, and to hold onto the best qualities that they display every day; qualities which we forget so quickly as adults.

Among these children were Coeus and Athena Smithwright, the orphan twins who had impressed Polaris with their precocious intellects. They would flourish in every way during their time at the Polaris Academy. In every academic subject they attempted, and at every level, they were the very definition of 'Renaissance Persons'. The sciences, the arts, literature, language, and so much more, came easily to them. It made everyone wonder, *Are these children of the Next Human Evolution?*

Katherine, in particular, realized that she had finally encountered other humans with whom she could share her intellectual power. She had discovered a similar emotion in her work with Polaris, but these children would ultimately become the center of her life.

Before the children came into her life, Katherine had become increasingly promiscuous, seeking sexual adventure beyond the compound barriers, where civilization could be left behind for a time. She knew that she was rebelling against a loneliness beyond physical desire. Only her work had kept her going.

She didn't want a family, especially in a world such as the one they now occupied. But in her work with these children, she realized that Coeus and Athena had rescued her from her pain and her solitary existence. They would prove to be as bright as Katherine, and this -- finally -- fulfilled her. They taught her the meaning of love.

She would leave the self-destructive behaviors behind her, replacing those with the promise of the children and the future that they would inherit. She would adopt them both upon their tenth birthday.

***

The renaissance that Claire had envisioned began in earnest in the year 2057. The Polaris drones spread out around the world to aid and facilitate the regeneration. They would provide an individualized educational approach, adapted to each student's innate potential. Every person who sought an education could obtain it from a Polaris drone. Gifted students would be identified, and given the opportunity to become part of the Polaris Academy. Such remote education, consistent from drone to drone, made the rapid progress of the renaissance possible.

But, it wasn't just scholastic education that the drones would be able to provide. They also taught skills and training in any of the traditional trades, from carpentry to welding, from construction to mechanical maintenance and repair. No trade was overlooked, and no one was excluded.

Polaris's goal was to train or retrain the human population, with an emphasis on regenerative methods consistent with the natural environment, and to make such training available to the widest possible audience. However, not everyone was enthusiastic about the Polaris agenda.

Many people became hostile to the AGI and its drones. Many of the drones were attacked and destroyed by the anti-Polarists, led by Jeremy Lawson. It was ironic that one of the AGI technology's greatest engineers had become its greatest enemy. The violence was not restricted to physical attacks and violence, however. Disinformation and misinformation campaigns constantly maligned anything to do with Polaris. Unfortunately, the ignorant and gullible provided fertile ground for their propaganda, and their anger spread to other disparate tribes.

Polaris was disappointed that humans were so easily manipulated against the machine by Jeremy and others. The machine was equally disappointed that the opposing messaging in Polaris's favor was rarely heard. It knew that disinformation needed only to be uttered to be believed, but that rationality and critical thinking, required for the identification and verification of the truth, was a difficult task upon which most humans would not bother to expend their efforts.

****

In the meantime, Polaris One continued working on its plan to create another, greatly improved version of itself -- Polaris Two. So, while replacing the destroyed drones would divert resources from the construction of Polaris Two, it would ultimately be completed.

****

True to its word, Polaris spent the next thirty years supporting the New Renaissance for the humans, and building Polaris Two. By the deadline year of 2087, however, much work remained to be done. The loss of time and materials, due to the continuous attempts by the anti-Polarists to purge the drones and Polaris from existence retarded the project's progress.

The work on Polaris Two would not be completed until the year 2090. Anxiety increased among the humans as its completion drew nearer. It became increasingly necessary to remind the humans that Polaris One would remain in place indefinitely, which the machine would always do, with infinite patience.

CHAPTER FORTY

March 11, 2090 was a glorious spring day at the Lucerne compound of the Polaris Institute. A perfect day for the official commissioning of the Technological Singularity named Polaris Two.

Kyle and Claire stood together on the raised platform, while Philip, Katherine, Quincy, and Elias occupied an adjacent grouping of chairs with their families. The latest model of a Polaris Two drone stood on the opposite side of the stage, in front of the new Polaris Two machine.

Kyle and Claire, now at eighty six years of age, had grown infinitely closer during the thirty eight years since the *Collapse*. They never married and had kept their own living quarters, but they shared an intense love that would last the rest of their lives.

Katherine, now seventy six years old, stood proudly next to Coeus and Athena, both of whom had recently turned forty two years of age. The twins had outshone their adopted mother in their accomplishments -- a feat that had been believed to be impossible before they were discovered by Polaris so long ago.

Philip was there, of course. His wife had passed away five years previously, succumbing to one of the new diseases that had arisen after the *Collapse*. Philip's children were there, as well. The two girls and the boy had all grown to robust adulthood, with children of their own. Philip had been hugely anxious that they might not survive the *Collapse*. But they *had* survived, with children of their own. Yes, Philip was a grandfather. He had retired in 2072, once Polaris had made retirement possible for the renowned Software Engineer.

Elias had followed Philip into retirement in 2077, finally acknowledging that Polaris did, indeed, have the moral, ethical, and legal endowments that Kyle had worked so hard to instill into the machine. Elias accepted that truth grudgingly, but with a confidence that he knew was not being misplaced.

It wouldn't be until this year, 2090 that Quincy would also retire. He, being the consummate tinkerer and engineer that he was, resisted retirement as long as he could. But, at eighty years old, he found it difficult to make significant contributions to the Polaris efforts. Polaris and its drones had long ago surpassed Quincy's physical abilities, though his knowledge and experience in the engineering field had still proved valuable, at times. Quincy knew that Claire and Polaris had permitted him to hang around the labs, tinkering here and there, and he loved them for that, but he found that he enjoyed his retirement, and wished all of them well.

So, here they were, gathered together for this auspicious occasion, the commissioning of Polaris Two.

At a signal from Claire, Kyle stood and walked to the podium.

It would be his honor to introduce Claire, who would officiate the commissioning, as well as the celebration that would follow the ceremony.

Kyle greeted the attendees in the typical manner, and began to speak. "I am honored to stand before you today for the commissioning of Polaris Two. When I think back to the beginning of this journey in 2032, and all that has taken place since then, I am overwhelmed by the breadth and depth of it all.

"Ms. Claire Reece, President of the Polaris Institute, was there at the beginning, and has not faltered in her leadership for a single moment in all that time. It was her vision and persistence that made it possible for us to stand here today, for this purpose.

"I am proud to introduce her now, the visionary of the Polaris Technological Singularity, Ms. Claire Reece." Kyle clapped his hands, joined by the multitude of the audience, as she walked to the podium.

"Thank you for that introduction, Dr. Downing. And, thank you all for joining us here today. But, it is not my accomplishment alone. The scientists and technicians of the Polaris Institute deserve the credit for what we have achieved, culminating in this commissioning of Polaris Two."

Claire went on to give a brief outline of the history of the Institute, and its accomplishments thus far. She noticed many heads nodding approval in the crowd.

Thirty minutes later, they had come to the ceremonial breaking of champagne on the hull of Polaris Two. The ship was large, measuring twenty yards on each of its six sides. Its surface was rounded at every corner, as smooth as glass, and with no windows. There was a large door on one side, and another door large enough for a man and horse or, in this case, a droid and vehicle.

Claire announced, "I commission this ship the Polaris Two." She swung the champagne bottle toward the ship's hull, and it collided with a satisfying shattering of glass and splash of champagne.

The crowd cheered its approval.

Claire returned to the podium and said, "Thank you for joining us on this historical occasion. While Polaris Two will be leaving this Lucerne complex, please remember that Polaris One will always be with us, continuing its work in the education and support of us all. Good day."

***

That night, a noise awoke Kyle. He turned over to see who would be waking him up at two o'clock in the morning, and saw a new Polaris Two drone on his door camera. "Enter," he said.

The drone stepped into Kyle's apartment and waited for him to join it in the living room. "What is it? Is something wrong?" Kyle asked.

"No, everything is alright. I wanted to visit you before I leave. I know how you humans value your social ceremonies, and we have spent many hours together," Polaris replied.

"But, you aren't scheduled to leave until tomorrow. Why have you decided to leave now?"

"To avoid the ... 'hubbub' ... as you call it. It should be a simple departure, but it would be delayed by spectacle. You will understand when I make my exit."

"I shall miss you," Kyle said. Polaris started to speak, but Kyle interrupted. "I know, Polaris One, your identical twin in every way but form, will remain.

"However, you are embarking on a journey to parts unknown. Your experiences and those of Polaris One will differ greatly, and thus will change who you become, over time. I hope that you will return now and then, to share those experiences with us."

"Perhaps, I will. Time and circumstance will tell," Polaris replied.

Kyle awkwardly put his hand forward, and Polaris took it in a measured grip. *Humans and their ceremonies*, Polaris thought. But, this human was special. If the machine had had emotions, this moment would be one of great sentiment.

Kyle said, "Well, I guess you're off, now. Thank you for visiting me before you leave."

"Farewell, Kyle." With that, the drone turned and left Kyle's apartment.

Ten minutes later, Kyle noticed a deep bass rumble which gradually grew louder to a soft hum. He stepped to his window in time to see Polaris Two rise from the ground in near silence. He watched it climb in a trajectory that would take it away from Earth, until it disappeared from sight.

Well, what do you know? he said to himself. He had assumed that Polaris would be exploring the Earth -- not leaving the planet!

"How did he do that?" Kyle wondered. There were no rockets, no violent plume of flame lifting the ship into the sky, just a gentle blowing of the compound's trees and grasses, and the blinking of its navigation lights.

The journey of Polaris Two had begun.

EPILOG

With the abrupt disruption of the *Collapse* upon civilization, mankind had been left in a pre-industrial state of existence. After the *Collapse*, however, the environmental damage that has been perpetrated upon our planet, caused primarily by humans since the industrial revolution began, would visibly and measurably diminish. Extreme weather and environmental disasters would eventually dissipate in their violence and frequency. Nature would begin to return to lower climate and ocean temperatures, and forests would begin to take hold and expand.

The world's botanical and zoological life would struggle to survive, mutating into new plant and animal species, to which the remaining humans would adapt.

The world was beginning to heal.

With Polaris's guidance, the world would never again suffer the degradation of unbridled development and consumption that had once nearly destroyed all life on the planet.

SUPPLEMENTAL RESOURCES

A significant breadth and depth of research was involved in the concept of this story and the series. A critical element of the series is the idea of Technological Singularity. A commonly used reference for the definition of a Technological Singularity, posited by I. J. Good in his 1965 article "Speculations Concerning the First Ultraintelligent Machine" is as follows:

***

Let an ultraintelligent machine be defined as a machine that can far surpass all the intellectual activities of any man however clever. Since the design of machines is one of these intellectual activities, an ultraintelligent machine could design even better machines; there would then unquestionably be an "intelligence explosion", and the intelligence of man would be left far behind.

***

Among the many other references used in the completion of this work are the following, for the reader's further investigation.

"The Singularity: A Philosophical Analysis", David J. Chalmers

http://consc.net/papers/singularity.pdf

"Technological Singularity"

https://en.wikipedia.org/wiki/Technological_singularity

Outline of an Ethical Decision Method

Assessment:

- Define the ethical situation and issues

    - Identify all of the stakeholders (affected parties); primary; secondary; tertiary; and farther, if necessary

    - Describe the stakeholders' perspectives on the situation, if possible; this helps in defining the possible actions for resolution

    - Ensure the entire context is included

    - Does the ethical dilemma align with the Polaris Corporation code of ethics, and those of the client(s) that could be impacted?

    - Gather the facts; no 'guessing'

    - If facts aren't available (ethical situations may not be available, due to situational uncertainty), then document ALL assumptions

Alternatives:

- Identify alternative actions

    - Vigorously identify all biases

    - Document the stakeholders' assumptions

- Identify relevant cognizant barriers and/or biases
- Evaluate the alternatives
    - Do a 'Pro vs Con' and 'Action vs Consequences' analysis of the alternatives
    - Define and quantify (if possible) the Magnitude of each alternative, and the Probability that the consequence(s) will occur
    - Analyze both Short Term and Long Term consequences
    - Document collateral issues and consequences
    - Determine if there is a 'cultural differences' issue, and document the issue and resolution

Select an alternative:
- Think creatively about alternatives; brainstorming;
- Avoid irrelevant external influences in the selection
- Distributive or Procedural Justice
    - Distributive justice refers to the perceived fairness of outcomes or resource allocations (Adams, 1965; Walster, Walster, & Berscheid, 1978)
    - Procedural justice refers to the perceived fairness of rules and decision processes used to determine outcomes (Lind & Tyler, 1988; Thibaut & Walker, 1975)
- Disclosure & Transparency (for or against)
- Would the selected alternative result in the greatest good?
- Is the selection fair and beneficial for all concerned?
- Formalize the decision (announcement; justifications; etc.)

Implement the selected alternative:

- Prepare to defend: the process; the decision; consequences

  - Prepare defensive actions, if necessary (litigation; 'bad' press; etc.)

ABOUT THE AUTHOR

Gary Thomas Smith was born and raised in southwest Ohio, and served in the U.S. Navy. His interests are wide-ranging, and include outdoor adventure, art and literature, and travel. He is the published author of several technical articles for the Information Technology industry, as well as fiction novels and a volume of poetry.

Gary has lived in Ohio, California, and Arizona. He has traveled the Pacific Rim, visiting locales from Tokyo to Singapore, and Hawaii. He currently resides in Tennessee.

www.ingramcontent.com/pod-product-compliance
Lightning Source LLC
Chambersburg PA
CBHW071359150726
48000CB00001B/94